KRISTY'S STORY

A novel

Additional Titles by this Author

Novels
The Language of Bodies

Children's Books
Jamie the Germ Slayer
The *Rumplepimple* Adventures

Other Books

Holding on to Hope: Help for friends and family of transgender people

Reaching for Hope: Strategies and support for the partners of transgender people

Where True Love Is: an affirming devotional for LGBTQI+ individuals and their allies

Transfigured: a 40-day journey through scripture for gender-queer and transgender people

I Don't Want Them to Go to Hell: 50 days of encouragement for friends and families of LGBTQ people

Pro-Life, Pro-Choice, Pro-Love: 44 days of reflection for finding a third way in the abortion debate

A Theology of Desire: Meditations on intimacy, consummation, and the longing of God

Sex With God: Meditations on the sacred nature of sex in a post-purity-culture world

Sleeper, Awake: 40 days of companionship for the deconstruction process

KRISTY'S STORY

A novel

Suzanne DeWitt Hall

DH Strategies

First Edition

ISBN-13: 978-1-7347427-7-0
Printed in the United States of America

This is a work of fiction. Names, characters, businesses, places, events, and incidents are either the products of the author's imagination or used in a fictitious manner. Any resemblance to actual persons, living or dead, or actual events is purely coincidental.

When the nightmare of my past neared its peak, Lee asked what the hell I'd been thinking. But if I could pull you with me through time to see what led to that moment, maybe you'd understand.

Aren't stories exactly that? Ways to travel through time?

Here's mine.

PROLOGUE

Beep. Beep. Beep. Hour after hour.

I couldn't stand it any longer. "Thayer," I said. He didn't respond, so I shook him. "Thayer!"

His eyelids fluttered and blinked as he tried to come out of it. "Lee…" he finally said, the word a faint whisper of breath.

The baby in my womb rolled as if responding to Lee's name. A low keening escaped my clenched teeth.

Thayer grimaced when I stood up from my perch on the bed beside him.

"Did that hurt?" My voice was thick with sorrow.

Beep. Beep. Beep.

I'd watched the nurse adjust settings on the bags dripping nutrition and narcotics into his bloodstream. It wasn't complicated. I reached for the morphine pump, turning it up. "The pain will be better in a minute," I said.

His eyes drifted closed.

Beep.

Beep.

Beep.

PART ONE

PART ONE

CHAPTER 1

It's funny being six when your mama abandons you. First you think it's the greatest thing that ever happened because she's bossy and grumpy and makes daddy upset. But then you find out life is a lot more complicated once she's gone.

I should have known something was up that day because she made our favorite breakfast: sausage, eggs over hard because I couldn't stand snot, and cheesy grits. She always did her makeup so that wasn't surprising. But she had earrings on.

The earrings should have been a dead giveaway.

When I try to remember mama back then I mostly catch a whiff of perfume along with a quick sensation of glamour and disapproval. But I *do* remember the people showing up and taking her with them. And Daddy crying when he came home.

It was still early when they knocked on the door. Mama had sent Daddy out for butts and baloney, but that was nothing new. Daddy used to say he was her knight in shining servitude. They knocked loud, even louder than the cartoons I was watching. I looked at Mama because we didn't get visitors much, and especially not at 8:00 on a Saturday morning. But she just breathed a dragon stream of smoke and squished her cigarette out then went to the closet and pulled out her big old ugly brown suitcase.

I loved *my* suitcase. It was small and covered with pink and purple flowers.

This time the banging rattled the door on its frame. "Mama? Someone's here." I wasn't supposed to get the door.

"I'm coming."

Mama lurched toward the door with the suitcase. It pulled her body sideways as she dragged it, which didn't make sense because I'd picked that thing up in the closet. It was almost bigger than me, but not heavy.

She opened the door and a man and a lady stormed in. They were wearing fancy clothes, like the people I saw in The Shyster's office when Daddy had to get himself out of trouble and Mama didn't want to watch me. The man was wearing a white shirt with a jacket and a tie which must have been tight because his face was red. The lady was wearing a long, loose dress covered in small flowers with buttons down the front. She looked like an older, meaner version of Mama, except her face was squinchy and her hair sparkled around the ears. I thought the dress was pretty.

"Are you ready? Is he gone?" The man's head swung back and forth looking around the trailer. I thought he should slow down and be careful because with a tie that tight his head was likely to pop right off. Mama just nodded and pushed the suitcase toward him. His eyes finally landed on me. "So that's the little hell-spawn."

"Papa," Mama said.

But he didn't stop talking, this time to me. "If it weren't for you, my daughter would have finished University. She'd be advancing in her career by now." He glared like I should know what he was talking about.

"Looks just like him, doesn't she?" This time it was the lady. She was staring at me. What she said didn't make much sense because Daddy always said I looked like Mama. "Should have known nothing good could come of a man with eyes that color." She shook her head in disapproval, then realized I was watching her watching me. "Keep your peepers to yourself, young lady!" she snapped. I whipped my head toward the TV.

"And this place!" The man started flinging his head around again.

"You've been living in a dump." His face looked like my bus driver's when someone throws up on the ride home.

"Hey!" It's all I could come up with in protest.

I knew all about dumps. We had to take our trash to the big bins at the end of the trailer park where it got picked up by the garbage trucks. That place smelled gross and had flies buzzing and weird puddles of mystery juice on the ground. Our trailer was *nothing* like that. Our couch was soft and comfy and Daddy's chair tipped back so he could rest his eyes, and Mama hated stinks so it always smelled good. I had no idea what he was talking about. Clearly the man was crazy.

"Let's just go," Mama said, which made no sense. Why should we leave with these mean people, especially since I wasn't even dressed yet? She never let me leave the house in my nightgown. She moved closer to the door. "We'd better hurry."

"Mama?"

She turned back toward me. Her face looked really tired. "Goodbye Kristy."

She never even hugged or kissed me. Just followed the mean people out the door and closed it behind her.

"Mama?" None of it made sense, but it was like I was glued to my spot on the floor in front of the TV. I decided there was nothing to do but wait for Daddy to get back.

We moved not long after that. To another trailer, in a different town. Daddy said he didn't want her to be able to find us when she came back. I liked the new place better.

It didn't take long to get used to her being gone. There was a lot less arguing and sighing going on. But I did miss her cooking. Mama sure knew how to cook.

Daddy was sad though. I didn't understand why he missed her, but he did.

The new trailer park was great! Tons of kids lived there, and there were woods all around. Daddy made friends with a bunny who hopped out of the bushes and into our side yard each night before darkness fell. Daddy took to bringing it lettuce and carrots. I was glad when the rabbit came, because that meant Daddy started buying vegetables. I didn't love eating them, but I knew you were supposed to. I knew *he* was supposed to, and a lot of the time, I didn't like the way he looked, and hoped vegetables would help. He didn't cook them though, so once in a while I'd grab a couple of carrots and pretend to be Bugs Bunny, trying to get him to eat one too.

Rabbits weren't the only animals at our new place. Squirrels came to visit, but they'd dart away quick because of the cats living under our neighbor's trailer. Birds were always singing, and the cats watched them too. One time a turtle the size of a cereal bowl was hanging out in the shadows under the car. Daddy got a broom and pushed it out of the way. He kept the broom on the porch after that, and every time we went to the car Daddy would yell "Ahoy, all ye turtles!" and we'd bend over and look under it before getting in.

The one animal I wished would come into our yard never did: an armadillo. I saw plenty of dead ones on the side of the road, but I never saw a live one. I guess that's good though because Daddy told me I shouldn't touch one.

"Why not?" I asked. "I want to see what the armor on their back feels like!"

"They can give you leprosy."

"What's leopardsy?"

"Leh-prah-see," Daddy corrected. He liked teaching me new words, and said vocabulary kept us from sliding hellbent into heathendom. "It's a horrible disease. In the Bible days if you got it, you'd be ostracized."

That cured me. Ostriches were cool, but I didn't want to be one.

I spent a lot of time in the side yard and the empty lots down at the end of our road. Before I made friends I watched the neighborhood kids playing. One trailer had a basketball hoop out front, and kids hung out down there. You could hear a basketball thwacking almost any time of day and night, and in all seasons. In hot weather, the rhythm just got slower.

One day I made an excellent discovery. The grass down in the empty lots was soft and green, except in July and August when the sun baked it brown and prickly. I was sitting there in late spring, watching the basketballers, and feeling the softness beneath my palms. The warm sun made me sleepy, so I lay down with my head on one arm and looked at the grass sideways. Some of it was spiky and tall. Some was silky fine and bendy. And some was short and made of three circles with a white stripe running through them. Some of the circles looked like hearts.

There were also bugs. Little flying things would buzz through, and ants would come tramping by. But they didn't bother me. I picked a piece of the round leaf stuff and chewed on it. It tasted sweet.

I chewed and peered through the green forest and wondered about the three-circle grass, and probably fell asleep. When I opened my eyes again, I got a surprise. A piece of circle grass was right in front of my nose. But it didn't have three leaves. It had four.

Daddy had to see this. I plucked a few of the normal three-leafers along with the special one, and ran home, carrying them carefully. I burst into the house with a bang of the screen door.

"Krispy, you rascal, I almost jumped through the ceiling!"

"Daddy, look what I found!" I ran to him and unfolded my fist. The leaves looked fine. I was glad I hadn't smashed them. "What is it?"

"That's clover. Looks like you found a four-leafer!"

"I did! There were zillions of the three-leaf, but I found one that has four!"

"Well, that's good luck for you. Congratulations."

"Why is it good luck?"

"Come here and let me tell you." He sat back down in his tippy chair, and I climbed on his lap. His body was warm. He wrapped one arm around me, and I rested my head near his throat, where I could hear his words rumbling from the inside. I loved it when he told me about things. He was a really good teller.

"There's an ancient Christian legend about four-leaf clovers."

"There is?"

"Yes. You remember who Eve was?"

"That first lady. Adam's wife."

"Well, they weren't actually married, but that's another story."

"Will you tell me it sometime?"

"Maybe. When you're older."

"Okay."

"Well after the snake tricked Eve into biting the forbidden fruit, and she and Adam got into their first argument, they got kicked out of their beautiful garden."

"I sort of remember." I'd learned a few things in Sunday school. The Baptist church sent a bus around to pick kids up Sunday mornings so they could teach us about Jesus. So far they'd talked about Adam and Eve, Noah, and a guy who got swallowed by a whale.

"That place was paradise, and boy were they upset when God made them leave," Daddy said.

"What's paradise?"

"It's another version of heaven really. Where you don't have to worry about anything. All your food is right there so you don't have to work. Everyone gets along. The animals talk to you." That heaven sounded a lot better than the one my Sunday school teacher described, which was a city with streets made of gold bricks where people sang hymns all the time. "When Eve had to leave paradise, she took a four-leaf clover with her," Daddy continued. "So, the legend is that anyone who has one has a little piece of heaven."

"That's cool!" I lifted up my own bit of paradise so we could look at it.

"Each leaf has meaning. One is for faith, one for hope, one for love, and one for luck."

I touched the leaves as he counted them off. "It's like magic, isn't it?"

"Yep. Some people even think having one lets you see fairies and recognize evil. It's like magical protection."

I thought about that for a while. "I'm so glad I found this one!" I decided to find more of them, but first, I wanted to snuggle with Daddy. I yawned. He yawned. We fell asleep, with me right there on his lap, thinking about paradise and what evil might look like and how I could protect him from it.

As the days and months passed, I searched for four-leaf clover. Each time I found one I tucked it in the pages of Daddy's old copy of *A Wrinkle in Time*. It was my favorite book. I wished Daddy's problems could be solved by tessering to another planet and battling evil, though that would be scary. He couldn't seem to shake off Mama's leaving. I could make him smile, but his sadness always came back. I didn't know how to fix it, but figured having a bunch of magical clover couldn't hurt, and so I made finding them my mission. By the time I was done, there could have been a hundred in that book. Maybe even more.

CHAPTER 2

It was a lot easier to make friends in our new place than at our old trailer. For one thing, there were more kids. For another, there was no Mama to stop me from being outside all day. Daddy talked about "rugged individualism" and an "independent spirit," but she wasn't a fan of either one.

When I was eight, I had my first sleepover at my friend Karen's trailer, five doors down, next to the place with the basketball hoop. We came in for supper after playing hide and seek in the woods with the gang. Her parents didn't smoke like Daddy did, but her house smelled like farts and old kitty litter.

Karen's mom greeted us. "I hope you like hotdogs and beans, because that's what we're having."

"I like hotdogs with bread and ketchup!" I blurted.

"Do you like hotdog rolls?" She asked.

"What's that?"

"It's a bun. That you put your hot dog in." Her eyes looked funny when she said it.

"Oh, those! I love those!" I thought they were just for rich people, and wondered if Karen's family might be rich.

We all ate together, then Karen and I played in her bedroom until her mom told us it was time to go to sleep.

It was strange getting ready for bed in someone else's house. I'd brought an old tee shirt of Daddy's to sleep in. It was long, and felt like home, and when I sniffed really hard, I could catch a whiff of his aftershave, which smelled like if a pine tree and a leather belt had a baby.

Karen was brushing her teeth. "Where's your brush?" she asked around a mouthful of foam and bubbles.

Daddy didn't pay much attention to things that needed brushing, so it wasn't my priority either. "I forgot it," I said. "But I know you're supposed to brush every seven days."

Karen's mom was passing by the bathroom door right then. She stopped in the doorway and looked at me funny again. "We have some extras. Here you go." She opened the medicine cabinet and handed me a blue one.

"Thanks!"

"You should really brush your teeth every day. A few times a day," she said.

That made me feel embarrassed, so I showed them I knew how to do it. I squirted a quarter-sized dollop of Aquafresh on the brush. I was pretty excited to try it because I'd seen the ads, but all we ever had in the house was Ultrabrite which was so strong it burned my tongue. Mama had told me to brush for as long as it took to sing Happy Birthday, so I scrubbed at my teeth, and hummed really loud, marching around in a circle. Karen and her mom watched and had weird looks on their faces by the time I finished the song, so I figured I'd better run through it again.

Falling asleep was hard without my beautiful Strawberry Shortcake comforter. I wished I'd brought it along.

CHAPTER 3

The thing about living in Missouri is tornadoes. Once winter is over you come to expect the big storms twisters love to hang out in. Every time a thunder boomer blew in, Daddy turned on the radio and made sure it had batteries in case the power went out. We tuned it to the weather station but turned the volume down low because Daddy liked to listen to the storm itself.

There were a lot of storms, so you'd think I'd get used to them, but one night was really scary. It was the loudest thing I ever heard, with light suddenly filling the room, and crazy bangs of thunder booming right afterward. Water pounded the roof of the trailer and blew sideways against the walls. I peered out the front window during a break in the rain, and saw a lady's face peeking back from behind her curtain across the street and one door up. She was wearing some sort of blue scarf over her hair. She smiled at me. She didn't look scared, but I sure was. Scared for us and for the bunny and the turtles and the next-door cats.

I went back to the living room and crawled up into daddy's lap where the world felt safer.

He snuggled me in. "Don't be scared, little Krispy."

"Seems like we *should* be scared. Did you hear that last one?"

"I sure did."

I didn't like how he'd been looking lately. His skin wasn't the usual color, and his eyes always looked tired, like they stole all the pink from his face. Plus, he must have changed cigarette brands because he even smelled different; like stinky cleaning products even though he hated housework.

But he was still Daddy. I snuggled in closer. "What if the roof blows right off?"

"If the roof blows then we'll feel the pounding of the rain on our skin and turn our mouths up for a drink."

"I think it would pound my tonsils out. Maybe even my teeth." Daddy laughed, but it didn't make me feel better. "I'm scared."

"Fear is a useless emotion, Krispy. If it's your time to go, it's your time and no amount of fear will prevent it. And if God wants you to keep living, there's no storm big enough to kill you. He's got a time for me and for you, so it doesn't make any sense to worry."

"But what if there's a tornado?"

"If the siren goes off, we'll hightail it down to the fire station. Otherwise, we'll sit tight and wait to see what happens."

I just sighed because none of what he said made me feel better.

"Can you imagine a more glorious way to enter eternity? Being picked up by a tornado is almost the way Jesus, Elijah, and Elisha did it. Rising up into the air!"

"Who are Elijah and Elisha?"

"They were two men who tried to teach people about who God is. When their work here was done, God rose them up into the air and took them to heaven."

I made big eyes at him, the kind that usually made him laugh.

"When it was Elijah's turn, a chariot and horses made of fire came down, and away he went."

"Cool!"

"Doesn't that sound kind of like a lightning-filled tornado to you?"

I thought about it for a minute and had to admit it did. "But that wouldn't make it any less scary, if you were really in one."

"Think about it Krispy… Imagine what it would feel like to be at the center of all that power." Daddy went on to weave a story about feeling the wind and the pounding of the noise against your eardrums as you became one with the force, and the oddity of the things you'd see flying past you; uprooted flowers and lake-fulls of water and maybe a billy goat, and your neighbor's house. "And you wouldn't care because it would all be so deafeningly glorious that nothing else would matter." His words began to fade into the storm and join with it, until eventually I fell asleep in the encircling safety of his arms and his voice. When I woke up the next day I was in my bed and the storm was over.

From then on, I respected tornadoes and bad storms, but wasn't quite so frightened by them. But I still hoped God wouldn't decide to take me for a while. Daddy needed me.

CHAPTER 4

Daddy wrote poetry. Some of it was silly; jokes about peanut butter sandwiches or tickling the bellies of pill bugs. Others were beautiful; verses that read like songs without music, describing the greens of spring or the way the ocean never stops singing. I think he always wanted to be a writer.

Here's one I memorized.

> A little tickle
> upon my cheek
> my eyes fly open
> to take a peek
> and there she sits
> the wee pipsqueak
> my pretty Krispy Whiskerton.

He left poems on scraps of paper around the house. Each time I found one, I'd slide it carefully under my mattress. I liked to think about lying on them while I was falling asleep, safe on a bed of his words.

CHAPTER 5

Karen was a pretty good friend. She was the only one I did sleepovers with, and they were usually at her house after Daddy started getting grumpier. But I ended up having an even better friend, and believe it or not, he was a boy.

His name was JB. I don't know what the letters stood for. I never thought to ask. He'd lived in the trailer park his whole life and was a legend. He kept mostly to himself and never played basketball, so you'd think the other kids wouldn't like him. But he was everyone's hero. Especially mine.

Maybe he didn't play basketball because half his hand was missing. One Fourth of July JB blew his fingers off with an M-80. I didn't really know what an M-80 was, but apparently you had to have guts to light one. And apparently he lit one but didn't throw it away fast enough. So BOOM! Bye-bye fingers.

The first time I met JB I was lying in the grass down near the sewage pump, taking a break from searching for four-leaf clover. The field had just been mowed, which was great because the tall weedy stuff was gone but the clover was short enough to escape.

When I looked for clover, I got kind of lost in it. I crawled on hands and knees with my nose close to the ground and scanned back and forth while concentrating on not concentrating. When I passed a clover with four leaves, my brain caught it before my eyes did. I'd have to go back and find what my brain knew was there, because my eyes had already moved on. The process was kind of tiring, and so I lay down on my back to watch the clouds for a while.

"Hey."

I hadn't even heard JB coming. *That's* how deep the search for clover sucks you in. I sat up because it felt weird to be lying down when someone was standing over you. "Hey," I responded, all cool and relaxed. I hoped.

"You're Kristy."

"Yup. And you're JB."

"Yup." He sat down a few feet away from me. "You looking for something?"

I explained my clover collection, trying not to look at his hand, because that would be rude.

"So how many do you think you have?" he asked.

"I don't know. I've never counted them." I told him about keeping them in *A Wrinkle in Time* and how much I loved that book, and how it would be great if your dad was this amazing scientist and your mom made soup on a Bunsen burner. That's how I found out he was a good listener. He just stayed there and listened, nodding and hmming at the right times. Like he cared about what I was saying. Like he might want to read the book too.

He was cute up close. His black hair was straight and really shiny, and his nose turned up at the tip. And of course, he was tanned real dark like most of us were from spending so much time outside.

Mostly I liked his eyes. They looked like they really saw you.

From then on we were friends. We rode bikes together, and went for walks. On bad days I'd ask him to tell me stories, and he'd weave tall tales about swamp monsters and heroes who carried giant axes. Once in a while it would be him who had a bad day, and I'd be the one to tell the story. Mine were usually about real stuff that happened because I wasn't good at making things up.

There was a small pond down the slope behind JB's trailer where turtles liked to hang out, so he kept some treats ready in case one passed by when we were there. He let me feed them and taught me how to not be scared of their pointy beaks.

He taught me a lot about not being scared of things.

CHAPTER 6

Daddy kept getting sicker, which meant he couldn't work as much, which meant he worried about money a lot. When he worried about money, he stayed out with his friends more. I didn't like them. I was eating cold hot dogs with lots of ketchup one night when he didn't come home for supper and noticed that the end of the wiener looked like an inside out dog's butt. And kind of like a star. I dipped the star butt in ketchup and pressed it on my bright white paper plate. The first press resulted in a tiny red mountain. The second and third began to look like stars until the ketchup eventually faded away to nothing. I took a bite and pressed the bit end in the ketchup again, but the shape wasn't so satisfying. I kept going with the other hotdog, wishing I had more, I needed to save a couple for another day. The plate was covered with red stamps, and I wondered what the texture felt like. I touched the stars and slid my fingers around to change the patterns, but it needed more ketchup, so I glumped out a pool on the plate. I made a river, like if Buck Creek turned to blood or fire, flowing through a white field of starflowers. I made fiery trees to hover over the flowers on the banks. That's when Daddy walked in.

"Hey Krispy," he called when he saw me. His words sounded bleary which was never a good sign. Then he saw my ketchup painting. "What the hell are you doing?" He came to a standstill next to me at the table instead of walking straight to the fridge for a can of Walky's Best, which was another sign of trouble. It was never a good idea to get in the way of that first beer, especially when he wasn't feeling well, and I could tell by the way he was walking and flinging his fingers around that it was a not-feeling-good day. Maybe even a dark day.

"I made some flowers. For you." I hoped that would soften him up.

"Flowers? What is this, Mother's Day?" He chuffled like that was funny, even though I could see he was still mad. His laughing gave me hope, because sometimes it led to him ruffling my hair. But he stopped laughing. "What I'm seeing is a waste of money."

I hadn't thought of that. "Sorry daddy."

"Sorry doesn't buy another bottle of ketchup, now does it?" I shake my head. "No, it doesn't," he said. "So, what are you going to do about it?"

I scrambled to come up with a solution. "Scrape it back into the bottle?"

"After your fingers have been all through it?"

I just blinked in response, then looked at my hands. They *were* pretty dirty.

"What you are going to do is eat it. We don't waste in this housh. House."

I looked back from my hands to his face. He wobbled a bit and grabbed on to the chair next to him.

"Go on now. You got that ketchup out, so go ahead and eat it. It's good for you. Helps you see in the dark." This time he laughed out loud.

I tried smiling back but it was hard. He was in the dark place for sure. I didn't want to eat the ketchup, especially after I'd looked at my hands. But his darkness was scary, and there was no talking him out of anything when he was in it. I picked up the plate and started licking.

"That's it. Clean it up. And get all of it." He watched me for a minute. I kept licking. "You look more like your saucy little bitch of a mother every day, don't you? Like to see *her* licking that plate, tell you what." He was still facing me, but his focus was somewhere else, and I think he was talking to himself. He scratched the zipper on his jeans, then shook his head as he moved to the fridge, grabbed a cold can, and walked to his chair. I knew I was in the clear when he turned on the TV.

I kept at the ketchup. Eating it that way was different. You could taste it more. It was salty and sweet and sour all at the same time. And I found out I could make patterns with my tongue too.

By the time I got the plate clean I almost hated ketchup.

I thought about those patterns for the rest of the night, and how my fingers felt moving through the red slickness to make pictures. I wanted to paint with real paint sometime, and I fell asleep watching patterns forming and shifting behind my eyelids.

I'm not sure how long I'd been asleep before the door banged open. Daddy stumbled in and moved toward the bed.

"Come on Lisa. I need you tonight honey."

Lisa was my Mama's name. "Daddy?" I saw motion behind him, where the mirror was. For a minute, I thought it reflected Mama, right where I was sitting on my bed, but then I realized it was just me.

"Thass right. I'm your big daddy." He slid me over on the mattress, climbed up and sat right next to my head. "I need it Leesy. I'm hurting tonight." His words were smeary, like his tongue got stung by a bee. "I'm not in a good place."

"What do you need, daddy? Maybe I can help."

He laughed then, almost a giggle, and the joy of it nearly split my heart. It was hard to make him laugh these days.

"Oh honey, you know you're the only one who ever *could* help me. Are you sure Leesy? Are you sure?" His voice was strange. It reminded me of how I sound when the ice cream truck drives through the park, but sad at the same time.

"Of course I'll help you," I said.

"Thank God." He rose up on his knees and undid his belt. Then he unbuttoned the brass button of his jeans and tugged down the zipper.

"What's the matter? Did a spider bite you?" A spider got stuck in my underwear once. I think it came in when the laundry was on the line. It bit me right on my butt and hurt like a B-word. I cried and cried.

Daddy giggled again, the sound strange and foolish. "Oh, I got bit by something a'right." He yanked at his jeans and started to tip over, so he rested one hand on the wall above the headboard. He used the other hand to pull down his underwear.

"What are you doing daddy?" I'd seen him naked before, plenty of times. But this was different. He was so close. Plus his thing wasn't hanging like normal. It was sticking out and up. It was bigger. I wondered where the bite was.

"Come on Lisa. Come on baby. Don't tease me now." He put his hand around his thing and pointed it toward my face.

"Why are you calling me that?" The beer sweat gathered around him like a cloud with a stronger stink coming from beneath his lifted arm. But there was another smell too. It was like his bed but stronger. Like the scent of a skunk and cheese and the bleach we use when we washed the sheets.

"Daddy?"

"Why don't you stop calling *me* that." He grabbed my head and pulled it toward his thing, which was waving at me. I didn't know what he expected me to do. I didn't see anything that looked like a bite, but Daddy sure acted like he was in pain and his thing was sort of scary. "Do it like you did that plate out there, baby."

He couldn't mean it.

But he did mean it.

Afterward, after he made that awful noise and fell over and I thought he might be dying and wondered if I should call an ambulance, after I choked and spit and then threw up all over my bed with chunks of hot dog and bright red goo messing up my beautiful Strawberry Shortcake comforter, after I ran out of the room to brush my teeth for like an hour and then wadded up my bedding and threw it on the ground, after he stumbled his way down the hall to his own room, after all that, I heard him crying.

The sound was awful. I grabbed the orange and green afghan from the couch, the one I didn't like because it was made of holes which my toes poked through. I crawled back into bed and covered my ears.

I'd hoped it would help him, like he said it would. But he was in there, crying.

I remembered the ketchup and the plate and the pattern and the sharp, salty, sweet taste of it that just wouldn't stop. And I knew one thing for sure. I was *never* eating ketchup again.

The sounds of his sniffling continued, so I got back up and went to Daddy's room. He seemed to be asleep, but the tears were still wet on his face and his chest shuddered the way babies do when they cry really hard. I patted him on the back and pulled the blankets up to his chin.

"I'm sorry Daddy," I whispered. "I'll do better next time."

CHAPTER 7

It was hard not to notice when the men in the trailer park started noticing me. It was as if their gaze had weight, and I could feel it resting on my chest or my butt. I'd been invisible when I was a nine-year-old, just one of the tribe of kids that roamed the place. But when I turned ten it was like I took off an invisibility cloak and everyone blinked, surprised to see me standing there.

They also stared at my eyes. I never thought much about them because they were the first eyes I remembered, looking at me from Daddy's face. When I saw them in the mirror, they just seemed normal. I didn't like the stares, and I didn't like them looking at my eyes the way they did. When I found an old pair of sunglasses at the dump, I kept them. One lens was a bit cracked but the crack was in the corner, so it didn't make it hard to see. Wearing them made me feel like a movie star, or a secret agent.

On hot days the men walked around with no shirts on. Most of them had beer bellies and beards. Most of them squinted because the sunshine was so bright. Most of them smoked. Almost all their eyes followed me as I rode my bike, or walked toward Buck Creek with JB. They'd raise their faces from the inside of the car engines they were trying to fix, or stare at me from their front steps where they sat drinking beer. They even watched me when they joined in the kids' basketball games, looking at me when they tried to make a basket. Talking trash to each other and looking at me.

It got to be very uncomfortable, all that watching. And then it got worse.

It was a short walk to the place with the dumpsters. A path was mowed through the weeds of the field that separated our road from trash headquarters. I liked walking through there in the summer, because the weeds grew high on each side, so it was like moving through a tunnel. You could hear birds rustling in it, and insects chirping, and once in a while a grasshopper would jump in front of you. I tried to remember to take the garbage out before the bag got too full, but I'd waited too long this time, and the bag was heavy and bounced against my leg with each step. You couldn't drag them because the plastic would rip, and stuff would leak out along the path. I'd learned that the hard way.

"I do believe you get prettier every day, Kristy." The voice startled me. A man stepped out from behind one of the dumpsters just as I reached them. His eyes roamed up and down my body. They rested on my chest, then moved down to where my butt had started pushing out sideways, making my shorts too tight and too short.

"Thank you Mr. Baker." I hated how he was looking at me, but Daddy said you should always say thank you when you got a compliment. His face was red and sweaty. I never liked him. He had a weird thing growing off his back that looked like a long nipple, and that was just disgusting.

"Tell you what. Let me get rid of that for you and we'll take a little walk into the woods over there." He jerked his head toward the trees near the sewage processing building and reached for my garbage bag. I handed it to him because it was heavy and would be hard for me to throw in the dumpster.

His eyes had that hungry look like Daddy's sometimes did, only meaner. I was pretty sure he wanted me to do things to his penis. It was bad enough having to touch my dad's junk. It would be so gross to have to get anywhere near this guy's. "I have to get back," I said, turning to go. "Daddy might need me."

"Your Pa is so toasted he wouldn't notice if you grew two heads and disappeared for days. Not to mention, he owes me money." He grabbed my arm and started pulling me toward the woods. "Let's go."

"I don't want to!" I tried to pull away, but he was strong.

"I'll make it worth your while. And you can tell your father his debt's been cancelled." Mr. Baker made a grunty snort, which I figured was supposed to be laughter.

I wasn't sure what to do. I was supposed to be obey adults. But Mr. Baker was so creepy. He had no right to force me to touch him.

"Let her go!" The voice came from behind me, but I'd recognize it anywhere.

Mr. Baker looked away from my face to stare at JB. "Why don't you mind your own business?" He let go of my wrist, and I jumped away from him.

"Kristy is my friend, and my friends *are* my business."

"How about I make it my business to kick your skinny ass?"

"How about I go tell Rose Jean where you're at? I'm a fast runner."

Mr. Baker's face turned even redder. His fists curled into tight balls and then released, repeatedly. He looked back and forth at JB and I, then shook his head and started walking away.

"You're gonna regret that, son."

JB watched him leave, then turned back to me. "Let me know next time you need to take the trash. We can go together."

"Okay. I will."

"Promise?"

"Yes."

We walked back to his trailer, and hung outside for a while, watching his turtle.

I had a hard time falling asleep that night. I kept seeing the hungry look on Mr. Baker's face, and the feel of his beefy fingers wrapped around my wrist. The TV was on in the living room, which meant Daddy was still up, so I went out to check on him. When he saw me, Daddy waved his hand to come over. He looked pretty good. Didn't seem as sick as some nights.

I settled in on the floor in front of his chair and rested my head against his knee. He put his hand on my head, and I felt his heat, radiating. He stroked the hair back away from my face, and the touch was soothing. Warm, like a bath. Soft. I sighed, leaned in further, and tried not to think about Mr. Baker.

CHAPTER 8

Daddy started bringing women home. I could hear them at night. Daddy made the same noise he made when he had me help him. It was kind of a relief; I didn't like helping him and his voice was always sad when he called me Lisa. Sometimes I heard them making noises like "oh, oh, oh!" at the same time. And there were bouncing sounds, like they were jumping on the bed.

Sometimes the women turned into girlfriends. They'd come over to hang out and stay overnight, bringing their kids with them, which could be fun, depending on the kid. One kid was especially *not* fun, because he was too little. The night he stayed over, I heard Daddy and the lady up after midnight laughing in the living room. Walky's Best bottles were clinking, and the smell of butt smoke and that other scent floated around the hallway and crept under my bedroom door. I woke up late the next day; it was almost lunchtime, and when I came out the girlfriend's kid was playing on the floor near the couch. The kid seemed happy to see me. Right next to it was a pile of poop and a pee puddle. I couldn't believe it.

I knocked on Daddy's bedroom door to tell him.

"Go away Krispy. My head is killing me. I need to sleep." His voice was blurry and sort of weak, like he was sick. Sicker than normal. I heard the woman's voice mumble something.

"I'm sorry Daddy, but it's almost lunch time and there's this baby out here, and you wouldn't believe..."

"Give it some crackers. I'll be out in a little while."

I could tell he meant it, and the girlfriend didn't seem to want to help, so I guessed it was up to me to figure it out. Her bag was on one of the kitchen chairs. It's rude to go through someone else's purse, but I didn't really have a choice. There was a diaper near the top. It was tempting to look further, but I forced myself to just grab the diaper and put the bag back down. I'd never changed a diaper before, so I unfolded it to figure out how it worked.

I got a few paper towels wet then pulled down the kid's pants to try to clean him up. I expected to find poop everywhere, but he must have been potty training and took off his own pants before going right there on the floor.

"I suppose I should tell you 'good job'?"

The kid giggled. When he smiled he was kind of cute. "Next time come get me and I'll help you use the toilet." He just giggled again, as I wrangled him into the clean diaper. I took him to the table and poured us some cereal. Luckily we had milk, and it even smelled okay.

The sun was shining and the adults were still sleeping, so I figured we might as well go out to play. I helped him get down the stairs and then walked to the back to get my bike. It was leaning against the big shed Daddy bought. He called it his man hut. It smelled weird once I got close to it, like chemicals and stink. That same smell he carried into the house. I pushed my bike out to the driveway and hopped on, then rode up and down the street. The kid ran along after me, his flip-flops flapping and sliding sideways, but staying on his feet. Daddy always said exercise was important for kids, and boy did that kid get some.

I rode by a doll which had been left in the road. It had a plastic head with a cloth body and was all bedraggled from the rain. I left it there and told the kid to leave it alone in case whoever lost it came looking for it. It felt weird to just leave it lying there in the street, naked and helpless, but it wasn't my doll and it seemed like taking it would be sort of like stealing.

When we passed the place across the street and one trailer up, I saw the lady with the blue scarf watching me again and looking peaceful. I smiled at her, but I doubt she saw peace on my face. Daddy was starting to scare me. He wasn't working on his poetry, and he was getting really skinny. He must be worrying about something, because I could hear him grinding his teeth at night which was a pretty horrible sound. I wondered what he could be worrying about, and wished I could fix it.

CHAPTER 9

Even before we were friends, I'd see JB walking up the road Saturday mornings with a fishing rod over one shoulder and a bag in the other hand. He'd come back down in the afternoon carrying a string full of fish. I decided to ask him about it. He'd just gotten home and was trying to hold a huge fish down on top of the big green transformer box in front of his trailer. The thing was flapping like crazy. I came down the porch steps and passed Daddy's man hut. He was in there with some friends. Music was playing and the air was full of stink.

The road doll had changed position and lost its head. A black pattern of tire tread ran across the cloth chest. The head was in a ditch on the other side of the road. I guess I should have rescued it when I had the chance.

JB saw me coming. He was holding the giant flopping thing down with his bad hand and pulling his hunting knife out of its holster with his good one. Offering to help seemed like the polite thing to do, but that thing had whiskers.

"What are you going to *do* with that?" I asked.

"Eat it. What do you think?"

"You can *eat* those things?"

"Sure! Haven't you ever had fish sticks?"

"Of course."

"Well, what do you think they're made of?"

That startled me. I never realized fish meant fish.

"Tuna too. Do you eat that?"

"Sometimes." I wasn't a huge fan. Tuna smelled. I watched him as he began working on the thing. He whacked it so it stopped wriggling, and then used the knife blade, cutting off the head and tail. My next-door cats circled JB, and he threw them the stuff he cut off. It was pretty gross.

"So, you eat fish," he said. "And fish looks like this before it ends up in a box or a can."

"Huh."

"The best part? Totally free. I just dig up some worms and head off to Buck Creek or the river and come home with free food."

That got my attention. With Daddy getting sicker, he sometimes forgot to grocery shop. He never had an appetite, so he probably didn't think about it. If I knew how to fish, I could bring food home myself.

By the time JB was done, he was left with a pile of pinky white sections of meat. They didn't look too bad.

"Will you teach me how to fish?"

"Sure. We can go tomorrow if you want."

"Okay."

Turned out JB was not just a good listener; he was also a good teacher. He showed me how to put a worm on the hook, impaling it a few times so it wouldn't get loose, but not killing it because the fish liked them alive. He showed me how to cast and tease the fish when you got a nibble. He taught me how to reel a fish in and be careful not to snap the line. He taught me how to pull the hook out of the fish's mouth. That part was hard.

We caught a bunch that first day. JB carried them home in an old five-gallon plastic bucket, half filled with river water. When we got back, he pulled up the stringer where three fish I'd caught were wriggling. His own fish were swimming around loose in the bucket. They seemed to like the extra room.

"Keep them cold and wet until you are ready to clean them."

"Okay." I took the stringer inside. I was hungry already and thinking about fish sticks. I carried them to the sink. Their gills were still moving. I looked at the worn scrub sponge in the sink and wondered which parts of the fish were dirty. I hadn't paid that much attention when JB was working on that big old catfish, and realized I'd better get another lesson. So I went back outside to ask him. He came right over, and walked me through it, step by step. Turns out you didn't have to wash them.

"Do you have oil for frying?"

"I think so."

"Best way to do it is dip them in milk, then roll them in cornmeal mixed with salt and pepper. Then just fry them in an iron skillet."

"How do you know when they're done?"

"They'll start falling apart. After you do it a while, you'll know to pull them out right before that happens. But for now, if you see one starting to come apart, you'll know it's ready."

We finished turning the fish into meat chunks, and JB went home.

I'm not a great cook. I'd only been able to use the stove for a year or so. The Crisco started smoking as little bits of crust fell off the fish and burned.

That's when Daddy came in the door.

"Jaysus H. Christ, Krispy! Are you burning the place down?" But I could tell he wasn't mad. He came over to see what I was doing and helped me finish up. We sat down to try it. Turns out it was good! Daddy even liked it. When he was done, he sat back in his chair and looked at me.

"That was delicious. You're turning into a regular little Suzanna homemaker." His eyes smiled at me in a way they hadn't in a long time. He almost looked the old Daddy. The one I missed. It made a ball form in my throat, like I wanted to cry. I wondered if I'd eaten a bone and it got stuck.

That night the air was cool. Daddy left the outside door open to let the breeze in and the fish stink out. He stayed in a good mood and seemed to feel better than normal. He told me stories about fishing with his granddaddy, and the different kinds of fish that lived in the ocean near his Aunt Hildy's house. Huge bugs attached themselves to the screen door, drawn by the light. Or maybe they were drawn by his voice.

When it was time for bed, I went to look at the bugs through the screen. From behind the protection of the door, I could examine their underbellies; places you don't get to see during the light of day. I felt sorry for them because I didn't think they'd like being seen that way.

CHAPTER 10

A few days later a big, bearded man banged on the door. I opened it and he said, "I'm here to take your shed." He gestured toward Daddy's man hut. Daddy had been getting mad about it for a few months because notices were left in the mailbox about payments. He wasn't home so I didn't know what to do. I couldn't stop the guy, but I wondered how he'd be able haul away something that big.

He walked over to the man hut's door.

"What about all his stuff in there?" I asked

The man tugged on the padlock, but it was clicked shut. "Ain't nothing I can do about that, honey. Got to take it this way."

"Daddy's going to be mad!"

"I can't help that. If he wants his stuff, he has to go to the office and pay what he owes."

The guy rolled a forklift off a big trailer attached to his truck. He jacked up the front of the hut and stuck the forky parts beneath it, then started backing the shed out to the street. It was a tight squeeze between the trailers, and a crowd gathered to watch. JB came over and sat with me on the steps. It felt good to have him there.

"I'd go gentle if I were you," Mr. Baker called from the back of the group. "That thing's a meth lab. No paycheck's worth getting your face blown off."

"What's that supposed to mean?" I asked JB.

"I'll explain it later," he said.

Daddy's friends yelled at the bearded guy and called him names. Some kids joined in, imitating them. I felt bad for the man. I wouldn't want that job.

After the truck pulled off and the crowd wandered away, I asked JB again. "What did he mean about the shed exploding?"

JB sighed, and his face looked like he didn't want to talk about it. But he did anyway. I didn't like what I heard, but it explained a lot.

When Daddy got home, he stomped around and talked about how much money he'd lost and yelled about why his boys didn't stop it when they knew, and ranted about blood-leaching-money-grubbers. His hands twitched and his skin looked extra pale. He even picked up a lamp and threw it, which was really scary. He hated violence. He'd see a woman with a black eye then shake his head and tell me to never settle for a man who hit me. Which seemed like a weird thing to say, because why would anyone do that? He'd say men who hit women were cowards, and that violence was for people who didn't have the vocabulary to work out their anger in healthy ways. So throwing the lamp was strange and scary, but maybe the meth had something to do with it.

Daddy finally sat down in his recliner and dropped his head in his hands. His shoulders were shaking. I went to give him a hug, and I kissed the top of his head. His curls smelled dirty and weird, with that pissy, chemical stink. I wanted to tell him to wash it but didn't think it was the right time. All I could do was hope it wouldn't explode.

He left a while later, and I made myself some mac and cheese. The kitchen clock kept ticking while I yawned and waited, but I didn't want to go to bed until he got home. When he finally walked in, he smelled all boozy. Not like the Walky's Best smell, but something different.

"Hey there, Krispy Kreme." He stumbled a bit on his way to the fridge, and his words were smeary again, and sad.

"Hi Daddy."

"Why are you still up?"

"I was waiting for you."

"Well, I'm here now. Go to sleep." He grabbed a cold one and headed toward his chair.

"Aren't you going to bed?"

"Nope. Just gonna sit here a while. You go on. And click off that light for me, will ya?"

I turned off the light and scooted, but didn't like leaving him alone. I listened for a while, to make sure he was okay. He didn't turn on the TV, and that was a worry. Just went back and forth to the fridge a few times, and that was also a worry. Eventually I went back out to check on him.

When he saw me coming, he said "Hey, Leesy Lou. C'mere." His voice had gotten even more mushy.

"Don't call me that." I didn't like it when he called me Mama's name. His getting sick was all her fault, and I didn't want to be associated with her.

"Okay, okay. I remember when you used to like it. Before you got so uptight."

I didn't know what he was talking about and just assumed it was the beer. Or the meth. But I went to him.

"You sure look pretty." I didn't know how he could know, because his eyes were barely open. "Oh, Leesy Lou, it was a shitty day."

I sat on the arm of his chair. "I'm sorry." He flopped his head over to rest against me.

"I sure have missed you." His thing started rising up the way it did. I sighed, but figured he didn't need that pain on top of everything else, and so moved down so I could help him. Afterward, he finally fell asleep, which was a relief. Sick people need sleep. He needed sleep.

I went to the bathroom to brush my teeth and pee. There was a circle of burn marks on the linoleum surrounding the toilet. They were brown against the dirty cream-colored surface, and looked like poop streaks. But I knew it wasn't poop, because I tried to clean them and they didn't come off. There were 15 marks tonight. Last week there were only 12.

There was too much to worry about for sleep, so I went outside and sat on the front steps. The sky was a deep blackish blue, and the stars were bright and numerous. They shined and blinked, and all of a sudden I saw a pattern. First, a big pot with a long handle like the one I made mac and cheese in. And then a little pot with an even longer curving handle, right across from it.

I couldn't believe no one had noticed them before. I decided not to tell anyone about them, not even Daddy. They'd be up there above everyone, floating secretly in plain sight, just for me.

CHAPTER 11

He kept getting sicker. Maybe it was AIDS. Kids in the neighborhood joked about people getting it from fudge packing. I didn't think Daddy ever worked in a chocolate factory, because he would have told me about something that awesome, so I figured you must be able to catch it other ways. I just hoped the meth helped.

He used to be handsome but had gotten really skinny and had sores on his face. His teeth were even falling out. I found one where he'd tossed it toward the bathroom wastebasket but missed. Grownups weren't supposed to lose teeth. Something was very wrong.

I didn't like him driving. He was twitchy and uncoordinated, and driving seemed dangerous. One morning when he was leaving the house to go see The Shyster he seemed especially clumsy.

"Can't you cancel the meeting, Daddy?"

"Not if you want me around the place, Krispy. I have to go."

"You seem kind of sick today. That's all. So, I was thinking maybe you shouldn't drive." Saying this last part was risky, because it could trigger him getting really mad.

He turned to look at me, but his face was sad rather than angry. "I've got to go." He grabbed the keys from their hook and started toward the door. "Besides. We're out of milk. I have to get milk for your infernal cereal consumption."

"I can do without cereal! We have bread, right?"

He just shook his head and stumbled over the threshold.

"Don't forget to check for turtles!" I couldn't stop him from going, but I could at least try to make sure he didn't crush a turtle. He'd never forgive himself for that.

The door closed behind him. I ran to the front window to watch him leave. The woman in the headscarf, across the street and one door up, was also looking at him from her window. It felt good to have company watching over him.

CHAPTER 12

He got home safe, but he forgot to get the milk.

Every day after that I'd rush down the hill from the school bus to check on him. Some days he was just knocked out on the couch. I'd try to get him to eat but he wasn't hungry. He stopped writing poems. The man hut stink was in the living room lots of mornings. I wondered if it was his sickness seeping out of his pores.

As he got sicker, his thing didn't seem to bother him as much, which was a relief. But I would have traded having to do it a million times over if he would just get better.

One Friday I went to hang out with JB after I'd checked on Daddy. Daddy seemed okay that day; he was watching TV when I came in after school. I made him some toast and left it with a cold one on the table next to his recliner. His wrist bones stuck out so hard and sharp they looked like they hurt. But his eyes were open, and he smiled when I brought the food.

JB was waiting out front on his bike. We decided to take a ride down the back road outside the trailer park and get some apples from the trees overhanging the fence a mile or so down. There was a lot of fruit that year. The boughs were low and heavy, and bees buzzed around the fallen fruit which collected beneath them and was starting to rot. My bike had a basket, so I loaded a bunch in there. JB brought an old grocery bag and filled it until it bulged. I should have brought a bag too. When we were done, we sat down some distance away from the trees and the bees.

"How was he today?" JB asked.

"Better, I think."

"Good." He nodded. "I was thinking about doing some fishing tomorrow. You in?"

"Sure! What time?"

"I'm going to go early so I can be there when the sun rises. You come when you're up and ready. I'll have your gear." He grabbed his backpack and pulled out two margarine tubs and two big spoons. "Help me find some bait."

I took a tub and spoon and started poking around in the dirt, wishing there was a way to know where the crawlers were so you could dig carefully around them. I hated cutting them in half. But there was no way to know, unless maybe you were a bird and could hear them. So I just dug around and hoped.

It was a good spot. We got a whole bunch. The fish would be happy.

When we were done, we wiped our hands and spoons on the grass, and loaded the tubs back in JBs pack. They were heavy with dirt and worms, and with the apples he was weighed down pretty good for the ride home. But he was strong, and never complained.

We got to my trailer and I pulled into the driveway. The car was there which meant Daddy was still home, and I was glad about that. He didn't leave a lot lately, but I still felt better when I knew he was home safe.

"See ya in the morning," JB said as he rolled away.

"See ya."

I went inside and made some soup for Daddy. He didn't want much, so I ate most of it, even though Daddy's stink turned my stomach.

CHAPTER 13

I was asleep when the storm hit. September wasn't normally a tornado month, but the wind whipped, and thunder cracked the sky open with sound and light, and cracked my ears into awakeness. I flew upright, my heart pumping, and ran out to the living room. Daddy was in his chair, in the dark, but he saw me coming.

"Leesy! C'mere." He held out his arms. I ran the rest of the way into them. "You are so beautiful. I swear, you look younger every day." His eyes were swimmy, trying to focus on me. "How do you do that?" He smelled awful. The beer, and the bleachy piss smell, and the rot of his teeth. He swung me up onto his lap and reached to touch my boob. Ever since they started growing they ached, and his hand hurt.

"Daddy."

"Are your boobs shrinking?" He giggled, but it didn't sound funny.

"Daddy!" I pushed his hand away.

"Why're you calling me that Leesy?"

"Why are *you* calling *me* that?" My heart was still pounding, first from the storm and now from this. But I needed him to know. "I'm not Mama. I'm Kristy." His face stayed fuzzy for a minute, but then his eyes went wide open and all his face parts tightened. I swear, it looked like they turned to stone.

"Krispy?"

"Yes, Daddy. It's me."

"Krispy? Dear God." He pushed me back off his lap.

"*Yes*, Daddy." I was getting irritated.

His face changed again then, turning from stone into something liquid, like melting wax maybe. He pulled me up against him, tucking me under his chin. "Dear God. Dear God, Krispy. I'm so sorry."

"It's okay Daddy." I needed him to pay attention to the storm.

"No. No it's not okay. It's *so* not okay."

I just sighed. I needed him to snap out of it, whatever this was. "Let's listen to the weather station. This storm is *bad*." But he didn't move or let go of me. I finally wriggled loose and went to turn on the radio myself. Lightning flashed and filled up the room as if it were daylight. By the light of it I could see him watching me. His face looked like he'd just run over a turtle or something. "Tomorrow I'm taking you to the doctor," I said. "Something's really wrong with you."

He laughed again, and this time it definitely didn't sound funny. It sounded like a laugh you'd hear in one of the scary movies Karen liked. He dropped his head into his hands and the laughter changed until it sounded like crying. Thunder boomed so loud I let out a shriek and ran to him.

"Get your shit together Daddy! I need you." I'd never said anything like that to him before. It felt good and seemed to do the trick. The crying turned into real laughter for a second. He raised his eyes to look at me and I've never seen a face that sad. Not when I had to tell him Mama left. Not when they took his man hut. Not even when he found his rabbit dead in the side yard. He looked at me with that saddest face ever. And then he nodded. Three times. And he held out his arms, and I climbed up in his lap again.

"Tell me about those tornado guys." I said.

"Who?"

"The ones in the Bible who got lifted up into the sky."

Lightning snapped and thunder boomed, and in the space that followed Daddy told me again about how everyone dies only at the time God ordains. That if it's your time and a tornado is there, then off you will go on the adventure of your life. His voice got high and scratchy a few times. He talked about what it would be like to be in the center, with all the energy and the stuff of life spinning around you.

I started to blink. It was late, and I was tired. The booms were still banging and the bolts of light flying, and the wind still shook the trailer. But I concentrated on his voice and the pattern of his words. Sometimes they sounded like his poetry. I blinked again, imagining Daddy and I in the center of that spinning funnel of energy. I blinked again and was asleep.

When I woke up, the storm was over, and I was in bed. Daddy must have carried me there, but I'd been too deeply asleep to know it. I stretched and tried to remember a dream about four-leaf clover, but it kept drifting away, so I thought about the day ahead. First, I'd grab something to eat and then go meet JB at the fishing hole. I wondered how fish reacted after a storm like that. Would it make them extra hungry? Or would they be scared and hiding out like I'd wanted to? When I got back with a bunch of fish, I'd talk to Daddy about making a doctor appointment. I sighed with satisfaction at the day. It felt like something had shifted. Like something new was beginning. Like the storm had knocked something loose.

I got into my fishing clothes and brushed my teeth, then headed to the kitchen to look for some food. I could see the top of Daddy's head resting against the back of his recliner. "Morning Daddy." I said it softly, in case he was still asleep. He didn't answer, so I got some cereal and poured it, real quietly. Sick people needed rest, and we'd been up late. I ate my cereal, washed out my bowl, and was ready to go.

I walked into the living room. The normal stink was strong, but there was also something else today. Something smelled really bad. I looked at Daddy.

There was puke all over his shirt. His skin was gray.

"Daddy?" I put my hands on his cheeks. They were cold. He didn't answer.

"Daddy..." I sank to the floor.

Of course he didn't answer. He couldn't.

I'm not sure how long I sat there. Maybe five minutes. Maybe five hours. Sometimes when you're crying the pain in your eyes, throat, and heart is so strong that it blocks out everything else. I cried so hard I threw up my cereal, and that added even more to the stink of the room. Eventually I wiped the tears and boogers off my face, then went to the phone and dialed. My hands were shaking.

"911. Do you need police, fire, or ambulance?" The woman's voice sounded calm.

"I… I don't really know."

"What is the nature of the emergency?"

"My Daddy. I think he's… dead."

"What's your name?"

"Kristy. Kristy Lamberton."

"What's your address, Kristy?"

I told her. She said they'd send someone right out and asked if there was anyone else in the house to stay with me. I told her no. She said if I needed her to call right back.

I sat on the floor across from Daddy, and waited. Then I scooted over to rest my head on his knee so he could touch my hair the way he always did, but he couldn't. His knee was bony against my temple.

The ambulance guys got there first, but it took twenty-five minutes. I knew because I watched the clock. They came in with a rush and a bang, pulling a rolling bed and moving immediately to where Daddy was still sitting. They apologized for taking so long.

"He's dead. You couldn't have stopped it. No one could," I told them. I thought about last night's storm. It wasn't fair. If it was his time, why couldn't he have been caught up in a tornado? And maybe taken me with him?

They looked at each other and then look around the room, and I saw a weird glass tube that looked burned on one end, and a bag of crystally stuff on the table next to him. They moved Daddy down to the ground and took out black paddles and put them on his chest and pressed a switch that made his whole body jump, and I wondered if that meant he was coming back to life. Then they pressed on his chest and breathed in his mouth, and I kept thinking how gross that would be with his teeth the way they were plus the puke. They did that for a while and then the police walked in.

The cops made me move to the bedroom and kept apologizing saying it took forever to get there because the storm knocked branches and whole trees into the roads. I didn't want to listen to their words or answer their questions. I wanted to listen to the ambulance guys in the living room. I wanted them to use the shock machine and jolt Daddy back to life, even though I knew it didn't seem possible. I'd seen dead things before. Dead birds. Daddy's rabbit. I knew that once you die, that's it. When God said it was time, it was time. But I still hoped in the electric magic of those paddles and wanted to listen.

After a few minutes, one of the cops went back out to the living room. I could hear the noises shift, and movement. Their voices trailed into silence which meant they'd gone out the door of the trailer. When one of the cops came back in, he told me he was sorry. He said they'd been too late.

But that wasn't news.

CHAPTER 14

The cops took me to a children's shelter. The people there were pretty nice, but I don't remember much about that whole stretch of time. It was like I was on vacation in some other universe, like there *had* been a tornado and it did carry me off, but I'd just been sleeping when it happened. The shelter smelled weird, like paper and old stew. Everything was clean and tidy, and I didn't know what to do with myself. They had some cool toys and nice ladies who kept trying to talk to me about Daddy and asking me to draw pictures. They had Disney movies on video. There were other kids, and most of them were quiet like me. I kept worrying about making a mistake, like maybe using the wrong kind of cup, or not brushing my teeth long enough.

But mostly I couldn't think about anything because I was too busy crying. My eyeballs burned like they were squirted with onion juice, but my heart hurt a whole lot worse.

After being there a few days, *she* showed up.

"Well just look at you. You're growing up," she said.

"Mama?" No one told me she was coming. I wasn't sure whether I should be mad or happy to see her. She looked mostly like she did when she left, though her hair was cut shorter, and she wore more makeup. Her clothes looked fancy, like she was someone from a magazine. I wasn't sure what to think.

"Come on. Get your stuff. Let's get out of here." She handed me a bag.

I didn't have stuff, other than the clothes, comb and toothbrush they'd given me. I went to the room my bed was in and gathered those things up in two seconds. The nice ladies were out in the common room when I returned. They hugged me goodbye and acted like I should be thrilled she was there.

"Where are we going?" I asked Mama as we went out the door.

"Back to New York. You'll be living with me now."

"But I don't want to."

"None of us have a choice about that, now do we. Your Daddy went and killed himself. Now he's burning in hell, and the rest of us will be living with the hell he left behind." Her statement shocked me. He hadn't killed himself. He'd just been really sick, and I hadn't gotten him to the doctor in time. But I knew better than contradict her. "I just hope it's a lesson to you about what happens to people who do drugs."

Her unfairness left me shook. He only took the meth because he was so sick.

"Let's go. We have to stop by the trailer to get some of your stuff." I was happy to hear that. I wanted my things. "We have to hurry, or we'll miss our plane. You haven't flown before, have you?"

I shook my head because I hadn't and didn't want to my first trip to be with her. My eyes teared up as I tossed my plastic bag into the back seat and got in the car.

She wouldn't let me get out when we got to the trailer. Just slammed the door and told me to stay put.

"I need my sneakers and my *Wrinkle in Time* from the living room and Daddy's poems from under my mattress."

"Let me worry about what you need."

She went in. The car smelled new and was super clean. I looked around hoping to see JB or Karen, but school hadn't gotten out yet and the street was empty.

It didn't take her long. She came back carrying a bulging black trash bag. She tossed the bag in the back seat and got in the car with a big sigh. "Well, that was unpleasant."

"I told you I could've gone in."

"No. That wouldn't have been appropriate." She looked at the clock. "Oh my gosh. We have to rush." She started the car and backed out of the driveway. As we started up the road, I saw the curtain draw back on the trailer across the street and one door up. The woman's face peered out, surrounded by a white so white it seemed to glow. She wasn't smiling this time though. Her face was still soft, but she looked really sad. Her eyes followed mine as we drove past. I lifted a hand to wave to her.

"Did you get my *Wrinkle in Time*?"

"What?"

"My book. It was on the shelf in the living room."

"No. I didn't know you wanted it."

"But I *told* you! How about the poems?"

"What poems?"

"*All* his poems! Under my mattress! I *told* you!"

Mama just shrugged. "We can get you more books."

"Turn the car around. We need to go back."

"There's not enough time. We'll miss our flight."

I cried and begged, but when Mama said no, she meant it. She just turned on the radio to block the sound of me. I turned my face to the window, mad at God for deciding Daddy's time was so early. Mad at Daddy for choosing her as my Mama. Mad at Mama for being so mean.

Eventually I stopped crying and watched the scene around me. The drive took a long time. We drove past the huge arch in St. Louis. I'd never been so far away from home before.

I never *felt* so far away from home before.

INTERMEZZO

Thayer was dead.

I hadn't *meant* to kill him.

Okay, fine. I meant to, but I stopped in time.

Didn't I?

PART TWO

PART TWO

CHAPTER 15

I dreamt of Daddy a lot that first year. In the dreams he looked like he did when I was little; handsome and strong. But dream Daddy didn't have any teeth. His smile was like a baby's, empty and pink. He was still Daddy though, so I looked forward to dreaming, and wished he could find a way to come back and rescue me from life with Mama.

Her house in Rochester was on two levels, split at the front door with a half set of stairs going downstairs and another half going up. It felt like a mansion compared to the trailer.

Everything was very clean. There were no piles of papers or books lying open on the couch. Shoes were kept hidden like secrets in bedroom closets. It smelled like lemon Pledge and air fresheners.

On my first day, Mama led me to the room which would be my bedroom. "You'll stay in here," she said. Her eyes showed she wasn't happy about it. "Steve insists." It was pretty. All the furniture matched, and the curtains were the same purple and yellow as the comforter, which went with the lilac walls. She put a hand up to stroke the drapery fabric. "I worked very hard on this room."

"It's nice."

"It was supposed to be for guests. Actually, it's *still* for guests, so you can't go messing it up with your toys." I didn't have any toys, so didn't think that would be a problem. "When we have visitors, you'll have to sleep downstairs."

I nodded quickly, eager for her to leave me alone. "Yes ma'am."

"Don't call me that. It makes me feel ancient."

"Yes ma…" I bit back the response which had come out of habit. She gave me an eye-rolly look, but left, which was a relief. I poked around, opening the dresser drawers (which were empty) and looking in the closet (which had her clothes hanging in it.) I saved the bookshelves for last, like dessert. And there, in the middle of the bottom shelf was a copy of *A Wrinkle in Time*. It felt like a miracle. It wasn't the same version as Daddy's, but it was better than nothing. I moved it to the bedside table, where it could keep me company at night.

My new life was different in every way. Daddy was gone, and even though at the end he was pretty messed up, I knew he loved me. Plus, JB seemed to like me a lot, and the lady in the scarf who used to watch me must have too. At Mama's no one loved me. I was nothing but a problem. Bombs seemed to be hidden under every conversation. Being the new kid sucked, but the school had activities at the end of the day, so I joined the page-turners club, the cooking club, and robotics so there'd be reasons to stay late. After dinner I went straight to my room.

For a while I called Mama Mother because Mama seemed too warm. But any word associated with being a mom seemed like a lie, so I started calling her Lisa which ended up sticking. She liked it because she could pretend she was my aunt or a nanny or some other poor sap stuck taking care of me.

My daydreams were filled with Daddy coming to get me, even though I knew he was dead. I'd seen the death with my own eyes and felt its coldness with my own hands. I imagined him reviving somehow; wanted to believe it was all faked, like something Lisa dreamt up to get revenge on him. Stealing me to hurt him. I wanted him to come, wrap me in my beautiful Strawberry Shortcake comforter, and take me home.

I knew he couldn't come for me, but still believed he might somehow come for me.

Death is weird that way. Weirdly hopeful. At least for a while.

Mama's husband Steve was pretty nice, which proved love is blind, at least to meanness. I needed someone in my camp, so I figured I'd better get on his good side. It didn't take long before I had my chance. She taught at the community college, and sometimes had to go to events at night. After she pulled out of the driveway one evening, I joined Steve in the living room. He was holding a book.

"Hi Steve."

"Hey." His smile made it seem safe to be there. "Want to join me for reading time?"

"Sure." A bunch of magazines were arranged on the coffee table. I picked one with a painting on the cover and sat down on the couch right next to him. He looked at me a little weird, but I ignored it. He wasn't used to having kids yet.

The article about the painting was full of pictures. It would be amazing to be able to create something that beautiful. The artist's name was Van Gogh, and I loved his painting of a night sky. It reminded me of the sky at the trailer park where there were so many stars. If you lay still and watched them, you could almost see the whole thing moving. Thinking about the Missouri sky made me sad. I put the magazine down, slid closer to Steve, and rested my head against his shoulder.

He looked up from his book.

I wondered if he would want to do the things Daddy did. Maybe it was something all men had to deal with, and if so, I was glad to be a girl. It was hard to picture Lisa being helpful if Steve's thing bothered him. She didn't care about anyone but herself.

"Do you need any help?" I asked. The thought of touching him made me feel gross, but it seemed like the best way to get him to like me.

"With what?"

"You know. With your thing." I pointed at it. "Does it bother you? Because I could help."

"*What?*" His face changed, and he looked at me like I was crazy. He jerked upright, tossed the book on the table, and walked a few feet away. "No, Kristy. I don't need any help." He left the room, shaking his head. That made me figure it wasn't a problem for all men. Maybe just some. Maybe just Daddy. Maybe it was part of his sickness.

There wasn't much reason to stay in the living room at that point, because my hope for getting Steve on my side hadn't worked. He seemed irritated at me now.

When Lisa got home, I heard them talking, then her stomping steps headed toward my door. She wasn't very big, but she sure made a lot of noise with her feet. The door slammed open and bounced off the wall, almost hitting her in the face. She looked super mad, and the door thing didn't help. Her face was red, and her lips were pulled together into a tight, ugly little rosebud.

"What the hell is wrong with you?" Her voice was a cross between a growl and a hiss.

"What did I do now?" My mind went through my list of chores. Dishes? Check. Table set for breakfast? Check. Backpack put away? Check.

Her expression shifted to show she thought I was full of crap. "What did you *do*?"

I just gave her an "I have no idea what you are talking about" face. Because I didn't.

"Steve. That's what." She crossed her arms over her chest and stuck her chin out like it could knock me down.

"Wasn't I supposed to read with him?" I knew she liked to keep the living room clean, but I hadn't messed it up. Maybe it was because of that book he'd left on the coffee table. I guessed I should have straightened it.

"*Reading?* Is that what you call it?"

Now I was just plain confused. What else *would* you call it?

She finally spelled it out. "You told him you would take care of his penis for him."

Her words were a shock. I thought you weren't supposed to talk about stuff like that. I don't think Daddy ever told his girlfriends. "Oh! That." A wave of shame hit me in my chest and crawled its way up into my face.

"Yes, *that!* What kind of a sick little bitch are you?" I knew she didn't like me, and she'd said some stuff before that wasn't very nice, but calling me a bitch was a new level altogether. Plus, she said I was sick. Was I? I didn't know how to answer. "Well?" she asked.

"I just thought he might need some help. Sometimes they hurt." I didn't want to talk to her about Daddy. I hated what she said about him, and if she found out what he did to me her words would likely get worse.

She laughed then, but it was more like a witchy cackle. "Listen, Kristina."

I pulled my eyebrows together to show I was listening.

"Don't you ever. Ever. *Eve*r think you need to be concerned with Steve's penis. You got that?"

I nodded fast.

"Don't you *ever* try to make another move like that. He's *my* husband! Got it?"

I nodded again, eager to have the awful conversation come to an end.

"I didn't hear you."

"Yes ma'am. He's your husband."

She stood staring at me for a minute which felt like ten, then shook her head and went back out the door, muttering. I heaved a huge sigh of relief, trying to shake off the tension. I'd made a pretty bad decision, obviously. I'd just have to find another way to get on Steve's good side. It's not like touching him was something I *wanted* to do. I saw how he looked at her when she was on one of her rants. Maybe we could team up for protection.

They were already at the table when I came down for breakfast the next day. "Good morning," I said, hoping to start things off the right way. Steve said hello, but Lisa just glared at me. I helped myself to some toast. The one good thing about being there was the food. Both of them cooked, and both of them were good at it.

"We've been thinking," Lisa said. "And we think you should call Steve 'Daddy'." I stopped chewing and stared at them. He was smiling in his gentle way. His eyes were kind, but Lisa's shot icicles. "We think it would help you remember the role he's playing in your life now," she continued.

I didn't know what she meant by that. For some crazy reason, he'd decided to marry her. Maybe he hated himself. He went to work and made delicious roast chicken and liked pulling weeds in the back garden. Those were his roles. What I *did* know was that he wasn't my Daddy. That was not his role.

"I can't." He was nice. I liked him. But he wasn't Daddy, and never would be.

"What do you mean you can't?"

"I can't call him that!" My chest felt like there were big rubber bands around it, tight and squeezing. It was hard to breathe.

Steve looked worried. "How about 'dad'," he asked. "Do you think you could manage that?"

Lisa whirled around to glare at him. She wasn't going to back down. "Okay," I finally said.

"Good!" Steve said, sounding all jolly like we were a happy family, and it was Christmas morning. "That settles it! A compromise."

Lisa made her eyes go all squinty and looked like she was going to start hissing. But Steve put his hand on her back, so she gave me a final glare and turned back to her breakfast. I finished my toast so Lisa wouldn't rage about wasting food, even though it felt like I'd never be hungry again.

When Lisa left us years before it had mostly been a relief, which made me realize she'd never been good at momming. My feelings toward her until Daddy died were pretty bland. I didn't like that she'd hurt him, but that was about it. After Daddy died, that all changed. If it weren't for her, he'd still be alive. If she'd taken care of him, if she'd done to him what he needed me to do, maybe he wouldn't have started taking meth and I'd be back home playing with Karen and fishing with JB. She didn't care about Daddy, and she didn't care about Steve. She only cared about herself.

I hated her.

CHAPTER 16

Daddy warned me about creepers who would tell you their puppy was missing and ask you to help find it. Then once you hopped in their van they'd take you away and you'd never come home again.

It felt like that was what happened to me, except death was the creeper and his van was the rental car Lisa drove to the airport. I'd feel him behind me and turn to look, and there was Daddy on the floor again, with the ambulance guys pushing on his chest. I'd be asleep and dreaming of my room with Daddy's clover fluttering around my head like tiny butterflies, and the door would open and the only thing outside it was darkness and emptiness and no Daddy.

The creeper liked to show up when I least expected it: at school, in the bathroom, or when I was watching cartoons. I never knew when he'd come, and he wouldn't leave until he made me cry.

CHAPTER 17

Lisa was still mad when school broke for summer vacation. It was going to be rough staying out of her hair for that long. Kids at school talked about the camps they were attending, but Steve and Lisa hadn't pick up on my hints, so I was surprised when Lisa waltzed into my room after the last day of school.

"Pack your stuff," she said. She was carrying a small black suitcase with wheels and sounded cheerful for a change.

"What? Where are we going?"

"Not we. You. You're going to visit your great aunt Hildy."

That shocked me. Daddy told me about his wacky aunt who encouraged him to write poetry. He'd visited her when he was a kid like me, and she'd taken him to the beach. She didn't have children of her own. He'd loved Hildy. It was a shock to think Lisa would actually let me see her.

I jumped off the bed where I'd been reading. "When do I leave?"

"Your plane takes off at 10:00 tomorrow morning. Figured you wouldn't get up to any good with school out of session, so I hunted her down and gave her a call." She pushed the black suitcase toward me. "You can use this."

"I wish I had my flowered suitcase."

"It would have been too small."

"Still. I wish you'd brought it for me."

Lisa flicked her head as if my wish was a mosquito buzzing near her ear and changed the subject. "Hildy didn't know your dad was dead. But she wants to see you."

That made me feel warm inside, for the first time in months. I got up and started stuffing clothes through an open gap in the zipper of the suitcase. Any place with anyone would be better than staying with Lisa. Being with someone who knew and loved Daddy would be fantastic.

"Slow down! I didn't buy you those things so you could treat them like trash. Fold them and put them in neatly."

"Yes ma'am. I mean Lisa." I plopped down on the floor next to the suitcase and unzipped it all the way around. It wasn't pretty like my old one, but the wheels made it kind of cool. I refolded the clothes and tucked them in carefully. Lisa was 99% mean, but she did buy me some really nice underwear. It had the days of the week printed on it.

"Don't forget your bras." She knew I hated the way the band dug into my back and the straps pulled at my shoulders. But my boobs were growing fast, and she liked me to keep them strapped down.

"I won't."

"Don't pack your toothbrush until tomorrow."

"Okay." I wanted her to leave so I could try to remember Daddy's stories about Aunt Hildy and swimming in the ocean. "What about a bathing suit?"

"She'll get you one."

I nodded, imagining what the sand would feel like squishing between my toes. Daddy said there were lobster pots washed up on the shore. It was strange that people would lose cooking pots while they were out in boats. Hopefully Aunt Hildy would explain it when I got there. I couldn't wait to smell the scent he'd described; a smell that was filled with salt and seaweed and a hint of fish and yet still smelled clean.

She finally stopped laser beaming my packing and headed toward the door. "Come downstairs when you're finished. Dinner's almost ready."

"Yes ma'am."

She sighed loudly.

"I mean, yes Lisa."

I was so excited I hardly slept that night, thinking of all the stories Daddy told me, and wondering what she looked like. Did she look like him? Would she look like me? Of course, she was old; she was Daddy's aunt. He said she was older than his parents, who died when he was in high school. It must run in our family to grow up without parents.

Maybe Lisa would die next.

Hildy had moved to Missouri to take care of Daddy until he graduated, and then went back to her house by the ocean. I couldn't wait to meet her.

Lisa lectured me on the drive to the airport about how to act and who to talk to and not talk to on the flight. She waited with me until the plane boarded and then gave me to a flight attendant who was a heck of a lot nicer than Lisa was. I got settled in my seat and watched the clouds once we were up high, trying not to act scared during the bumpy parts and the landing.

The flight attendant stood next to me once we got off the plane and walked through the tunnel to get inside the airport. But we didn't have to wait long. A roundish lady came barreling toward me, then bent down and swept me into a big hug. She smelled clean and the scent of coffee was on her breath. She was padded and even though the squeeze was tight, it was all softness and warmth. When she pulled back, I got to check her out. Her eyes were deep blue like mine, but her hair was thin and cut short like a cap. She looked at me and her face was sad and happy at the same time. Then she shook her head, slowly.

"My word. You are so very lovely." I smiled even harder. "Come along. Let's go find your bag." She reached for my hand. I didn't know I could smile that hard. Her hand was as warm as the rest of her, and the skin was like velvet. "Now what does it look like?"

On the drive to her house, I discovered she liked to talk. Her stories were full of unimportant details and would have been boring if her voice wasn't so soothing. Just ordinary stories about when she was in college and took tennis lessons, or what it was like the day she played in her first concert. But I thought they were wonderful.

Her house sat on the bank of the Merrimack River, and was full of antiques, ornate rugs, and musical instruments. Scattered here and there were pictures of a younger Hildy with another woman. "Who's that?" I asked, holding up one example.

"Her name was Keetah." She took the frame from me and ran her finger along the woman's cheek.

"Is she dead too?"

"Yes. She died three years ago. I still miss her every single day." I missed Daddy like that. She set the frame back down on the desk and looked at me. "Just one more reason your coming to visit is such a joy and a blessing."

That made me smile. Her expression was sad, but somehow still sprayed me with warmth. Her eyes reminded me of Daddy's. They had the ability to send out love.

"Now let us perambulate along the water."

"What's perambulate?"

"It means to walk. We need to sweep our hearts clean of sorrow and embrace our future. Together." She reached for my hand again. "Shall we?" We walked to the back door, arms swinging.

Our days were filled with adventure. Aunt Hildy was the oldest person I knew, but the most active. She loved the beach, and we went at least once a week, at times when not many people were there. We'd watch the sun rise over the horizon, and sort through the stuff that collected at the high-water line. She taught me about tides and the pull of the moon, and how to tsk tsk about litterbugs.

But that's not the only thing we did. Aunt Hildy played the cello, and we went to rehearsals and concerts, to the theater, book readings, and art shows. I loved it all. Especially the art shows.

On one walk along the river, we came across a man who sat on a little stool painting a picture of the bridge and a little island nearby it. Aunt Hildy knew him, and they chatted for a few minutes about the nature of the light that day, and the need to protect the plovers on

Plum Island. I couldn't stop looking at his painting. He'd captured the sun resting on the clouds so that the tops were white, but their undersides were gray. He'd included the wild roses growing along the bank. You could almost hear the bees in the picture buzzing along with the ones near us, hovering over the masses of pink. His paint smelled wonderfully of pine, licorice, and something oily.

I kept thinking about the painting on the walk home; how the waves on the water were sometimes little swirls, and the texture of the paint stood up, so you wanted to feel it. It reminded me of the day I'd made stars with the hotdog and ketchup. It made me think about that night being the first night of what happened in the dark with Daddy. I wondered what Aunt Hildy would think if I told her, and decided not to risk it.

"So, my Kristina. I take it you liked that painting," she said, bringing me back to the memory of the man and his easel.

"Yes! I wish I could paint like that!"

"Each painter has his own way of painting, just as each singer has his own voice. But you could paint your own way of seeing."

I thought about that for a minute, wondering what my way of seeing might be. "Why was he painting outside?" I asked.

"Because he has to *look*. He was trying to capture the essential elements of each thing in his view."

"What if what you're seeing is inside your head?"

"Then that is where you must look."

When we got back to the house, Aunt Hildy went in to get her purse and then took me to the art store. She bought a sketchbook and pencils, a watercolor kit, a few small canvases, and some acrylic paints. She said I could work my way up to oils. I didn't know what that meant, but it didn't matter, because I was in heaven.

The night before I left to go back to Lisa's we looked through photo albums. Aunt Hildy showed me a picture of Daddy when he was little, standing with his parents; my grandparents.

"She was my little sister. I miss her so much."

"Daddy's Mama?" Aunt Hildy nodded. "What happened to her? To them?"

"She had breast cancer. They discovered it too late."

"How about him?"

"He died in a car accident a few years later. Never got over her death. He turned to alcohol to soothe his sorrow and it ended up killing him. And then look what happened to your papa." She shook her head. "Addiction runs in this family." Her eyes were so sad it made my heart hurt. She turned to look at me. "But that is the end of that cycle, do you understand me, Kristina?" Her expression turned fierce. I'd never seen her look like that, but I wasn't scared. She wasn't mad at me. "You will *not*, under any circumstances, turn to substances when you are struggling. Am I making myself quite clear?"

Daddy drank Walky's Best and took meth when he struggled with being sick. I didn't want to end up dead like all those others. "Yes, Aunt Hildy. I won't turn to substances."

"Do you promise?"

"Cross my heart."

"All right then. We have an understanding." She went back to turning the pages of the photo album, and I snuggled into her soft side, listening to the story that went with each picture, in all its wonderfully boring detail.

I didn't want to go back there. To Rochester. To her. But Aunt Hildy said I needed to be with my mother, so we had a chance to heal our memories. I was quiet on the drive to the airport, and even quieter as we waited for my flight.

"You will come to me again next year. And we shall find a way to live our lives in the in-between times. Yes?" She held me by the shoulders and bent to look directly into my eyes.

"Yes ma'am."

"Yes. And we shall thrive because we know we have each other waiting at the end of a plane ride and will have much to share when we reunite. Yes?"

"Yes ma'am." I blinked to try and push the water back into my eyeballs.

"Yes. And you shall know how very dearly you are loved, and I shall know that you also love me."

I nodded. The love stuff wasn't making it any easier.

"Oh, my dear, dear child." She pulled me into her arms, wrapping me in her soft, scented warmth. I took a deep breath, determined to remember her smell and the feeling of that moment so when Lisa glared at me, I could call it up and wrap Aunt Hildy around me like a blanket. She released me, taking a deep breath and breathing it out again. "Enough with the maudlin, and on with the practical." She sat down in the chair beside me. "Lisa has never been an easy woman, and it's unlikely she's going to change any time soon. You are kind and obedient, so I don't need to counsel you about your behavior. But you'll need to develop an inner armor. You will find as you continue to mature that at the end of the day you are the only person upon whom you can fully rely. I hope you can learn to love your mother and I pray she can learn to love you. But during the time that takes, you need to be well girded."

I wasn't sure what girding meant, but I got most of the rest.

"How do I do that?"

"Prayer is one of the best ways. Remember that you now have two fathers in heaven. One the great and mighty creator of all that is, and the other the creator of the lovely and unrepeatable you. You can pray to both of them, remembering always that they love you."

I nodded. I'd gone to Sunday school with the other kids in the trailer park, but with Aunt Hildy I went to church, where there was incense and priests in long robes. They talked about our father in heaven in both places.

"Remember your heavenly mother as well, and turn to her when you are in need of consolation and succor." She meant Mary; baby Jesus' mother who the women at church prayed about with their long beads. Aunt Hildy handed me a blue velvet drawstring bag. I pulled it open to find a set of those beads and a tiny instruction book. "I should have taught you the rosary, but you can teach yourself. While you are away from me, and when you are in need, turn to this prayer. It will comfort you."

The announcement came for boarding my plane. I threw my arms around her. "Thank you, Aunt Hildy. I'll miss you so much."

"And I will miss you, Kristina. But we will be reunited in just nine months! And I shall telephone you. Now off you go."

I put my rosary and the booklet back in their pouch, put the pouch in my pocket, and moved toward the walkway. She was wiping her eyes when I turned to look back, but she waved at me with a smile, and love radiated from eyes like Daddy's.

CHAPTER 18

There was a surprise waiting for me once I got back to Lisa's house.

"This is Thayer. Your cousin." Lisa waved toward a tall teenager with blonde hair and muscles who stood next to the kitchen island.

"Hi," I said, feeling kind of shy.

"Hey, kid." He smiled at me. A real smile.

"How old are you?"

"17. You?"

"11."

"Huh. You look older."

Mama harrumphed and rolled her eyes. "She sure does," she said.

If *I* was 17, I'd run away and hitch a ride back to Aunt Hildy's.

"We've made a few changes while you were gone," Lisa continued. "Thayer's going to be staying with us for the school year."

"Doesn't your family want you either?" I asked.

"Kristy! That's very rude!"

Thayer didn't seem to mind. He just laughed. "It was partially that. They thought if I left town for a while things might settle down." I must have looked puzzled because he continued. "Someone tried to blame me for something I didn't do. I got framed."

"Oh. What was it?"

"Kristy!" Seemed like all Lisa wanted to do was yell my name that day. "Stop pestering him."

"Yes ma'am." I figured I could ask him more about it another time. Meanwhile, turned her attention back to him.

"You'll have to watch out for this one. She is precocious, and not in a good way. Let me know if she acts… inappropriately with you, okay?"

I had no idea what she was talking about, and Thayer just looked surprised.

With Thayer there, I was moved to the basement, which sounds worse than it was. It had been turned into a rec room and was all dark paneling and wood furniture, with a bar. It smelled vaguely of mildew and old beer, and I slept on a lumpy pullout couch. I liked it a lot better than the guest room because I didn't have to worry so much about messing anything up. Lisa hated it so she only came down when it was absolutely necessary. They kept all their guests upstairs, when they had any. I liked being kept company by Christmas decorations and the ghosts of old parties.

I liked being left alone.

CHAPTER 19

Thayer and I were in the backyard eating peanut butter sandwiches one weekend. The grass was soft beneath my hand; softer than it had been in Missouri, but still scattered with clover. I unfocused my gaze and let my brain do the searching while the blades tickled my palm.

"What are you doing?" he asked.

"Looking for four leaf clover!"

"Why?"

"I love them. Used to collect them."

"You do know four leaf clover are just genetic mutations, right?" I wasn't clear on what genetic mutations were, but it didn't sound flattering. I shrugged. "They're the fucked-up ones." He said. "Clover is supposed to have three leaves. The fact that there are four means they're mutants."

I scrunched my brow to think about it, then decided not to care. They were special. Different. Daddy always said different was better. "Anyone can be the same old, same old. It takes someone special to be different," he said.

"All the best people are mutants," I finally responded.

Thayer snorted. "If you say so."

Thayer was becoming my second-favorite human, but I wasn't going to let go of my love for four leaf clover. I wasn't sure I still wanted to collect them though. Without my book to keep them in, it just wouldn't be the same.

CHAPTER 20

The basement was always cool, so it wasn't the heat which kept me awake that night. Maybe it was the loneliness. Maybe having someone in the house who was friendly had me agitated. Whatever it was, sleep wouldn't come. Thayer's cracks about the clover made me sad, but I decided not to think about it. Instead, I thought about my collection back in Missouri, and how you had to turn the pages of *A Wrinkle in Time* carefully because the fluttering would puff the leaves out into the air. I remembered the copy in the guest bedroom and decided to go up and get it. Thayer would be asleep, so I'd have to sneak in.

Light glowed from the crack under the door. I considered turning around but figured he liked me so he probably wouldn't yell. I knocked really lightly, hoping Lisa wouldn't hear. It seemed unlikely because twin snores rattled down the hall from Steve and Lisa's room on the other side of the bathroom. First his deeper rumble, then her snortier version.

"Come in," Thayer said.

I pushed the door open. He was in bed with the TV turned on low. "I just came up to get a book," I said.

"Okay," he shrugged. "Come on in." I moved to the bookcases which framed the television, but could feel him watching me. "Can't sleep?" he asked.

"No."

"Me either."

I found the book and turned toward the door.

"What did you decide on?" I showed him the cover. "Hmm. Never read it."

"You should. It's good!"

"Let me see." I walked to the bed and handed him the book. He took it and read the text on the back cover. "Sounds interesting." He set the book down and looked at me. "Want to watch some TV?" He patted the bed.

"Sure." I climbed up next to him. He moved over a bit to make room. He'd mowed the lawn earlier and the green smell lingered on him. I breathed in, deep. The scent reminded me of home and of Daddy. *Thayer* somehow reminded me of Daddy, because he looked at me like he actually saw me, the way Daddy did. The thought made me cry.

"Hey, what's up? Why are you crying?" Thayer put his arms around me.

I wanted to be back there, back in our trailer. Back before Daddy started getting sick. Back when he used to brush my hair and write me poems. If I could be back there, I wouldn't even mind him coming to my bedroom and thinking I was Lisa. I stopped crying and snuggled in tighter against Thayer's grassy warmth. His arms felt strong, like Daddy's. I reached down for him, and when I touched it, his whole body stiffened. He pulled back to look at me.

"Kristy!"

I slid down to reach it better.

"Kristy, you're too little."

I grabbed it through his boxers. He groaned and it wasn't like Daddy's groan, but it was enough, so I kept going.

Once he felt better and was lying on the bed breathing heavy with his eyes closed, I got up and put my hand on his cheek. He wasn't Daddy. I missed Daddy. But he was my cousin and his penis seemed to cause the same trouble Daddy's had, and he smelled like grass, and for a minute it all didn't hurt quite so much.

A Wrinkle in Time was lying on the floor, and I took it back down to the basement with me. The sound of Lisa's and Steve's snores followed me down the stairs. I fell asleep with the book tucked under my pillow.

CHAPTER 21

Lisa liked to talk smack about Daddy. She'd look at me, shake her head, and talk about what hell must be like for him. I worried a lot about that. About hell.

"If he was so bad, why did you marry him?" I finally asked.

"Who said I married him?" She stopped peeling apples and raised her eyebrows at me. But at least she wasn't yelling.

"You never got married?" She shook her head. "But you had me."

"Marriage is not a requirement for impregnation," she said. She went back to peeling apples, then continued talking. "He was very handsome. And a bit of a badass. Plus, his voice was wonderful." She paused to look at me again. "You have his voice. Husky. Sexy." I was kind of shocked to have her use the word "wonderful" for anything having to do with me. "You look like him too." Mama had dark curly hair and curves, like me, but her eyes were brown and didn't sparkle or smile very much. Daddy had blonde hair and blue eyes, with dimples. Thayer looked a little like Daddy. I didn't think I did. But she was still talking. "I was going through a rebellious phase. I knew Mama and Pop wouldn't like him, which made him even sexier."

It was kind of fun to annoy Lisa, so I sort of understood that. "How did you meet him?" I asked

"I was in college. Washington University, in St. Louis. Economics major. I had a lot of dreams, but then you came along."

"Was he a student too?"

She laughed. "Hardly. The man had no aspirations. He was a bartender at the place we all hung out. I'd go there with my friends, and he'd write little poems on my cocktail napkins." Her face softened when she described it, and her voice trailed off. "But he never did anything with his life. I got pregnant with *you*, and dropped out of school when you were born, and we moved down to that little hellhole of a trailer park. I've never hated anywhere as much as I hated that place."

I never hated her as much as I hated anyone. That place was my home. "That's why you left?" I asked, hoping my anger would contaminate her like radiation.

She nodded. "That and a thousand other reasons." She piled sliced apples into the waiting pie crust.

"I didn't hate it there." She looked at me and I felt like one of the bugs the mean boys at the trailer park used to put under a magnifying glass until they started to smoke. "Sorry, but I didn't!"

She snorted and said "I'm sure you didn't. You're your Daddy's child, through and through." I nodded, happy to agree with her. For once. "I figured he'd straighten out after I left. For you. He loved you like crazy. Too much, maybe."

Not too much, I thought. Just the right amount.

"I was wrong about that though. Obviously." She put the pie in the oven. "Let me wash my hands and I'll show you something."

She took me to the living room and looked through the video tapes in a cabinet, then popped one in the player. There were a few segments on the video. The first was when Daddy was young. He was sitting on a stage in front of a microphone, reading his poems. It was wonderful to hear his voice again. She stopped that tape and put another one in. The next few clips were of Daddy playing with me when I was a baby, and then as a toddler.

"See how much he loved you? See how he took care of you? I knew you'd be okay."

I wasn't sure why she'd decided to tell me all this and show me the tape. It's not like I didn't understand why she loved him. He was wonderful. He was perfect.

It sounded like she felt guilty.

She *should* feel guilty.

Mama's leaving had ended up killing him.

CHAPTER 22

One good thing about living in New York State was that the storms weren't bad. Springtime in Missouri meant severe thunderstorms all the time, and you never knew when a tornado would spring loose.

Lisa and Steve were out at a work party one night when the first big storm I'd seen in Rochester broke out. It was the kind of storm where the lightning struck with an immediate bang, and the lights flickered out for a minute. Thayer and I were watching TV, but he said we should turn it off in case the lightening zapped it. I'd never heard of such a thing, and so I hurried to turn it off, wondering if the blast would travel back through the remote and hit me. I curled back under his arm, shivering.

"Hey... what's the matter?"

"I don't like storms."

"It's going to be alright."

"Where do we go if the siren goes off?"

"What siren?"

"The tornado siren."

"We don't have those here."

"Then how do you know if one is coming?" I sat up, nearly panicking. "I should go down and get my radio!"

"Wait, Kristy. You don't need the radio. We don't really get tornadoes here. Plus, we can turn on the stereo. Listen to some music."

"That won't get zapped?"

"Not like a television screen. It will be fine."

"Oh. Okay." I went to Steve's fancy stereo system and turned it on. I tuned it to a news station but couldn't tell if it was local.

"Come on back here." He held out his arms and I went and cuddled into their warmth. "Jeeze. Sometimes I forget how young you are."

"Let's talk about something," I said.

"What do you want to talk about?"

"I dunno. How about your school? Back home."

"School is school," Thayer said. "It sucks but you have to be there so you can eventually get out."

"How about your house? What is it like?"

"It's bigger than this one, and newer. Mom keeps it like a showplace which is a pain in the ass. Actually, *she's* a pain in the ass."

"I wonder if all mothers are?"

Thayer laughed. "Maybe."

"How about your dad?"

"Dad? He's not around much. He works a lot. He's Mr. Big Finance Guy, and wants me to follow in his footsteps."

"Are you going to?"

"I don't know yet."

"I'm going to be an artist."

"You are?"

"Yep. Probably a painter."

"Better plan on a side gig then."

"What does that mean?"

"It means if you want to eat, you'll need a way to make money."

"People will buy my pictures."

"Good luck with that."

I didn't like his negativity, but luckily the storm had calmed. "Think we can turn the TV back on?" I asked.

"Should be safe." He switched the set on and began flicking

through channels.

"Need any help with your thing?"

"Let's just say I had a *very* good afternoon. So, no thanks." He watched the screen for a minute. "Hey, how about this one?" It was an action movie with car chases and women showing off their boobs.

I shrugged. "Okay." It wasn't very interesting, but it took my mind off the dwindling sounds of thunder.

We went to bed before Lisa and Steve got home. For some reason I kept thinking about the woman who lived across the street and one door up at the trailer park. The one in the blue headscarf who used to watch me. I wondered if she missed me like I missed her.

CHAPTER 23

I decided to tell Thayer about the pots in the sky. They'd been my special thing, my secret. Daddy didn't even know about them. If I'd told him, we could have sat on the steps and looked at them together. He would have been so proud of me for discovering them.

That's one of the things you don't know about death until it comes; all the stuff you should have done. It piles up on your shoulders, heavy and invisible.

The air was cool and the sky full of stars when Thayer and I were on the back deck.

"Want to know a secret?" I asked.

"I guess that depends," he said. "Is it personal? Then no."

"It's not personal. It's… cosmic!" I'd heard the word on a television show and figured it was time to test it out.

"Cosmic? I guess you'd better tell me then."

"Look up there." I pointed into the starry sky. "Right there. Do you see it? The big pot?"

"Yeah. I see it."

"Now look over to the right. There's another one!"

"Of course there is. Ursa minor."

I had no idea why he was saying I was a minor. It had nothing to do with the stars. "But don't you think that's cool? Why aren't you excited?"

"Why should I be?"

"Because there are two pots made of stars!"

"Dippers. They're called dippers."

That stopped me in my tracks. "You mean you knew about them?"

"Everyone knows about them!" Thayer laughed, shaking his head. "You really did crawl out from under a rock, didn't you?"

I didn't have an answer for that, so I just sat there pouting, and missing JB. He would never make fun of me like that. I could feel Thayer watching me.

"Did you know there are more shapes up there?" He must have felt guilty for making fun of me because his voice changed to nice.

I kept up my pout, only harder to see if the niceness would increase.

"There are lots of them," he continued. "Look. I'll show you." He tapped under my chin. I reluctantly obeyed. "See those three bright stars?"

I tried to follow the path of his outstretched arm, straight off his pointed finger. "I think so."

"That's Orion's belt. He's a warrior."

"I don't see him."

"Let me go get something to write with. I'll draw him for you." He went in and returned with a pad of paper and a pencil, then looked up at the sky and started making points and connecting them with lines. When he was done, I could see the shape: shoulders, an arm raised high where he said Orion was holding a sword, and a shield in front. "The bright one is called Betelgeuse."

"Beetlejuice? Like the movie?"

"It's spelled different but sounds like that. Makes it easy to remember." His explanations reminded me a bit of Daddy's stories, though Thayer wasn't as good at telling them. "The dippers and Orion are called constellations," he said. He tried to point out a few more, but they were hard to see.

Later that week he brought home a stargazing handbook and gave it to me.

I loved that book. I loved him.

CHAPTER 24

Lisa and Steve went out again not long after that, so Thayer and I ate pizza in front of the TV. I took advantage of the chance to snuggle up against him, because Lisa would have a fit if she saw me getting too close. He smelled like the blue-striped soap from the shower.

It had been a hard day. Lisa made me wash all the glass in the French doors to the sunroom, and I hated that job. It was impossible to get the glass clear in all those corners, and she wouldn't let me stop until there were no streaks. But that wasn't the worst part. Each pane was like a mirror. My face was reflected, but it wasn't very clear so all I saw were Daddy's eyes peering back. My heart ached with missing him, but I couldn't cry because Lisa was behind me, dusting the spotless tables and mantle and if she heard me crying, she'd just tell me it was stupid to mourn a drug addict who didn't take care of me.

It was a relief to not have to hide from her after all that. I sighed with the freedom of it and snuggled in closer. Thayer wrapped his arm around my shoulder. His thing started pushing up against his pants, which was frustrating because the movie we were watching was good. I figured I might as well hurry up and get it over with so we could get back to the movie. His irritated him a lot more than Daddy's had. He needed help a couple times a week.

"Did you know there are other things you can do? Not just with your mouth?" Thayer said.

"I never really thought about it." Now that he mentioned it, I wondered about the noises I'd heard when Daddy had girlfriends over. That sound like they were jumping on the bed. "Do you mean my hands?" Maybe there was some sort of thing where he would bounce while I held it?

"Do you have your period yet?" I was speechless, because it wasn't something I'd talked about with anyone except girls at school. He must have thought I didn't understand, because he kept talking. "You know. When you bleed every month." Blood was rushing to my cheeks, but I couldn't come up with a response. "Lisa hasn't had the talk with you, obviously. And you don't have sex ed until next year. Haven't any of your friends started yet?"

"I'm still making friends." It was embarrassing to have to admit that I was still an outcast at school, but at least it was slightly off topic.

"It's related to the way women have babies," he said.

"It is?" This part was news to me.

Thayer laughed. "God, you are a savage." I just kept my head down and picked at my fingers. "So have you had one?"

"No! Never."

"Oh. Okay. Good."

You can say that again. I hoped it would never happen to me.

"Then let's give this a try." He rotated toward me and pushed me back on the couch.

Afterward, once the movie was over and I'd gone to bed, I thought about it. I was sore, and kind of pissed off because apparently doing it that way made you have a period. I didn't know what to do about that, so just stuffed some toilet paper in my underwear. It turned out to be enough, because I wasn't bleeding in the morning. Periods weren't that bad if they only lasted a few hours.

The best part was when he held me, and his breathing was soft against my ear. I didn't really like the kissing. His lips were wet, and he kept sticking his tongue in my mouth which was just gross. When he stuck his thing inside me also seemed kind of gross. He had to spit on it, and then spit on me, and it seemed like the whole business was about spit. Then he pushed in, and I thought I was going to rip in half.

He said it wouldn't always hurt, but I hoped next time we could just go back to using my mouth.

With more snuggling at the end. The snuggling was the only part I liked.

INTERMEZZO

The Little Guy picked up on my anxiety and started wailing as I fumbled him from one shaking arm to the other getting the keys out of my purse. "Shh…" I said. "We'll be in the car in a minute." He loved rides, though the drive to the police department would be quick. Too quick.

"Does he look like his father?" the short cop asked from where he stood leaning on my front bumper.

I pretended I didn't hear him. The baby's cry made good cover.

"Let's go, Detective Burke," the female officer said.

He didn't respond, just stared at me buckling the Little Guy in like I was equal parts disgusting and delicious. But he pulled his butt off my car and walked to where she stood waiting for him. They climbed in, backed out, and waited.

They were obviously going to follow us. I'd hoped they'd just meet me at the station because I needed time to think through how to handle questions about what happened in the hospital room. I pulled out and started down the street. The police car trailed accusingly behind.

The sound of the motor and hum of the wheels performed its usual magic, and the Little Guy was asleep before we'd gone very far.

I wasn't sure what to do. Tell them the truth?

PART THREE

PART THREE

CHAPTER 25

Forgetting chores was a bad idea in Lisa's house, so I was about to set the supper table when I heard Thayer's voice coming from the kitchen.

"You mean you didn't know?" he asked.

"It's been a long time. I just forgot," Lisa said.

"How could you forget? You gave birth to her."

"I know that. Don't be ridiculous." The last time Mama was around for my birthday was six years ago, so I hoped she might make an exception to her usual snottiness and be nice to me for the day. There'd been no celebration for my 11th birthday, because it didn't seem right to ask Mama for a cake so soon after Daddy's death. Now I was turning 12, which is kind of a big deal because it was my final year before becoming a teenager.

"Well, what are we going to do? We can't just ignore her birthday." My heart glowed a little bit. He'd remembered.

It had been such a relief when Lisa told me he wasn't going back home at the end of summer. She said something about "routine," and "better safe than sorry," and a few other phrases, but I thought she just liked having him around as much as I did.

"How about this," Mama said. "We'll tell her we'll celebrate this weekend."

"Fine. But I'm going to go get a cake." Keys jingled, so he must have taken them out of his pocket.

"There's no time. Dinner will be ready in five minutes."

"I don't care. You can either slow it down or put the food on the table and tell Kristy I'll be right back."

"All right," Mama sighed. "I'll stall as long as I can."

The door slammed, which made me smile because she hated when we didn't close doors carefully. I went into the kitchen to get the plates and silverware.

"There's the birthday girl."

I didn't bother playing along. "Want to guess how old I am?"

"Old enough to set the table. So go do it." She must have needed time to do the math.

Dinner was awkward, with Mama announcing to Steve that we'd have a real party on Saturday, and Steve trying to control his face, so the surprise wasn't too obvious. Thayer did a good job though. He got me an ice cream cake. Probably because there was a Baskin-Robbins just a few blocks away. I didn't care why. The cake was really good.

It tasted like love.

CHAPTER 26

Thayer was funny. He made jokes about Lisa behind her back, but when she was there, he acted all respectful and nice, giving her compliments about her hair or her dress. She slurped it up with a spoon; her cheeks turned pink, and she did this weird thing with her shoulders. She was a lot nicer to me with him around, but I knew I was his special girl. I kept watch for him if he had a girlfriend over while Mama was gone, hoping they'd help him with his thing so we could just be snuggle buddies.

Sometimes his sense of humor was directed my way though. "I'ma git sumpin to drank. Wuhnt anythang?" Thayer said, head wagging at me while he spoke.

"I didn't say it like that!"

"Yes you did. You sound like a hick."

Lisa made fun of me too. She was always complaining about something; my voice, my accent, my hair. She called me embarrassing.

"Do you want anything or not?" I asked.

"Yes. Bring me back a Coke."

I brought him his drink. "It's not my fault. That's just how people talked where I came from."

"Maybe so. But you can change it if you want."

I didn't want to sound like the people in Rochester; all rushed and squatty, with drawn out letter "A"s and weird word choices. The people I was used to sounded friendlier. But if Thayer didn't like it then I figured I shouldn't either. "How?" I asked.

"It's all about imitation. Pick someone whose voice you like and figure out how they say different words."

"Well, it sure ain't gonna be Mama."

"Isn't. Saying 'ain't' is the hallmark of a hillbilly."

"Isn't." I debated about asking him what greeting cards had to do with being a hillbilly, but figured he'd just laugh at me for not knowing.

Music awards were on that night, and when I heard Madonna's speech, I knew she was perfect. I tried to memorize her words, and then repeated what I could remember over and over again. "I have been so incredibly blessed this past year. And I have much to be thankful for. And I learned so much. I will never forget it. The experience." She sounded like the Queen of England, who no one could consider a hick. After practicing in the basement for a while, I started using Madonna-speak around the house and at school.

"Would you please hend me thet lest piece of toast?" I asked Thayer at breakfast. He made his eyebrows scrunchy at me, but gave me the toast. "Thenk you. So veddy much."

"Who'd you pick? Princess Diana?" he asked.

I scowled at him.

"You sound good, but you might want to dial it down a notch."

"If you think this is easy you are ehz crazy ehz a coon." I delivered the insult in Madonna-speak, and thought I sounded excellent.

"I guess we'll also have to work on the phrasing. Raccoon references aren't exactly mainstream."

I rolled my eyes and crunched my toast, then flounced off, deciding there were some days he was just impossible to please.

On days like that I really missed JB. He wouldn't make fun of me. He'd tell one of his crazy stories to distract me from being upset. But missing him didn't help, so I shoved the idea of his story telling away as something not safe to think about. Like Daddy's poems, and the clover, and my Strawberry Shortcake comforter.

CHAPTER 27

Thayer gave me the signal that night at dinner. We'd worked it out a few months before. When he wanted me to visit his room, he'd look down at his lap and make hubba-hubba eyebrows. Sometimes it was hard to stay awake that late, so Thayer bought me an alarm clock with a not-too-noisy beep which wouldn't wake up Lisa and Steve. I set the alarm for 1:00AM.

When I turned the corner upstairs, Lisa was coming out of Thayer's room. She had a strange smile on her face, like if she were a cat and just finished a bowl full of cream. Sort of sleepy and sort of happy and generally untrustworthy. But when she turned and saw me, her face went through a whole series of shifts. Her eyes went wide and then squinty and frowning.

"What are you doing up here?" she asked.

"What?" I'd been so busy thinking about her weird expression that I hadn't had a chance to come up with something.

Her face got meaner. "Why aren't you in bed?"

I glanced around the hallway, looking anywhere other than her eyes so she wouldn't see my lie hiding. My gaze landed on the light fixture in the ceiling.

"I was looking for you. I need a lightbulb."

"Since when do you need me to get a lightbulb for you? You know they're in the pantry."

"Yes ma'am. But I can't reach that shelf." I smiled with satisfaction at having one-upped her. She looked hard at me then, so I wiped the smile back off my face and tried to look sincere.

"Hmph. Come on then."

We went downstairs and into the kitchen. She opened the pantry door and reached for a pack of lightbulbs, looking at the shelf and back at me as she did, as if measuring the length of my arm. For once I was glad I was short for my age. She handed me a bulb.

"You could have used the stepstool."

I made my eyes go all big and surprised. "I never thought of that! Great idea!" She was looking at me too hard. It was time to get out of there. "Guess I'll just go put this in. Then I'd better get some shuteye." I punctuated this with a big yawn, hoping it sounded authentic. "Good night!" I took off but could feel her eyes on my back like two burning lasers.

In the safety of the basement, I swapped a random lightbulb in case Mama checked my trash and thought about the way she'd looked coming out of Thayer's door. What could possibly make her look that content"

I stopped Thayer on his way to breakfast the next morning.

"I'm sorry about last night." I whispered.

"What?"

"That I couldn't come help you."

"Oh. That's alright."

"Do you need me to meet you somewhere?"

"No. It's okay. I'm good."

That was a relief. I nodded, then decided to ask him about Lisa. "Did you get in trouble or something?"

He looked confused. "No. Why?"

"I saw Mama coming out of your room. That's why I couldn't come in. So, I wondered if maybe you were in trouble."

His face was pretty handsome, but for a minute, I didn't like the way it looked. For a minute his expression was a little too much like Lisa's. "I don't know what you're talking about," he said, and started heading toward the dining room.

I followed him. "Huh. I guess you must have been asleep." He didn't say anything. "I wonder what she was doing in there?"

"Maybe you should just mind your own business. Did you ever think of that?" His anger was strange, and it made me mad back. I gave him the silent treatment throughout breakfast.

It was hard to tell if he noticed.

CHAPTER 28

I went to Aunt Hildy's again the next summer. It was just as wonderful, but I missed Thayer something wicked. (Wicked was a word people in Merrivliet used when something was really good, or really strong, or really difficult. I liked it.)

While we were walking along the river, Aunt Hildy asked why I was talking so strangely, and I explained that I was trying to train the hillbilly out of my voice.

"Don't be silly. Your dialect is sweet. It's part of what makes you unique."

"Maybe, but I don't want to stand out."

"Perhaps you should try for a more cosmopolitan sound."

"What does that mean?"

"Cosmopolitan? It means you are comfortable with many cultures. Not stuck in any particular one."

That sounded good to me. Like what Madonna would be, with all her traveling and meeting fans from around the world, and staying in fancy hotels and eating strange foods. I nodded. "Cosmopolitan. That's me. So how do I sound like one?"

"In this case, cosmopolitan is a description rather than a thing. One becomes cosmopolitan, one does not become a cocktail."

"I'm confused."

"Part of it will come naturally. You bring a southern Midwest dialect with you, but you live amongst the speech of western New York, and you visit me here. People are natural mimics and pick up accents easily. You've already been practicing sounding British, obviously. Perhaps you can drop that and simply work on adding in a few Rochester and Merrivliet sounds into your own way of speaking."

The idea of getting to choose what you wanted to sound like was fascinating. If you could choose that, what else could you decide about yourself? How much of who you were was a matter of choice?

"All right then. I choose to be a cosmopolitan girl. A wicked cool cosmopolitan girl."

Aunt Hildy nodded, smiling. "That's the ticket."

"But I don't think I'll include a lot of Rochester. I don't like it there."

"I don't suppose you do."

I loved that she didn't make me hide how I felt about living with Lisa and Steve. She didn't make me pretend that uprooting my whole life was something I just had to shake off and move on from. She let me feel what I was feeling.

"I do love cousin Thayer though."

She tilted her head and looked at me closely. "You've mentioned him a few times."

"That's because he's awesome."

"You know how I feel about that word."

"Sorry."

"Something a bit more specific, please."

"He's... he pays attention to me."

"So, Thayer is attentive."

"Yes."

She was still watching me. A little too closely. It made me want to squirm. "What?" I finally blurted.

Aunt Hildy got quiet then. She pursed her lips before speaking again. "Has anyone spoken to you yet about relationships between men and women? About sex?"

I had no idea where this was coming from.

"Your father, before he died?"

That was a loaded question. "It's not something we talked about. But he had girlfriends, and I wasn't stupid."

"How about your mother?"

Her eyebrows shot up when I snorted in response. "The last thing she wants to talk about is sex. She turns the channel as anything racy comes on, and gives us all the death glare if someone tries to tell a dirty joke." I could see she wasn't happy that no one had explained the birds and the bees to me. "My friends talk about it a little."

"Well then, we can assume you know nothing. Or worse." She stopped at a bench and sat down.

"Plus, I'll have sex ed next year."

The tide was pushing water back up the river so fast you could see the edges creeping toward the high-water line. The air was filled with the scent of the brambly roses growing along the river path, and a tinge of sea salt and motor oil. I sat next to her. "You must be careful with this cousin. He is much older than you," she said.

"That's one of the things I like about him. Boys my age are so annoying."

"I'm quite sure they are. But that's not the point. They aren't the ones I'm worried about."

She was being very confusing. "Thayer loves me. He's not going to hurt me." What I did with Daddy had made me feel like my soul was bruise colored. But being with Thayer was different. He wasn't *that* much older than me. He wasn't my *father*. And I needed him.

"Since you've been taught nothing about sex, we'd better start at the beginning. Have you begun your menses?"

"My what?"

"Your menstrual cycle. Your period."

"Oh! I bled once. But it didn't last long."

"Just once? When was that?"

"Hmm. Maybe February?"

"Nothing since then?"

"No."

"Well that sometimes happens. It will return. Do you know what is happening with your body during menstruation?"

"I know it has something to do with babies, but that's it."

Aunt Hildy launched into one of her long speeches, but this time her voice didn't make me relax. This time she sounded like a teacher. She described the whole process and how it was a cycle that would take place every month. "I suppose we should get some supplies for when it comes back," she concluded.

I wasn't looking forward to that.

"Now that you understand how the female body works internally, we must move on to sexual relations." She launched back into her lecture, telling me some things I already knew, like about how penises fit into vaginas. She talked about getting pregnant, catching diseases, and emotional upheaval. She also said sex should be pleasurable.

This was kind of shocking. "You mean, for girls?"

"Of course. It should always be pleasurable. If it doesn't feel good, one or both of you is doing it wrong."

I stored the idea to think about later. "Did you ever have a husband?"

"No. I have never been sexually attracted to men."

I didn't know what that had to do with anything. "Then how do you know so much about sex?"

Aunt Hildy laughed. "It's a subject of endless fascination to humanity. And just because I wasn't attracted to men doesn't mean I didn't have a sex life. I'm a lesbian, Kristina. I love women, not men."

The pictures Hildy treasured finally made sense. "Oh! Keetah!"

"Yes. Keetah." Her eyes were sad. "But back to the subject at hand. Some men allow themselves to be driven by their bodies. Having a penis requires self-control, because it can be very demanding, particularly for young men. The drive to procreate is evolutionarily useful, but socially challenging."

I knew all about the demanding nature of the things, so I nodded, hoping she'd hurry up and finish. The conversation was getting awkward again.

"This cousin Thayer may have strong drives to release his sexual urges. You must be on guard. Just because he's family doesn't mean you're safe."

Family and safety had never been concepts I associated with each other. Until Hildy.

"If he makes any sexual advances, you must be firm with him and tell your mother. Immediately."

There was no way I could tell Lisa. She freaked out enough about Steve. But I couldn't think of a way to explain it all to Aunt Hildy. Obviously I was going to have to be careful with her. She'd helped explain why penises were so demanding, but she didn't seem to get how important it was to take care of them. She was a lesbian, so how *could* she understand?

"You're at a tender age, just blossoming," Aunt Hildy continued. "He might be attentive, but you should avoid being alone with him. You're a beautiful girl, and boys that age can be very selfish. Even when they're your cousins." It was nice to hear her say I was beautiful, but she loved me so much I didn't think she could be objective. "Are you listening to me?"

"Of course, Aunt Hildy! I always listen to you."

"You've gone uncharacteristically silent."

"I'm just thinking." It hurt to have to keep things from her; first what Daddy had done, and now the situation with Thayer. But it was for her own good. I didn't want her worrying about me because it wasn't *that* big a deal. I could handle it.

Maybe that's what growing up was all about; realizing you sometimes had to hide things from people you loved, for their own good.

"I suppose I *have* given you a lot to think about." Aunt Hildy stood up and stretched out her hand. "Shall we continue our walk?"

I jumped up and took her hand. "Let's shall!" I tested out the phrase. It was one of hers, and I figured it would work toward my becoming cosmopolitan.

Later that day we went to the drug store where she bought me an assortment of pads and a box of tampons, explaining how they were to be used.

It was a good thing she did; I started my period three weeks later.

CHAPTER 29

A year later I realized I was hot which was kind of irritating.

The first time I noticed, I was walking down the aisle of the bus to get off at school. A stream of kids headed out in front of me, and more flowed behind. When I glanced up toward the front, I saw the driver's eyes looking at me from the rearview mirror. He was an old guy, with thinning, greasy gray and black hair marked with lines from a comb. He had scars on his cheeks, the kind left by chicken pox or bad zits. His eyes were dark and intense, and he watched me walk up the whole way, not paying attention to any of the other kids. Not watching to see if they were up to something. Just watching me, with his eyes looking kind of hungry and kind of angry.

It felt like a challenge, so I held on to his gaze the whole walk down.

It made me feel weird and powerful to leave the bus without looking at him other than in the mirror. I could still feel his eyes though, watching as I walked into the building.

The second time happened the same year, at the fireman's carnival. The carnival was one of the best things about Rochester. I loved walking around watching the people and listening to the music competing from various rides. The smells were great too; Italian sausage with peppers and onions, the greasy sweet deliciousness of fried bread, and the soft melted sugar scent of cotton candy being spun, all undercut by petroleum fumes from the rides. I was walking along the midway with my friend Sarah when one of the carnies called me over. The sun was sinking, and we were going to have to leave soon because Lisa didn't let me stay out late.

The guy was in a shed with an overhang which made it even darker. It was the kind of game where you tossed rings over Coke bottles. Some of the attractions had lights all around them. This one didn't. I wasn't planning to play, but the prize was a giant stuffed teddy bear. The dude must have seen me eyeing them.

"Hey," he called again, looking straight at me. "C'mere."

I moved closer. Sarah moved with me.

"Yeah?"

"Meet me after closing and I'll give you one of those." He tilted his head toward the bears I'd been admiring. But his eyes were moving up and down my body.

"Hahaha." I choked out a fake laugh. He wasn't very old, but he was scrawny and with really bad teeth.

"Eww!" Sandra had a better handle on things than I did and pulled me away. I looked back and he was still watching me. "Gross," Sarah said.

"Gross!" I confirmed. "How weird was *that*?"

We didn't walk by his shed again, and left for home shortly after that. But I kept thinking about him. And about the bus driver. I kept feeling that power. I didn't know what to do with it, but I felt it.

And I kind of liked it.

CHAPTER 30

"Why do you talk like that?" Lisa started in on me right after I hung up the phone a few days later. She paid way too much attention to me, and her hatred seemed to expand by the week.

"What do you mean?"

"You sound like you're working one of those phone sex lines."

"I was talking to *Sarah*. And we weren't talking about sex, which you know, because you stood right there, listening."

She rolled her eyes toward the ceiling. "It's not the words. It's your voice." She dropped her tone and got all breathy. "Ooh, just tell me what you want, big guy."

"You're being totally ridiculous." She pissed me off so much. I'd worked hard on my grammar and speech, but there wasn't much I could do about my actual voice.

She hated my voice, and my eyes, and even my hair, which was odd because it was just like hers. After complaining about it being too long, she made an appointment at her salon, which turned out to be super fancy and smelled like chemicals and too much perfume. I'd never been to a place like it. Daddy and I just let our hair grow as long as it wanted to be. The plastic cape made me feel like an overgrown baby in a highchair.

The haircut guy started ruffling my curls around with his fingers. "Whoa! What a mane! Looks like it's been a while since you've had a cut. What's it going to be, princess?"

I figured it was going to be hair but shorter, so I wasn't sure how to answer. Lisa stepped in with a command.

"Chop it all off Edward."

He turned to look at her. "Are you sure? You don't want to leave some length for a ponytail? Most girls her age like it shoulder-length."

"Nope. All of it. Gone."

He turned back to look at me in the mirror. I just shrugged because:

A) I didn't really care

and

B) I didn't have a choice.

"If you say so," he said, and picked up the scissors. He gathered half my hair in one fist and hacked it off, then did the same with the other half. My remaining hair swung back to rest against my jaw. My head felt light. "Do you want to donate it?" he asked.

"Why not," Lisa said.

"Donate it for what?" I asked.

Edward explained about how your hair could be made into wigs if it was long enough, for people who go bald from cancer. I was glad Lisa said yes. He went back to snipping at my head.

"Shorter," Lisa said, after a few minutes.

"Pixie it is," he sighed and kept clipping.

When he was done, he squirted some goop in his hands and showed me how to tousle the top. He swooshed away the bib and brushed the loose hair off my neck.

"What do you think?" he asked. Lisa tipped her face out of her magazine to look at me. I peered at myself in the mirror. My eyes looked bigger and bluer. My lips looked even wider. It was as if the shorter my hair got, the bigger my facial features became. I liked it.

"Good God." Lisa didn't sound happy, which made me like it even more.

"She really is gorgeous, isn't she?" Edward sounded thrilled. "Some girls can't pull off really short hair, but this child…"

Lisa's sigh sounded like she dragged it up from her shoes. "Come on." She gestured to get moving. I stood up and followed as she walked to the girl manning the cash register. Edward followed us, acting kind of fluttery, like he knew she was pissed.

"You don't like it?" he asked.

"No. I don't."

"But she looks stunning!"

"Don't you have another client waiting?" Her eyes were in laser mode, and I was afraid she was going to slice his head off if he didn't shut up. He sputtered a bit more, then backed off and started sweeping the hair which had fallen like a circle of black snow around the chair. Lisa finished paying and headed toward the door. Even her feet sounded angry. As the door closed behind us, I could hear Edward's voice. "*That's* what she left for a tip? Bitch."

He was officially my hero.

Lisa never went with me after that. Edward greeted me like I was his favorite niece each time I came in over the next few years, and he gave me exactly the look I wanted. Once it was cut short on the sides and long on top and dyed pink. Another time I had him shave it all off, figuring it was time to try out bald. Sometimes I let it grow a bit longer. When I came home after a cut, Lisa would shake her head and raise her eyebrows, but not say a word. It seemed like she just gave up.

She didn't comment if I dressed goth, as long as my skirts weren't too short and my shirts weren't too tight, which was fine with me. I wore loose tee shirts featuring album cover art with torn black jeans, or kilts with black leggings. I realized later that the wackier I looked, the better she liked it. It was one of the rare things we agreed on. She said no makeup until I was 16, but that was fine too. The last thing I wanted was to look like her; a painted puppet.

CHAPTER 31

My favorite class was art, taught by Ms. Hyslip. She had a big smile full of crooked teeth, and dark wavy hair with strands of silver sparkling on one side. She dressed like a 1960s hippy chick in long patchwork skirts with chunky knit sweaters in the winter, or camisoles in the summer. I adored her.

Most of the kids in my art classes were there because they thought it would be an easy grade. There was a new batch of hopefuls each semester, but they found out fast she didn't work that way. We had regular homework—usually some sort of sketching in our sketchbooks—and she graded it. Some kids were super talented and made me feel lame. Others barely knew how to hold a pencil. But her grades weren't about beauty; they were about effort and thought.

When the bell rang, we'd stream toward our usual seats. She'd explain the project of the day, then turn on old rock music. We'd hum along while we painted or sculpted, entering into a quiet sort of group buzz. The room felt like a sacred place where nothing bad could happen. No one picked on each other in her class, despite the normal high school rivalries and caste system. It was strange and wonderful. I absorbed the peace and tried to carry it with me.

Ms. Hyslip taught us about light and seeing, and how art isn't about creating an exact replica. She said the artist's job was to capture what moved them. Sometimes that might be a realistic portrayal of a scene; the fruit and bread on a table, or the face of your table partner with all its zits and angles. But sometimes it might be the way the sun shines through the spaces between grapes, creating a pattern of light and shadow on the tablecloth. The pattern might be the most important thing about the scene for you at that moment, and might speak to you about the nature of the universe with all its chances for light to streak in. Or maybe your tablemate's eyes are what jump out. Maybe they look so profoundly sad that the rest of his face doesn't matter, but you can't paint that because he'd see it and know you knew. And so, you paint everything *except* his eyes, figuring that his wondering was better than his knowing. You go home and open your sketchbook that night and capture those eyes without the rest of his face, eyes so tired, dark, and filled with wordless pain they would drown you if you didn't get them out on to paper.

That particular drawing wasn't for an assignment. But when I turned in my sketchbook Ms. Hyslip gave me a 10/10 on it as extra credit. So you can see why I liked her.

Toward the middle of my junior year, she invited a few of us to a ceramics show at one of the galleries on South Avenue. I took a city bus to get to it. She greeted me with a big hug and introduced me to her husband, who looked like an accountant or a lawyer. I'd imagined him being funky like her, maybe sitting on a stool in the corner playing guitar for the gallery guests. But he was all business-suited up with short hair, greeting people with a firm handshake.

Ms. Hyslip handed me a program and pointed out the various sections of the show, then walked me to the refreshment tables. "Here you go," she said, handing me a chunky gray cup full of sparkling cider. "Take the cup with you when you leave," she said. They're thank you gifts for attending." We talked for a few minutes about the brown and gray glazing, and how glaze changes color when it's fired. Then a few new people arrived, and she went to greet them.

I walked around looking at the displays and sipping. When it was gone, I cushioned the cup with some paper towels from the bathroom and nestled it safely in my bag. Ms. Hyslip hugged me again when I said goodbye. Her embrace was warm, and she smelled of wine and something spicy. She held on a long time and I leaned into it. Hugs from women were rare to me, and wonderful.

I washed the cup when I got home, and put it on the desk in my room, knowing Lisa wouldn't want it with her collection upstairs. Besides, I liked having it close. The curving gray lines and flicks of brown glaze were like the touches of bird wings and reminded me of the pleasure of her hug.

CHAPTER 32

Thayer picked me up from school on his motorcycle when he was between girlfriends. I'd hear it coming long before it got there, the throaty hum growing louder until eventually he roared to a stop at the end of the sidewalk, right next to the art room windows where I waited at the end of the day. I loved grabbing the helmet and buckling it under my chin, loved hopping on behind him and driving off, feeling his warmth against my thighs and the rumble of the motor between my legs. He said I was a good rider.

Ms. Hyslip stopped me as I was getting ready to leave the room after art class one morning. "Hey Kristy, can you stay for a minute?"

"Sure." I turned back and watched as she organized papers on her desk until the last kid was gone.

She opened a desk drawer and pulled out a big floppy purse. "Let's go."

"Go? Where?"

"It's a surprise. Come on."

"But I have class."

She stopped moving to look at me. "Are you telling me you've never skipped before?"

I shook my head. "Nope. Never."

"Well then, it's high time you did. Let's *go*."

I shrugged and followed. "If you say so!"

She laughed, and we walked down the hall and out the rear exit as if it was normal. She pointed me to a beat-up convertible MG, and we climbed in. The sun was shining. It was hot enough that you could smell the blacktop, but not so hot you felt your brain baking. Perfect weather for a drive with the top down. She drove across town to a frozen custard stand. I stood staring at the menu.

"Have you been here before?" she asked. I shook my head. "She'll have a medium chocolate almond in a waffle cone," Ms. Hyslip said to the man behind the counter, then turned back to me. "Trust me," she said.

We got our cones and sat at a picnic table. The ice cream was creamier than anything I'd ever tasted, and the almonds added crunch and a bit of salt which cut the sweetness. "This is amazing," I said.

"Told you."

We ate ice cream and listened to the whispering maple trees above us. "So *this* is what skipping school is about? I always imagined there'd be beer."

Ms. Hyslip laughed. "Actually, I want to talk to you about something."

That didn't bode well. I decided to go with non-committal. "Okay?"

"It's Thayer."

"You know him?"

"He was in one of my classes a few years ago."

"Huh! I didn't know he liked art."

"He didn't."

"Well, what about him?" Another car drove up which gave me something to look at because I didn't like how she was trying to read my eyes.

She took a bite of her cone and crunched it while watching me. "You need to be careful."

"What are you talking about? He's my cousin!" The objection flowed naturally despite my disingenuity.

She raised her eyebrows and said, "I know."

I looked away again and slurped the pool of melted custard from the tip of my cone. If she thought sex with a cousin was bad, how would she react to hearing what happened with my dad?

"I saw him in action," she said. "He's quite a player. Did you know that?"

I let my expression answer for me.

"I didn't like how he treated girls. He was rude and inappropriate. Sometimes good-looking guys think they can get away with anything. He knows how to turn on the charm, which might have worked with some of his teachers. But it didn't work with me."

I just sighed in response and rolled the remainder of my cone in a napkin.

"I see how he looks at you when he picks you up after school. I know that look, and it's not very cousinly." That stopped me in my tracks. How did he look at me? She answered as if she'd heard my thought. "It was the same look he gave girls in class before making his move. They'd flutter and purr and go out with him for a few weeks, and then he'd dump them. They were always heartbroken too, which makes no sense. He's not a nice guy." I wasn't thrilled that he gave the same look to other girls, but figured he had to fake it, so they'd think he really did like them. Having girlfriends was key to keeping Lisa from getting nervous. "One of them got pregnant, Kristy. She came to me for advice and ended up having an abortion. It was really rough for her."

My head whipped around to face her. "When was that?"

"Maybe January of that year? I remember it was snowy."

I couldn't believe he hadn't told me about it. I thought he told me everything. "Maybe it wasn't his," I said.

"He was her first boyfriend. Her family is very religious, and she wasn't allowed to date. They were planning an arranged marriage once she finished school."

"What does any of this have to do with me?"

"You need to be careful."

"You already said that."

Ms. Hyslip sighed. Heavily. "I saw how he was with pretty girls, and you're in a league of your own when it comes to looks. You're going to have to deal with a lot of men who want to get you in bed."

"That's nothing new. I've been dealing with it for years."

She looked at me with sad eyes. "I'm sure you have."

I just shook my head. "It's no big deal."

"Sexual harassment *is* a big deal. If you don't learn how to handle it now, it will just follow you into jobs later and create all sorts of problems. So, I'm going to teach you a few things. First, for the guys who tell you that if you smile you'll look prettier, or the ones who talk to your breasts. Learn to flash them the death glare once they look at your face. And don't look away first. Stare them down. Practice looking fierce, like you're fully prepared to rip their balls off."

I huffed in surprise; she'd said "balls".

"That will take care of a lot of them. But you should also carry a can of mace." She reached in her big bag and handed me a small black canister. "You can use it if someone physically assaults you, but it's also useful if a guy won't back off verbally. Just pull out the can and point it at him. He'll get the idea fast." I hadn't liked her talking about Thayer, but this advice was pretty useful. "But all that is off the subject. Sort of. Because I really wanted to talk to you about Thayer. Be careful of him, Kristy."

"That's the third time you've said that. I get it!"

She looked at me. Hard. "Do you?"

Now it was my turn to sigh.

"It's the way you look at *him* that scares me. You look at him just like the girls in class did. Just like that poor girl who got pregnant. I don't want to see you having to go through that kind of pain and chaos."

"Like I said. He's my *cousin*." I wished there was some other objection, because saying the word was super uncomfortable.

"Good try, but I know that doesn't mean shit."

First balls, now shit. Ice cream apparently had a strange effect on Ms. Hyslip. I had to figure out a way to get her off the trail, so I made my face go all sincere and concerned, then started nodding.

"I guess you've given me a lot to think about. I'll be careful."

She didn't say anything in response. Just kept looking at me in a way that made me feel naked. She finally pursed her lips and nodded twice.

"Okay!" She jumped up from the table and tossed her chocolate-smeared napkins into a trashcan. "Done with the tough conversation, it's time for some fun. I don't have class until 1:00. Let's go for a joyride." She walked over to the car and opened her door. "Come on!"

I threw away my own napkins and climbed in. She drove us out into the countryside, down back roads where rows of corn were shin high and the air smelled like clean dirt. The roads were empty, and she drove fast with the wind whipping our hair around our ears. She put on sunglasses, and we joked about the lateness of the birds we saw pecking for worms in the fields, laughing above the sound of the wind.

CHAPTER 33

My teen years were a cycle. School years with Thayer, summers with Aunt Hildy. Each season had its comforts and its horrors. At home there were happy stolen moments with Thayer, but the torture of Lisa. In Merrivliet there was the pleasure of time with Aunt Hildy and seaside life, but the gnawing absence of Thayer. And of course, the hole that was Daddy lurked underneath it all. Throughout all that, I learned to co-exist with longing. And I got good at hiding.

Thayer was my hidden secret. The secret which was added upon the earlier secret.

He taught me about life, and how to handle Lisa, and what the golfers talked about. He taught me about birth control and took me to a clinic to get pills. He even taught me about sexual pleasure, eventually. Maybe he was bored, or just feeling charitable that day, because when we were done with him, he reached out and touched me. What had been just a suggestion of an itch turned into a swelling ache of hunger which grew so huge that it eventually exploded. Afterward he watched me panting. He wore his "master of the universe" smile. I hated that smile.

The experience changed everything. When we started to fool around, the slow burn began, and the itch grew and I learned how to push and wriggle so that it wasn't just him who got relief. He liked to brag about how good he must be because I could come every time.

He still had girlfriends, of course. Lisa would have suspected something if he hadn't. I understood how things needed to work, and that was okay. I'd always be his number one. I just asked that he use condoms when he was with them. I didn't want to catch anything.

I didn't have any boyfriends, though. Thayer wouldn't have liked it, and no-one could compare to him anyway. It would be like dating a kid. Guys asked me out a lot, and a few were friends, but that was it. I made up stories about becoming a nun. That generally shut them up.

Thayer and Aunt Hildy were my anchors through those years. They were totally different and provided opposite forms of safety and comfort. That's how I stayed balanced: her protective and encouraging guidance; his physical warmth and the sound of his groans in my hair.

When he left for college, I lost half my ballast. Thayer finished high school the spring of the year I began ninth grade, so we never overlapped. His gap year working at the golf course delayed the inevitable, but his parents threatened not to pay his way if he didn't enroll somewhere, and that pushed him into motion. He applied a few places and decided to follow in his father's footsteps by going into a business program close to home at UB. Buffalo was only a little over an hour away, but it meant I only saw him a few times a year. He'd come stay sometimes on school breaks, but during the summers I was in Merrivliet. He was terrible about communicating. I'd write him letter after letter and get a postcard or two in return. And he didn't want to say much in email because anyone could get access. He didn't trust me to be careful.

When I finally did see him, it was like I was on fire, and he was too. My body would droop like a plant that hadn't been watered, then he'd show up and all of a sudden, every part of me was alert and tingling. We'd go somewhere; out to a park where he'd throw down a blanket, or just in a dark parking lot, and I'd swarm over him like I was an army of ants, and he was a hunk of melon dropped at a picnic.

By that time, of course, I knew it wasn't right. Not just because of what Ms. Hyslip had said; I was old enough to realize Thayer could be a real dick. Plus he was my first cousin, which a lot of people considered twisted. But it didn't bother me enough to stop it. Apparently I was addicted. Daddy's little girl after all.

CHAPTER 34

I couldn't wait to graduate so I could move to Buffalo. Not only would I be out of Lisa's talons, but I'd also be near Thayer. Lisa said painting wasn't a career, so I got her to leave me alone by talking about becoming an art teacher.

When we got home from commencement there was a small silver car in the driveway.

"Who do you think that is?" Lisa asked. Steve didn't respond, he just pulled up beside the car and got out. Lisa and I followed. I headed toward the house. It was strange that no one was in the vehicle or at our door, but it was too hot for pantyhose and the car didn't belong to any of my friends.

"Wait, Kris," Steve said.

I turned back. Steve tossed something to me. It was a set of keys. Lisa looked puzzled, which was never a good thing. Confusion made her mad. "What?" She said.

I looked at Steve. He was smiling.

"Are you serious?" I asked. Aunt Hildy taught me to drive. I didn't get much chance to practice when I was at Lisa's because she didn't want me using their matching Lexuses. Hildy said she'd match however much money I saved so I could buy a car when I was ready to leave for college. I'd gotten a job at an ice cream shop during my junior year, and saved enough to be ready. I knew I could only afford a junker, but that was okay.

He nodded, still smiling. "Come see."

I ran to the car, climbed in, and started touching things. "Oh my God! I can't believe it!"

"Steve?" Lisa said. "You didn't."

"She deserves it. She's a good kid."

"You don't think this is something we should've talked about?" Her voice had that low, simmering anger that scared me more than any of her other kinds of irritated. Steve was in serious trouble.

"I knew what you'd think. Initially. And I knew you'd realize it was the right thing to do. So…"

"So you bought her a car." She pivoted and walked toward the house. Her spine was very, very straight as if she'd begun petrifying from the inside out.

"It's used!" Steve tried to explain.

She turned to look at us when she reached the door. I was afraid she'd say more, but she just went into the house and closed the door behind her.

Steve looked at me and made an exaggerated "yikes" face. He was trying to be funny, but we both knew an angry Lisa was no laughing matter. "Congratulations on graduating! And thanks for being such a great stepdaughter," he said. "Daughter," he amended. I smiled back at him. I was probably glowing.

"I can't believe it! This is so much nicer than I could have afforded."

"I couldn't let you go off to school driving something that might break down and leave you on the side of the road. This baby is just five years old, and reliable as a tractor. You take good care of her and she'll take good care of you."

I kept looking around the interior, turning on the lights and the radio, opening the glove box, checking out the cup holders. "I love it!" I jumped back out of the car to give him a hug, but stepped back fast because Lisa was peeking from the living room window.

"Aren't you going to take her for a ride?"

"Yes! Want to come?"

"I'd better not. I'm already in enough trouble."

"Yes, you are. Thank you so much, Dad! I'll be back." I got in the car, started it up, and pulled out of the driveway. It seemed incredible that the car was mine. I headed out to the farmlands where Ms. Hyslip drove when we skipped school, and passed the same corn fields. The stalks were high and swollen with ears. I opened all the windows and let the wind and the scents blow through. It wasn't quite the same as a convertible, but it was still pretty good.

The house was iceberg silent when I got back, so Lisa must have finished ripping Steve a new one during my drive. She wasn't done with me though.

"I guess you got what you wanted." She snuck up on me while I was doing laundry. The sound of the water filling the washing machine drowned out the slithering sound she usually made. I jumped, which I'm sure she enjoyed. "How'd you get him to do that?" Her eyes were all slitty and dangerous.

"I didn't get him to do anything! I was as surprised as you were."

She snorted and tossed her head, morphing from python to dragon. "Sure you didn't. Haven't changed, have you? Little hussy. Going after other women's husbands."

That was totally unfair. I hadn't gone after anyone's husband. There was the one time with Steve, but he'd shut that down and I was glad he did.

"I'm not after Steve. He's all yours."

"He's not good enough for you now?"

"I didn't say that! He's a great guy! He just gave me a car! You're super lucky to have him." The bitch was lucky anyone put up with her. I didn't say that part, but it was like her kind of dragon had mind-reading powers. She crossed her arms and clamped her jaw so tight it looked like it hurt. I suddenly had an inspiration. "Look. How about I give you the money I saved to buy one." The look in her eyes shifted from pure malice to calculation. I walked from the laundry section of the basement to my dresser in the opposite corner and pulled an envelope out of the top drawer. I took it to her.

"Here. There's almost two grand in there." She looked surprised I'd saved that much. She rifled through the bills. "I'm sure it's a lot less than the car cost, but it's all I've got."

She closed the envelope and slapped it against her palm, staring at me. I squirmed, feeling like one of those mice they sell at reptile stores. Or a feeble-minded villager too stupid to run even though the sulfurous breath of the dragon is singeing his beard.

"Okay," she said. "But not a word to Steve."

I shook my head. "Of course not."

"And if I ever. Ever. Catch you with him."

"You won't! God!"

"Don't take the Lord's name in vain." Her saying that was a relief. It meant she was simmering down to her normal level of bitchiness.

"Sorry. 'Gosh.'" She was still watching me though. "Can I finish my laundry now?"

"Drop the attitude. Would you like to be grounded for the week? Miss all the graduation parties?"

"No Ma'am. I'm sorry ma'am." My early training asserted itself when I was nervous. "I mean, Lisa."

"That's better." She started up the stairs. "And remember. Not a word."

I didn't respond. I was just glad she was leaving.

CHAPTER 35

College couldn't start fast enough. Steve offered to help move me into the dorm, but I said I could handle it, and so I packed up all my stuff in my Honda and drove off on move-in day. It was still dark when I left, and way too early because I hadn't been able to sleep. Lisa and Steve were still snoring, so I just left a note to say goodbye.

Thayer came to the parking lot to hang out with me while we waited for registration to open. We had a reunion quickie out there, because his dormmate was in his room and Thayer didn't want him talking. It was so good to be with him.

The campus came alive around 7:30, with volunteers directing students. I checked in, got my keys, and Thayer and I carried all my stuff in. My roommates hadn't arrived yet, so I had first dibs on beds and desks. I flopped down on a bare mattress with a big sigh of happiness. "I can't believe I'm finally here."

"I can't either. Welcome to Buff U." He checked his phone. "I've got to go."

"Already?"

"I've got a thing."

"Okay. Can I have a kiss?" I hopped up, thrilled that I now lived so close to him, thrilled that we were alone. Thrilled that I could have his kisses.

"Sure." He gave me a quick peck. "But things won't be much different here. We still have to be a secret."

I'd thought we could just pretend to not be cousins. "Why?" I asked.

"Don't be stupid. Someone could find out, and that would be weird. People are judgmental."

"I'm not being stupid."

"This is my hometown, Kristy. Remember? People know me here."

"Fine. You're *just* my cousin." I could tell he wasn't in the mood to argue about it.

"That's right." He walked the few steps to the door. "See you later, cuz." He turned to look at me. I was pouting. "Hey," he said.

"What."

"I'm glad you're here." His eyes broadcasted their signature warmth at me, and I felt wrapped in the safety of his Thayerness. My anger melted.

"I'm glad I'm here too. See you later?"

"Sure." He went out the door. I looked around at the heap of boxes and bags, feeling overwhelmed. Aunt Hildy picked up on the third ring.

"How is move-in day going?" she asked. "I'm so proud of you."

I described the room and told her I was feeling kind of lonely, despite being thrilled to be out of Lisa's house.

"When you're feeling at loose ends, the best thing to do is keep busy. Set yourself to making that space your new home." It seemed like good advice, so I told her I loved her and signed off.

Having blankets and pillows on the narrow bed warmed up the sterile room a little, but I couldn't help missing my Strawberry Shortcake comforter, even though my roommate would undoubtedly have found it ridiculous.

It was the first time I'd thought of it in years.

CHAPTER 36

Sometime during sophomore year, I started to wonder if it had been a good idea to go to Thayer's school. He was kind of a jerk, and a lot of the guys around campus were pretty cool. Maybe lusting after your cousin wasn't the way to have a successful life. But when I brought it up to Thayer, it didn't go well.

We'd just had sex. I planned it that way because he tended to be in a good mood afterword. His current girlfriend was pissing him off which didn't surprise me. She was another in a string of big-busted blondes, and when you chose your female companions by those two characteristics, you can't expect a perfect match.

"She's always checking out the papers on my desk and trying to see what comes up on my phone," he said. We were stretched out on my narrow dorm bed, cooling off and letting the sweat dry. He reached up to scratch his chin. He looked gorgeous. The mixture of post-coital relaxation and mild irritation looked good on him.

"I can imagine how you feel about *that*. You hate nosy people."

"Speaking of which, would you mind not wearing perfume? Her nose is super sensitive. She sniffs me after I see you, even though I shower."

"Sure." I'd knock off the perfume, but amp up the scented products. That way I'd technically be in compliance, but still irritate her. I waited to see if he was done talking. When he didn't say anything else, I figured the coast was clear. "So, I was thinking."

"Uh oh."

"I was thinking maybe I should be dating too."

Thayer sat up and glowered. "What the fuck?"

"Think about it. You date and it works as cover just like we agreed. But here I am floating around with nobody and having to keep saying no. Word's going around that I'm a lesbian, but if I was, I'd have someone in my life, so that doesn't even make sense."

"Who is he?" The mix of relaxed irritation was gone. Thayer's face was turning red, and his nostrils flared.

"There is no 'he'. I'm just saying maybe there should be."

"You wouldn't have brought it up if you didn't want strange dick."

"You're being ridiculous. It's not about dick. You're all the dick I can handle." I reached out to touch his, hoping round two would help calm things down. He jerked away and started pulling on his clothes.

"If you think I'm going to put my penis somewhere other dicks have been, you're wrong. Dead wrong." He zipped up his pants and started buttoning his shirt, fingers moving fast. "I'm not into sloppy seconds, Kris."

"I told you it wasn't about sex!"

"It's always about sex. Guys want sex. If you start dating, there'll be sex."

His words reminded me of Aunt Hildy's warnings from years back. He was right and I didn't know how to argue my position without admitting the idea didn't bother me. Fucking my cousin was not an optimal sexual outlet on any level.

"It doesn't have to be like that." I tried to object but couldn't come up with anything convincing. I should have practiced that part of the argument. But it didn't matter; he was jamming his shoes on, then grabbing his keys.

"Diseases Kris. Crabs. Do you think that's okay with me?" He looked at the floor and shook his head.

"Thayer..." I tried to reach for him, but he reared back and held me off with his arms out and a "how dare you" look on his face.

"You need to do some thinking. You need to think about this.

Hard."

I nodded, fast. "I will."

He left then, slamming the door behind him.

It hadn't gone well. But at least the subject was on the table.

I didn't see him for three weeks. By the time he showed up at my door I was torn between fury and gratitude that he'd forgiven me. It had been long enough that I'd just about decided it was over and started evaluating guys as potential beaus. But he was Thayer, and I couldn't stay angry. I wouldn't know how to say no to him even if I wanted to. I jumped up, wrapped my arms around him, and sniffed his scent deep into my lungs. Filling myself back up with his safety.

When we finished, he gave me a routine talking to, which I expected.

He'd graduate in the spring. All I had to do was wait it out.

CHAPTER 37

About that time I met Lee. She was a tall, pretty thing with long hair the color of copper. When she stood in the sunlight it looked like sparks were flying from her head. We met in a literature class. She was an English major.

I'm not sure what attracted us initially. It might have been a shared amusement at the prof. He was a pretentious little prick who liked to look down the shirts of female students. He had an arching spine, a protruding belly, and an English accent, though the rumor was he came from Illinois. The way he talked was an embarrassing reminder of my attempts to sound like Madonna during her "I'm so British" phase. Most of the students took him seriously, but I found his affectation hilarious. I caught Lee trying to hold in laughter one day during class and waited as she packed up her books afterward. We walked out together and hung out regularly after that.

She was calm and reserved. Her quiet felt like peace, though I realized later it might be something else. We were opposites: me all short, jouncy round parts and curls, and her all tall, fair-skinned, and smooth. I talked a lot, she was reticent. By then I'd moved away from wearing black clothes with skull belts and was usually dressed in lots of color and pattern. Lee tended toward long pastel cardigans paired with camisoles and tight jeans. She'd pull her straight, copper-sparked hair into a ponytail or wind it up in a bun, and she looked like a ballerina. Super classy versus my super sassy.

There was something about Lee's writing that drew me to her spirit. The first time I read her work it was an essay about a book we were reading for class. She wasn't sure if the piece addressed the essential question and wanted me to take a look. I could see why she was concerned, because it took an entirely different path from what most of us had centered on. Her language was vivid and magical. Once in a while she let me read a piece of poetry or fiction. Her face lit up when I told her she needed to be read, like it made her day.

We found out we had something in common while we were studying in a coffee shop one Saturday.

"Does your family live around here?" I asked.

"My mom does. Not sure for how long though. She's got itchy feet and big dreams, so who knows where she'll be heading now that I'm settled into school."

"At least she waited until you finished high school."

"Barely. She wants to go off on a spiritual journey to 'find herself'. I think it's because she got married so early. Never had a chance to figure out who she wanted to be before becoming a wife and mother." She shrugged. "So, we'll see. It's okay with me if she goes. I'd never move back in with her."

"What about your dad? I take it they aren't still married."

She shook her head. "He died. A long time ago."

"Oh. I'm sorry."

"Thanks."

"What happened?" I asked. She looked at me, her face careful. "You don't have to tell me if you don't want to." She still didn't say anything. I decided to change the subject and let her off the hook. "The coffee today tastes like they threw in an old…"

"I saw him die."

"You did?"

Lee nodded. "It was pretty much right in front of me. They were fighting. They argued a *lot*." I didn't say anything, just watched her and gave her space to tell her story the way she wanted to. "He was a terrible provider. Always getting a new job and then losing it again.

Always coming up with dreams for living on a houseboat or moving to a cabin out in the woods." Her gaze had drifted away from me, her eyes focused on the past, but she suddenly turned her green eyes back my way. "He was a painter. Like you. I have some of his paintings."

"Are they any good?"

"Not really. Not that I'm much of a judge. I'll show them to you sometime."

"I'd love to see them."

"So they were fighting and that was nothing new. I can't even remember what he did that time. Probably got fired again. Anyway, Mom was furious. He usually just shut up and let her get it out of her system when she started yelling. But not that day. That day he yelled back." Lee lifted her right hand to scratch her head. She scratched it a lot; I'd noticed it in class. I wondered if she needed to change shampoos. "And then suddenly he was on the floor."

"What was it?"

"Brain aneurism. Apparently due to some sort of congenital defect. Hopefully I didn't inherit it."

"Oh my God..."

"He died so *fast*. I had no idea people died that fast. He was there, glaring back at Mom and then he was on the floor. Gone."

"I'm so sorry."

"I know it wasn't her fault, but I've had a really hard time not blaming her." She pulled her hand back out of her hair, and started shredding a napkin into tiny pieces, which she pushed into a pile. "If she would have just let him be. Just accepted that he was a fuck up. Maybe the blood vessel would have held out a while longer." She glanced back up at me. "I know that's not rational."

"How old were you?"

"Seven.

I paused before responding, considering how much to say. "I was ten when my dad died. I still blame my mom too." I'm not sure why I said it, because I wasn't sure I was ready to talk about Daddy's death. Lee's face turned even sadder.

"What happened?"

"Lisa left us when I was six."

"That's your mom?"

"Yes. I have a hard time calling her any word that is associated with the concept of motherhood."

"That's understandable."

I paused, kicking myself for allowing the conversation to get that far. I needed to reel things back in. No one needed to know he was an addict. I could give him that dignity. "After he left, he started getting sick." Addiction was a sickness, right? "He just kept getting skinnier, and more confused. Afterwards I thought maybe it was AIDS." Her face turned even more sympathetic. "He liked women, but he donated blood a lot. And right at the beginning of the epidemic they weren't careful." I realized I was babbling. What I was saying made no sense.

She gave me an odd look, like she could see into my brain and watch the gears moving, but she didn't probe. That was one of the nice things about Lee. She was sensitive. Considerate.

"Anyway, I came out one morning and he was there in his chair. Dead."

"You found him?"

"Yes."

"God. I'm so sorry."

"I guess it's better than actually watching him die. You win on that."

"Suckiest contest ever." We both gave a sad little huff of laughter. "You were only ten?" she continued.

"Yes. That's when I had to go live with Lisa in Rochester."

"I see."

"So I know what you mean about blaming them. If Lisa had been there, she could have helped take care of him. He would have wanted to get treatment. If she'd been there, he probably wouldn't have even gotten sick." She looked at me with her calm, green eyes. Her stillness radiated peace, despite the content of our discussion. "I *know* it wasn't her fault, really. I know it intellectually."

"All we can do is keep repeating the intellectual knowledge until we actually believe it," she said.

"Either that or hate them until they die. I'm leaning toward that."

Lee laughed. "It's definitely an option."

We moved on to other subjects, but something happened that day. We became really good friends. I even told her Thayer and I had fooled around when we lived at Lisa's but realized I didn't want to expose too much about the thing he and I had. I ended up making it sound like we were just a couple of foolish kids playing doctor.

Although we got into disagreements about a few things throughout the years, nothing was able to shake our relationship. Not until I completely destroyed it.

CHAPTER 38

Thayer graduated, which gave me more freedom to date. I went out with a handful of guys, and a few of them ended up being semi-serious, meaning we had sex. None of them had the effect on me Thayer did, and even though I knew my relationship with him was all kinds of fucked up, I couldn't seem to stop it. I'd see him and get all fluttery and panting. I wanted to end it, but I just couldn't do it. We didn't see each other as much though, and he seemed to have gotten used to the idea that there would have to be other men in my life.

I met Jimmy Alexander in my senior year. Jimmy was different from the other guys. He was a senior too; a biology major who interned at a local biotech firm and planned to work there once he graduated. He fell for me fast, and I encouraged the fall. Jimmy was easy to love; kind, generous, considerate, gentle, and smart. He was also mature and solid, unlike the other guys I dated. Lisa would hate that he was black, but that was her problem, not mine.

He didn't fire me up like Thayer did, but I'd come to the conclusion that no one could. Jimmy was such a good person I thought his love could push my need for Thayer out of my system, the way I thought love could have saved Daddy if it had just come along in time.

We graduated. Jimmy went to work at a different company which gave him a better offer. I got a job teaching at an elementary school, but what I really wanted to do was paint. Jimmy said if I married him, he'd support me so I could focus on making art, but I wasn't quite ready for marriage, and the voice in my head wouldn't shut up. The voice sounded just like Lisa's and repeated her warnings about needing a real job. So I set up an easel by the window in my one-bedroom apartment, and told myself I'd paint around my school schedule. But I could never catch the light. I had to leave too early in the mornings for the early sunshine and got home after dark for most of the year. And even when the light was available, teaching made me tired and grumpy. The kids came in fired up and glad to be out of their classrooms, but a lot of them couldn't focus on their projects. I told myself it was more important to keep them engaged than to stick to the curriculum. But the tedium and the petty school politics wore me down.

My painting mostly happened during breaks and over the summer. Imposter syndrome was a constant companion for me, as an artist, and as a girlfriend.

CHAPTER 39

I held Jimmy off as long as I could, but we finally got married. After my bachelorette party I went to Thayer's apartment. It was meant to be the last time. He seemed pretty normal, but for me the sex was saturated with sorrow.

Lee was my maid of honor. She was gorgeous in the emerald gown we'd picked out together. Her skin glowed against the dark fabric, as did the copper curls cascading from her updo. She was uber feminine and elegant; the complete opposite of my own form of femininity. Thayer watched her during the reception in a way I didn't like.

Life with Jimmy was sweet and unremarkable. He was so besotted with me that he even found my irritating qualities adorable. In bed he was warm and cuddly, and our sex life was… adequate.

It didn't take long before the whole thing irritated the shit out of me. And of course, that led to sneaking off with Thayer. My guilt manifested as snarkiness toward Jimmy, who received it with a sort of wounded acceptance, multiplying my guilt. He'd hug me in bed after one of my outbursts and ask what was bothering me; so sincere in wanting to help. It made me want to scream.

After one of those evenings, I thought about the way Thayer looked at Lee on the night of my wedding. And I made a decision. I had to get the two of them together. Lee was nothing like his usual girlfriends. She was soft-spoken and gentle, kind of like a female Jimmy. Thayer usually went for curvy, giggly blondes, and she was super slim and thoughtful, but I felt like they might bring each other balance.

I also thought that if Thayer was with my best friend, neither of us would want to hurt her by fooling around behind her back. It was the only thing I could think of to make it stop.

Jimmy wasn't thrilled when I invited them both to dinner. "You sure you want to inflict slicky boy's shit on poor Lee? You know what a player he is." Jimmy was helping me set the table before they arrived.

"He's 29. He needs to settle down."

"Undoubtedly. But why Lee? I thought you liked her." Jimmy smiled to make it seem like a joke, but I knew he was serious.

"I adore Lee, you know that. I just think it could work. She's steady, smart, and classy."

"In other words, totally not his type."

"Exactly." I checked the wine glasses for spots before positioning them above the napkins at each setting. "And don't call him slicky boy."

"Hey; if the slick fits."

"Please?"

"Okay my love." Jimmy came and put his arms around me. "I know you want him to be happy. Maybe she can make a good man out of him." He released me and patted my butt as he returned to the silverware.

"I sure hope so." Jimmy glanced back up at me, apparently hearing something in my voice I hadn't known was showing. "My aunt and uncle deserve some grandkids, don't you think?" I continued. The move was kind of a cruel distraction. Cruel, but effective.

"Yes they do. And we should do our part by giving them some grand-nieces and nephews." He finished straightening the last dessert fork. "Let's go make one."

I manufactured a giggle and batted my eyes at him. "We don't have time, Casanova. They'll be here in fifteen minutes."

"You know I only need ten."

"Ten?" I raised my eyebrows at him.

"Three for me and seven for you. Let's go." He tipped his head toward the bedroom.

This time I giggled for real. "I wish I could. But I have to finish frosting the cake and get the coffee set up."

"I'll take care of the coffee. You do the cake. And if we finish five minutes early, you are mine. Deal?"

"Deal."

We finished five minutes early.

I was straightening my clothes when the doorbell rang. Thayer arrived first. He stepped up close, then came to a halt. He sniffed and his eyes hardened. "You've been busy," he said. I stuttered a reply. Luckily Jimmy came in the room and extended his hand.

"Thayer! Glad you could come."

"Wouldn't have missed it." He lifted his nose in a parody of his earlier sniff. "Smells great in here. What's cooking?" He looked at me.

"Kristy made her osso buco, because she knows you're a red meat guy."

"Yes I am."

Recalling that discretion was the better part of valor, I bolted to the kitchen.

"What are you drinking? Wine or a cocktail? I have a gorgeous Zinfandel breathing," Jimmy said.

"Scotch?"

"Sure. Rocks?"

"You know it."

The guys made their way to the bar Jimmy had arranged on the buffet. I heard ice tinkling, and the give and take of their voices, and I thought about how good a man Jimmy was. You could never tell he didn't really like Thayer.

The bell rang again, and this time Jimmy got the door. I came out fast because I wanted to be the one to introduce them. Or at least watch as Jimmy did it.

Lee was all sleek gorgeousness in a long, flowered sundress. She had sunglasses pushed to the top of her head, pulling her hair away from her face. Her skin was as flawless as ever, and her makeup was perfect. I watched Thayer check her out. I saw him swallow. Twice.

"Lee, this is Thayer. Thayer: Lee." Jimmy introduced them.

Thayer put out his hand to take hers, then bent to kiss it. "Enchantée," he said. Lee actually blushed.

"You did *not* just say that," I burst out. "That was the single corniest thing I've ever seen you do."

"Yes, I did," he replied. "I've seen it in the movies so many times, I thought I should give it a try. Seemed like the right time."

"I warned you Lee." I beckoned for her to follow me to the bar. "Red or white? I'm having pink. Discovered this luscious Moscato. It's bubbly and ridiculously sweet. I love it."

"White please. And ick."

"What can I say? Plebian tastes," I said. Jimmy and Thayer moved closer. "Except in men, of course." Both of them smiled. I poured her wine and returned to the kitchen calling Jimmy to come with me so Lee and Thayer could talk.

"Well that was lame," Jimmy said.

I just snorted. "Ridiculous. He's usually got a lot more game."

"I should hope so. But I sensed a spark out there." It felt like a knife went through my heart as he said it but forced a smile. "Maybe you called it right. Maybe they *are* a match," he said.

"Aren't I *always* right?" He laughed. "Here. Take this." I handed him a plate of marinated shrimp with goat cheese and mint. I didn't particularly care for goat cheese, but I'd seen the recipe in a fancy cooking magazine at the gynecologist's office, and figured it would be impressive.

I followed Jimmy back out to the dining room and sat down. He held the platter so Lee could serve herself, then did the same for Thayer.

"Interesting combination," Thayer said, scraping cheese off a shrimp before popping it in his mouth."

I piled a few shrimp on my own plate. "You're not a fan of goat cheese either?"

"Oh, I like chèvre. I'm just in the camp of seafood and cheese not going together. The aggressiveness of the cheese overwhelms the subtleness of the fish."

Lee was her typical quiet self. She took a ladylike bite and then a tiny sip of chardonnay.

"I think the flavors work really well actually," Jimmy said. You get the earthiness of the cheese, and the sweetness of the shrimp, and then an herbal hit from the mint. "It's great, honey."

"Thank you." I was used to Thayer's straight shooting, but it was still nice to have Jimmy's backup.

"It's funny how rules are always changing," Lee said. "With cooking and everything else. It used to be that you couldn't wear white before Memorial Day, now white jeans are everywhere. Purses and shoes should match, then they shouldn't, and then they should again."

"Red wine with beef and white with fish," Jimmy joined in.

"Now anything goes." I said.

"So you're saying the cheese and seafood thing is out the window?" Thayer asked. There was humor in his face and playfulness in his voice, which was a relief, because it could have gone the other way.

"Anchovy pizza coming up next!" I said.

Things loosened up after that. Lee's gentle loveliness softened Thayer's hard edges, and Jimmy's natural cordiality kept the conversation moving. Jimmy cleared the appetizer plates, and I brought in the main course. The wine flowed and Thayer told stories about when I was a kid.

All in all, the evening was a success. And I'd been right. Thayer and Lee ended up becoming an item. The succession of blondes halted. Their relationship seemed to be serious.

We saw them quite a lot. They became the couple we did things with. When I watched them together and saw the way Thayer looked at Lee, it made me edgy. It made me want. He looked hungry, but not in a sexual way. I knew *that* look, and this wasn't it. When he watched her, he looked like he was always yearning.

The whole thing was agonizing.

My tactic worked; I kept away from him because of her. It felt good knowing I wasn't having sex with my cousin, or cheating on Jimmy. Introducing them had been brilliant.

I held out for a long time.

Three years.

Three interminable years.

CHAPTER 40

Lee moved in with him a few months after our dinner party, which surprised me. She'd always said she was the hold-out-until-marriage type because statistics showed marriages didn't last when people lived together first.

Thayer's pestering started about a year after she moved in. He called and asked if I'd meet him for coffee, which was strange. I figured maybe something was up between Lee and him. But when we met, he just talked about work and family updates. Banal stuff.

When my cup was empty, I looked at my watch. "Guess I should head home and get dinner started."

"Got time for a little ride?" His eyes pulsed with the sexual power I knew so well. It hit me like a wave of Missouri summer heat, shocking in its unexpectedness. I just blinked and stuttered. Thayer laughed. "I know it's been a long time. But I've missed you," he said.

I stuttered some more and searched for my keys to buy a little time, heart and body demanding that I give in. It felt like my skin was expanding, opening up to receive him. But my intellect overruled all the emotion. "I've... I've got to make dinner. Jimmy will be home soon."

His eyes smoldered hotter. "Jimmy can wait. Jimmy always waits. That's one of his charms." He traced a finger across my knuckles, then slid into the cleft between my pointer finger and thumb. My pores flared wider. I jerked my hand away.

"Thayer... I can't. *We* can't." I stood up from the table.

The heat dropped from his gaze and his expression shifted to disdain.

"Well, why did you come today? Just felt like being a tease?" He nodded toward my cleavage. I couldn't deny it; I'd worn a dress that hugged all my curves and showed a bit of skin. I hadn't been able to help it.

"No!" I lied. "I thought maybe something was wrong. Thought you might need to talk."

"So that's your psychiatrist uniform. I get it."

"Look, I'm sorry. I wish I could, but I promised myself..."

"Go on." He looked away from me to the young barista behind the counter. "Just get out of here." He ran a hand through his hair, the gold strands shining in the light from the window beside him. His gaze traveled from her face to her chest and up again. He looked back at me. His eyes were flat and cold. "Time to get a refill." He picked up his cup and walked to the counter. My own eyes welled with tears. I turned to go before they fell but heard his voice as I went out the door. I couldn't make out the words, but I knew the sexy tone.

I drove away so he wouldn't see me weeping in the parking lot but pulled over in a park to cry it out before I went home. I'd done the right thing, but my body ached, and my heart was heavy with a complex guilt which felt centuries old.

Guilt that I hadn't helped him when he needed me.

I held out for two years after that. It was easy for a few months because Thayer avoided me, refusing invitations to come over for dinner or a game. Lee finally asked about it when we were shopping one weekend.

"Did Thayer and Jimmy have a tiff or something?"

"Not that I know of. Why?"

"It's like he's mad about something but won't explain it. It's all underground. But every time I suggest getting together with you guys, he rolls his eyes and makes excuses."

"He *is* a champion eye roller," I said, hoping to joke her off track.

"Yes, but this feels different."

"I'll ask Jimmy, but I think he would have told me." I quickly realized this might make her analyze things even more closely and decided to backtrack. "Who knows though? Guys have their own rules about talking. Maybe he just forgot."

"Maybe." We were in the men's clothing section, and she was pulling Oxford-cloth button down shirts from the extra-small section of a hanging rack.

"Who are you shopping for?" The size was much too small for Thayer.

She looked up. "For me." She tossed the shirt into her basket and selected two other colors.

"Since when have you been a button-down girl?"

"I don't know. Thayer just thought…"

I gave her a moment to continue, but she didn't. "Thought what?" I asked.

"That maybe I should tone it down a bit at work." Lee worked as a technical writer in a technology company. "You know. It's almost all guys."

"So what?"

"So he asked me to, and I didn't see why I shouldn't." I stood looking at her for a minute. "You know what he's like when he isn't happy," she continued. "And it's not that big a deal." She wouldn't look me in the eye, and her hand lifted to scratch her head, nervously. Her glorious, long copper hair was pulled back from her face with a headband. Her makeup was perfect as usual. She was exquisite, and somehow fragile.

"I *do* know what he's like when he's not happy." Understatement. "I suppose shirts are no big deal really."

"Exactly." She looked relieved.

"All set?" I asked. She nodded. "Then let's check out and grab some lunch."

While we ate, we talked more about Thayer's avoidance, and I agreed to stop at their house with her before going home. The thought made me very uncomfortable, but I didn't know how to get out of it. When we got there, Thayer was in the living room reading a newspaper and listening to music.

"Look who I brought!" Lee called out with false brightness.

"Hey," I said, coming over to him and dropping a kiss on the top of his head just as I would have back when things were normal. The scent of him went straight to my bloodstream.

"Cuz," he said, setting down the paper. "What brings you here?" His eyes were flat, but not as bad as the last time I'd seen him. I took it as a good sign.

"Just thought I'd stop by and say hello. Haven't seen you in a long time!"

"That you haven't."

I could tell Lee was uncomfortable. She fluttered around for a minute, and then announced she was taking her purchases upstairs. When she'd gone, I tried to talk to him.

"Come on, Thayer. Can't we be friends? We're cousins!"

He looked me up and down, eyes resting on parts of my body that made my knees feel like they were melting. "Did you miss me?"

"Of course I missed you. I love you. You know that."

His face finally slipped into a soft smile. He nodded. Slowly. "Oh, yeah. I know."

By that time Lee was on her way back down the stairs, which gave me something to look at other than his eyes.

"I know!" Lee said. "Why don't you and Jimmy come over for dinner tomorrow?" She didn't look at Thayer when she asked. I could feel nervousness pouring from her in waves.

"Sounds like a great idea. I'll grill us some steaks," Thayer said.

Lee turned toward him then, relief blooming across her face. "Sure!" I said. I didn't know how I was going to pull it off, but there was no other option. "We don't have anything going on. We'll bring the wine."

"Yay!" Lee's face was childlike with relief and pleasure.

We worked out the details and I left. My heart still pounded from the scent of his hair and the heat of his gaze. I wasn't sure it was a good idea to spend time together, but there didn't seem to be any way around it.

It became a kind of a game. I'd work out ways to delay getting the four of us together, then when it seemed to be getting too obvious, I'd try to arrange things so that being alone with him was hard. We'd go to the movies or have a picnic in a park. Dinners in our homes were tough, because Thayer would find ways to search me out when Jimmy and Lee were talking. He'd come up behind me without touching me and bend to breathe against my neck, or trail his cheek behind my ear. Or he'd reach for my hand and draw it to his mouth; one finger gently stroking my palm while he brushed his lips across my wrist. It was nothing raunchy and he never touched any of my parts which are typically considered sexual.

It drove me absolutely crazy. I'd pull away taking a few deep breaths and return to Lee and Jimmy with a smile and a joke, feeling simultaneously guilty and virtuous.

But my season of self-imposed exile finally came screeching to a halt, and it couldn't have happened on a worse occasion.

Thayer asked Lee to marry him. Thank God Lee called to break the news, because even though I knew theoretically it was going to happen, I'd refused to think about it. The thought of them walking down the aisle made me feel like tearing my garments like an Old Testament prophet and perhaps setting myself on fire. I feigned as much enthusiasm as I was able, assuring Lee I'd be her matron of honor, then got off the phone quickly to wallow.

My emotion didn't make sense. I was married; happily if boringly.

I wondered if Thayer went through what I was experiencing. And I was mad he'd given me no warning.

Thayer's mother, my aunt Lillian, threw them an engagement party. The last thing I wanted to do was pretend to be thrilled about the whole thing. But there was no way of getting out of it.

Jimmy was out of town at a biochem convention, so I went to the party alone. Lee was in her element, though she still didn't look like herself to me. She'd cut her hair very short a few months before, which was surprising. Her hair was her one vanity. Thayer suggested it, and she always did what he wanted so off it went. The pixie cut couldn't hide her beauty though. It accentuated the graceful length of her neck. Because it was a party, she wore a dress instead of what had become her new uniform of loose button downs and khaki pants. It was a simple knee-length shift with a modest neckline. She looked simple and gorgeous, and she glowed.

The food was rich and expensive to match my aunt and uncle's home. I found them stuffy and pretentious. When Lisa and Steve walked in, I lost what tiny bit of appetite I'd had, and grabbed my second cocktail. I watched Lisa's eyes slink over Thayer in that creepy way of hers, then go all hard and judgy as she looked at Lee. God, she was a bitch.

Lee's light seemed to dim not long into the party. She went from glowing to vaguely green. I couldn't tell if it was the richness of the canapes or if she was coming down with a bug.

"Are you alright?" I asked.

"Not really. I'm not feeling well."

"Do you need to go home?"

"I can't leave my own party!"

"But if you're sick…"

Thayer showed up then and took her elbow. "You stopped circulating honey. You okay?"

She shook her head. "I feel ill."

"You'd better take her home, Thayer. I would do it, but I'm a little buzzed already."

He looked at me, then at Lee, then back at me again. He nodded. "Go get your stuff. I'll run you home and then come back to explain to our guests."

"I'm so sorry, Lee said vaguely. She really didn't look well.

When she went to get her purse, Thayer took a step closer. His eyes zoomed deep into mine. "I'll be back," he said.

My heart thumped and I took a quick gulp of my drink, then looked around to regain my composure. I saw Lisa watching. Her lips were pursed, hard.

He left, and I got another drink, then wandered through the crowd, talking to people at random, trying not to think about Thayer and Lee being married. It was as if their marriage sealed the possibility of my ever being with him. My own marriage hadn't done that, but with Lee... Once they were married it would really and truly be over. He wouldn't and couldn't be mine.

By the time he got back I was feeling sloppily sentimental. I watched him come in and work the party. I watched people leave, Lisa and Steve along with them, thank God. Finally, it was just us and his parents. I helped clear up a few things, but Aunt Lillian said their service would get it in the morning. They were yawning, so we said our good-byes and left.

Thayer insisted on driving me home. He hadn't drunk much because he didn't like getting tipsy. It was a good thing, because I was pretty well sloshed by then. I felt like crying.

He turned on some music; an Elvis collection, full of sappy love songs. They didn't help with my emotion. When we arrived at my house he got out. I followed him, trying to figure out how I would say goodbye without breaking down. He took the keys from my fumbling hands and unlocked the door.

He took me into his arms as soon as the door was closed, running his lips against the skin of my throat, and I was on fire. I said his name and tried to say no but I couldn't because my heart was breaking. I was losing him, and I loved him so much and my mind was soft and fuzzy from all the alcohol I'd consumed. He pushed me against the wall and then we slid to the floor as our hands pushed up fabric and pulled down zippers.

When it was over, I lay with my head on his chest, breathing his scent and listening to the beating of his heart. I tried to feel guilty but couldn't.

After that, we became a regular, secret thing again. I told myself maybe it was okay. Maybe I was even helping Lee. Maybe I was protecting her. Thayer was bound to have affairs, and if he just stuck with me, Lee was kind of safe. I'd never try to steal him the way other women would. I was so much better than a stranger.

Wasn't I?

CHAPTER 41

The years moved along as they somehow manage to do whether you're a good person or not. Teaching gave me joy; the children's ingenuity was endlessly inspiring. They didn't have rigid concepts about what art should be, and the ideas they came up with were a delight. I tried to make the time in my classroom a place of peace and welcome the way Ms. Hyslip had, and the kids seemed to respond to what they encountered there.

Unfortunately, their inspiration didn't transfer to my own painting. Jimmy set up the guest room as a studio, saying we could always put my stuff away when we had people to stay. But the light wasn't right, and the space didn't motivate me. My brain was the problem, but it was easier to blame the room.

Jimmy seemed genuinely happy, and never saw through me after trysts with Thayer on those guilty mornings when I handed him his coffee cup. He'd ruffle my hair, kiss the top of my head, and swat my butt as I headed to the shower. He was a good-looking man. Great looking, really; broad shouldered and well-muscled, with a gorgeous smile. When his hair started to recede, he just shaved it all off, revealing a perfectly formed head. The little paunch above his belt was the only flaw, and it was minor. Most women would find him super sexy. But for me, he was more like a cuddle buddy. I'd watch him working around the house, and my heart would swell with gratitude and guilt, but never with the kind of love he deserved.

What we had seemed to be enough for him. More than enough, really. It wasn't enough for *me* though.

During that phase of life, there were only two times when I felt truly like myself. The first was when I went to Aunt Hildy's. There were a few weeks throughout those years when Jimmy had grueling projects over the summer, and I'd go solo. Being there took me back to that first trip when I was just a girl, bewildered by the new world into which I'd landed. Before Thayer came. In Merrivliet, I could paint.

The other time I felt authentically myself was when I was alone with Thayer. In those moments I also returned to an earlier stage of life, before I was married or knew Lee. With him I nestled into a cocoon of emotional comfort, which made no sense. He wasn't emotionally safe. He was frequently mean, and sometimes even a little scary. Especially the few times I tried talking to him about stopping. His eyes turned to ice, and he clenched his jaw so tight a muscle would start to tic.

"You think we should tell Lee?" He asked during one of these conversations, voice dripping with condescension. "Is that it? Confess our sins and all that?" His fists clenched and unclenched in time with his jaw.

"No! That's not what I'm saying. At all." If he told her, Lee and Jimmy's lives would be destroyed, and it didn't seem fair to do that to them. I know that sounds ridiculous given what we *were* doing to them, but Lee had conformed herself so completely to what Thayer wanted that I couldn't imagine what it would do to her. And Jimmy was so darned sweet and trusting. Telling him would be like beating a puppy. The thought of his face crumpling at the news was overwhelming. "I couldn't do that," I said.

"Well then." He came up and stood right in front of me, only inches away. "I guess you have a choice to make." I could smell his Thayer scent, tinged with anger. For the first time, though, his smell didn't turn me on. He scared me. "What's it going to be?" he asked, the threat clear in his eyes. I reached for his zipper. He nodded, slowly, not breaking eye contact. The threat was still heavily present. "Smart girl."

I felt a bit sick afterward, but it didn't take long for the sensation to settle into resignation, and within a few weeks the resignation turned into normalcy. I decided if I couldn't stop it from happening, I might as well enjoy it. My hunger for him rushed back like a dam finally bursting.

So that's how it went, for several years. A cycle of guilt and pleasure, with more of the former than the latter. Then something shifted. I'd been trying to figure out what it was, looking back, and I think it was mostly about Lee.

We met for coffee at our favorite place. It was filled with vintage kitchen appliances, fresh flowers and the smell of cinnamon and apples baking.

"I think I'll have one of those streusel muffins, and a café mocha," I told the kid behind the counter. Lee stood beside me, scratching her head and gazing into space. "What would you like?"

"Just an Americano," she said. "Black."

"Are you sure you don't want one of those chocolate croissants? You know you love them. My treat." She just shook her head, her hand still moving beneath the short cap of copper hair. "Are you okay?" I asked.

Lee turned and headed toward a table in the back. As she walked away it struck me that there was barely anything left of the girl I'd met during college. We sat down, and she forced a smile.

"You *aren't* okay," I said. "What's going on? Did something happen?"

"Nothing, really. Nothing new." Lee's hand crept back up toward her hair. The head scratching was becoming a compulsion. If she'd been one of my students, I would have checked her for lice. "Everything is just… the same." She used to be calm and confident. Quietly poised. Elegant. I admired that about her because my flaky flamboyance was such a contrast. But the stillness which used to convey calm and peace had become pensive.

"Is it work? Your talents are being wasted as a tech writer."

"No, work is fine."

"Are you doing any creative writing?" My questions were starting to feel like an interrogation, but I kept going. "Your poetry is gorgeous."

"I haven't felt inspired. I'm too tired to get up early enough in the morning, and Thayer likes me to spend time with him after work. Writing is a solo activity, so it's hard to carve out space."

"He should encourage your creativity. It's such a part of who you are." I thought about the support Jimmy offered and felt a familiar twinge of guilt.

"He should do a lot of things. But he's *Thayer.* You know that."

I did know. He was charming, demanding, and very hard to say no to. "I'm not producing anything either. Is it just a product of getting older? We set aside our dreams?"

Lee just shrugged again. Her spirit seemed defeated.

Another question rose in my mind, demanding to be spoken. It felt like a compulsion. Maybe like the draw of her scalp to her fingers. I tried to hold it back but failed. "How... how are things in the bedroom?"

The question didn't seem to faze her. Her expression of deflation didn't shift as she answered. "Not good."

"No?" My heart pounded from nervousness.

"I'm finding it hard to be with him lately. He expects me to... perform. It never feels like he's making love. It's just sex. There's no... intimacy."

"Have you tried talking to him about it?"

"A few times. And then I gave up. Now I just try to avoid it."

The information required processing. "I'm so sorry you're having to deal with all that," I said. My heart went out to her because she was clearly hurting. But my guilt about having sex with her husband eased a tiny bit. The less she slept with him, the less gross it seemed when I did. The topic was too fraught to continue. It was time to change the subject. "Tell me what you're writing about at work. Some top-secret device designed to shoot down Amazon delivery drones?"

Lee laughed. "Nothing *that* exciting," she said. "It's an optics system. The team is great, for a change."

"Not like your previous project."

"Not even close. Thank God." Lee told me more about the people on the engineering team, and I relaxed as she talked, promising myself to consider what to do once I was alone.

CHAPTER 42

Sleep was elusive that night, and it wasn't just the late afternoon caffeine which kept me awake. When the alarm played its annoying wake up song, I'd managed three hours of sleep but developed a plan.

The foil-backed packet of pills in my bedside table was a totem of my freedom. I stared at it for a long time, fingers itching to pop the day's tablet out and forget the whole mad idea. Jimmy had been bugging me about having kids for a long time. I'd held out because what kind of a mother could I be, given my background? I was also afraid of how Thayer would respond.

The thought of his reaction made my heart thump, and I pressed my thumb against the tablet's plastic bubble. But I couldn't keep watching the slow destruction of the person who used to be Lee, knowing the role I was playing in it. The only way to force a change was to get pregnant. Maternal instincts would kick in and all I'd want to do was nest and make a protective space for the baby.

I dropped the packet on the floor.

Pregnancy would calm down whatever it was within me that demanded Thayer. My connection with Jimmy would be strengthened because he'd be a fantastic father. It was the only answer.

I lifted my foot and let it hover above the silver rectangle for a moment in acknowledgement of the ways the world would soon change. The pills felt resistant under my heel when I stepped down, as if fighting on my behalf, but I pressed harder, twisting at the ankle, grinding my freedom into powder.

Google reported it should take a few months before conceiving after stopping birth control pills, which was good because I needed time to get used to the idea and figure out how to tell Thayer. Jimmy couldn't know because he'd go crazy and tell everyone, and I couldn't handle all the fuss. He never paid attention to my pills, so it wasn't as if I had to hide anything. Meanwhile, I made myself extra available to Thayer because they would be our last sexual encounters.

During that short season of farewell fucks, I avoided having sex with Jimmy, because I wanted there to be a kind of purity in the goodbye. When I told Jimmy I was too tired, or too grumpy, or whatever, he just gave me a hug or a kiss on the top of my head, or brought me a cup of tea. His kindness made my gut twist, but the guilt was tempered by the knowledge that it was almost over. A baby would be his reward for the deception.

When Thayer and I had sex, it felt like I finally had something over him. He'd always had the upper hand in our relationship, but finally I knew something he didn't, and had power over what was happening. I felt smart and virtuous while taping paper Jack-o-lanterns in the halls of the school, filled with certainty that life was finally going to normalize.

But autumn turned out to be the season when everything began to snowball. Just like when Daddy died.

INTERMEZZO

The police detectives escorted me to a small, bland room, sat me down, and offered coffee. I said yes, hoping the caffeine would kick my brain into high gear because I hadn't been able to formulate an alibi on the drive to the station. When they didn't return after ten minutes, and then twenty, I realized leaving murder suspects alone must be some sort of tactic to keep us on edge.

It was working.

I dangled my keys in front of the baby's face, moving them back and forth, and watching as his eyes worked hard to follow the glinting, jingling metal. I'd had no intention of falling in love with the Little Guy and couldn't imagine anything good coming of it. But it was happening.

The detectives came back in. The woman handed me a cup of surprisingly good coffee. I slurped it fast, ignoring the burn.

I thought even faster. I had to get my story straight.

INTERMEZZO

CHAPTER 43

We arrived at Aunt Hildy's a day after the phone call. Her house smelled like practicality and cinnamon, just like it had when she was alive. Grim, watery November light sifted through the sitting room windows. My lap was heavy with the photo albums I'd gathered and held on to the way I hadn't been able to hold on to her. I knew death was inevitable given Hildy's age, but she was so smart and vital that the news still came as a shock. She'd gone to lunch with friends and had a heart attack. I was listed as the emergency contact on her phone, but by the time they reached me, she was gone. There'd been no sitting by her bedside, no chance to tell her how much I loved her, no opportunity to say goodbye.

In typical Hildy fashion, she'd prepared all the details of her funeral and asked her lawyer to launch the plan when she died. All I had to do was show up and grieve. The service was lovely; full of incense and stringed instruments playing songs of sorrow and joy. She'd selected gorgeous Bible verses, and the priest spoke of her with affection. Several friends offered moving eulogies. They'd left room for me to say a few words, but when I went up to try, all that came out were tears.

She was my last connection to my father, and I hadn't been able to attend his funeral. It was like I was burying them both.

A box sat on the floor next to me, waiting to be filled with the photographs I gripped. There wasn't much from the house I planned to take back home, but the pictures would definitely go with me.

Jimmy poked his head in the door. "The estate sale people called. They'll be here in an hour to start sorting and pricing." Aunt Hildy's lawyer had informed me that the house was mine, and I couldn't imagine emptying it of her things. But Hildy knew even that; she prearranged a clear-out company to come in and auction everything off.

"Okay," I said.

"Want some help?" he asked.

"No. But thank you." I'd removed her intimates and the contents of the medicine cabinet. The pictures were the last thing we needed to attend to. The last hold I'd have on the place before it was turned over to strangers.

I started crying again, or maybe I hadn't really stopped. Jimmy dropped to his knees next to me and wrapped me in his arms. His warmth and understanding were gifts I didn't deserve, but I took them anyway.

On our way out of town, we stopped so I could spend a few minutes in the Mary chapel of Aunt Hildy's church. She'd loved it so much, and I thought maybe I could find her there. The place was empty, and I sat before the statue she'd called Our Lady. Peace wove around me along with the scents of candle smoke, roses, and centuries. I felt pulled out of time, out of that moment of grief and into an odd sense of calm. I couldn't sense Hildy's presence but still felt she was somehow there with me. I wished I'd brought the rosary beads she'd given me.

Jimmy watched me closely when I got back in the car. "It looks like it helped," he said.

I nodded. "It did."

"Ready to go home?"

"Yes," I said, though it wasn't exactly the truth.

The peace from the chapel didn't last, of course.

I didn't know what I was going to do about the house. I loved Merrivliet. It was like a healthy part of me surrounding a rotten core. As the days passed, I considered moving there and making a clean start of things. Leaving both Jimmy and Thayer behind. Jimmy would be better off without me. I could start over in the place where I'd only been known as Hildy's niece, carrying no baggage. No longer an adulterous wife and a lying friend. I could offer plein air classes to make money until I found a real teaching job, and pretend my life hadn't unfolded the way it had.

In the end I knew I couldn't do it. Jimmy deserved to be a dad, and to have an honest wife. And I couldn't imagine sullying what Merrivliet meant to me by bringing my broken reality into it.

The house became a touchstone though. If I couldn't take it anymore, I could always go there.

CHAPTER 44

With Aunt Hildy gone, my whole system of balance was broken. Tears weren't a big enough outlet. A few prayers in a church and at the side of her grave felt like tokens, fleeting and disconnected from the ongoing reality of loss. Several days were filled with nothing but Jimmy's pity and endless screen-scrolling. A story about ritual scarification as artform gave me the idea for how to vent the pain.

It took a while to come up with the right symbol. I considered a four-leaf clover, but they'd been my thing with Daddy, not with her. Roses and rosaries were too complicated. Hildy's love for music finally provided the solution. I googled the G-clef and drew the pattern on the top of my left wrist, referencing the image to make sure I got the swirls right.

The knife drawer in our kitchen held a collection of options, and I wasn't sure which would do the job best. The initial puncture was fairly easy, but I didn't expect the skin to resist the pull of the knife so much. I tried a sharper one, hoping it would go faster, but we weren't great about keeping our blades honed, and the second wasn't much better. I had to keep wiping away the blood and starting again. Sweat dripped into my eyes by the time I got the basic S shape done.

The cuts hurt. A lot. My hand shook as I finished making the big dot at the bottom. I went to the living room, grabbed a handful of ashes from the fireplace, and pushed them into the wound, making sure each line and curve was packed.

Ashes to ashes.

It stopped the bleeding. I wrapped my wrist and went to bed. When Jimmy got home from work, I kept my arm hidden beneath the sheet.

"Bad day, huh?" he said, kissing my forehead.

"It wasn't great." Normally I'd hug him back, but he was worried enough about my mental state, and would probably make me go to the ER which might mess up my handiwork.

"You want to get up? Come watch the news with me? I'll make you some soup."

"I had a snack a few minutes ago, so I think I'll take a nap, if that's okay." He stood watching my face, and I could tell he was about to try talking me into going downstairs. I yawned ostentatiously.

His sigh was quiet. Resigned. "All right. But it's not healthy to stay in here so much, honey."

"I'll have dinner with you tomorrow. I promise." My words seemed to work because he just stroked my hair and then went downstairs.

When he came up to bed a few hours later, I huddled in on myself and pretended to be asleep. I hid my wrist again when he kissed me goodbye in the morning. But he saw it that night when he made me get up to take a shower.

"Sweetheart! What happened?"

"You don't actually want to know."

"Let me take a look." He held my hand in his big, gentle grip, and tugged at the tape. There was no getting around it, so I just let him do it. When he saw the wound, he went silent, looking from my face to my arm and back again. I wasn't impressed with how it looked. The final line was kind of jagged. I could see why he wouldn't be impressed either. "What the hell did you do?" he finally asked, his voice sad and confused.

"I'd hoped it would come out better."

"What's the gray stuff?"

"Ashes. They're good for healing."

"You're either going to let me clean this out, or you're going to the ER. Take your pick," he said, shaking his head.

"But why? It's not swollen. There's no irritation. It looks like it will heal just fine."

"You aren't listening. Which will it be?"

"Fine. Clean it."

Jimmy took me by the good hand and led me to the bathroom. I sat on the toilet seat while he got out hydrogen peroxide and cotton pads, then worked on my arm. He was slow and gentle, and my heart swelled with a peculiar kind of gratitude-shaped love. But it hurt like a bastard, and I couldn't help grunting and jerking my arm from the pain. "Do you want to tell me what you were doing?" he asked.

"She was a musician." He looked up from my wrist, his eyes soft and sad. "I had to do something to honor her. Something sort of big."

"But why this?"

"It's an indigenous peoples thing. Mourning scarification." He shook his head and went back to work. "At least I didn't do it on my face."

"I suppose I should be grateful?"

"Definitely."

He finished cleaning it, all the while muttering about how we should still go to the hospital. But he admitted I was right; it didn't look angry, and the site didn't feel warm.

"I couldn't get all the ashes out." He slathered the wound with antibiotic ointment and placed a clean cotton pad on top.

"Good."

"We'll see how you feel about that in 10 years. It's not pretty now, and unlike you, it won't improve with age."

"It's not supposed to be pretty."

"Well then you achieved your goal." He put away the supplies, still shaking his head. "Sweetheart?" His voice shifted toward serious. "Do you think you should see a counselor to help deal with all this? Maybe join a grief support group?"

He wouldn't accept a brush off for this question, so I paused for a moment to look like I was considering it. There was no way I'd go into a counselor's office. They'd break through the shaky semblance of sanity I'd carefully assembled throughout my lifetime. "Maybe I will,"

I said, nodding with slow sincerity. "I'll give it some thought."

"Good." He heaved a sigh which sounded like relief.

My heart surged with guilt and gratitude. He was so much more than I deserved. "Thanks Jimmy. For being such a great husband."

"Thank *you*, baby. For being the perfect wife."

I halted a bitter laugh by squeezing my sore wrist. "That's me. The perfect wife."

The wound healed just as ugly as he'd predicted, with gray bumpy bits. The shape was a sign of the beauty that was her, and the bumps represented the ugliness of her absence. The ugliness of the things I needed to be punished for.

I hated it, and I loved it.

CHAPTER 45

The next domino fell the following week, once I'd returned to work. My phone rang at 7:45 in the morning. This time it was Lee.

"Talk fast; the kids are about to storm the fortress..." I started to greet her but stopped at the sound of her sobs. "What happened? Are you okay?"

"I've got to get out of here!" She choked out the words between deep, ratcheting wails.

"Honey, what's the matter?" She kept crying. "All right. Just cry it out for a minute." I sat listening to her storm of emotion and watching the clock. The bell for the next class was due to ring in five minutes. I had to find out what was happening and how I could help before it rang. Her sobs slowed. "Do you think you can talk now?"

"It's just that I've been holding it in all night. I couldn't let him know I was this upset."

So it was related to Thayer. "Do you need me to get a sub? I can get one."

"I just need to get out of here and I don't know where to go."

"What happened?"

"He's been cheating on me!"

Oh my God. How did she find out? Did he tell her? Why wasn't she screaming at me?

"Last night some bitch called here. She's been fucking Thayer.

Apparently he broke up with her and she's raging. He was cheating on me Kristy!" She broke down into tears again. "I can't believe it. I should have left him a long time ago, but I didn't. I couldn't. And now…" A new wave of sobbing broke out. "Oh Kristy, what am I going to do?"

I felt like I'd been punched in the temple. My thoughts were jumbled. I was simultaneously relieved, furious, and broken hearted that he'd betrayed me. Betrayed both of us.

"Kristy?" she said.

"Let me think…" I finally stuttered. "Let me think…"

"I have to get out of here."

"Yes. Yes, you do. He went to work, right?"

"Yes. He just left."

"Go pack your stuff. Then come to the school. By the time you get here, I'll have a plan."

"Okay." She sniffed hard, as if trying to pull her shit together by the sheer act of snorkeling up a nose full of snot. It didn't work. She broke down again.

"Shh, honey. It's going to be okay," I said. "This is horrible and he's a mother fucker, but we're going to figure it out. Text me when you get here." Lee calmed down again enough to hang up the phone, right before the bell rang.

The kids streamed in. I shut down my emotion enough to get the class started on their projects, and then called the office to get someone to come stay with them. I walked down to let the principal know there'd been an emergency. My face must have looked like a tragic mask because she was super nice. The news gut punched me, even though I shouldn't have been shocked. Thayer had cheated on all his girlfriends with me, after all, and that apparently hadn't stopped just because he'd gotten married. It was stupid to think he wouldn't cheat on me too.

The pain of it was lavish and stupefying. I'd told myself I was protecting Lee by being there for him sexually. Turned out that was bullshit. Turned out everything was bullshit.

When her car appeared I slapped myself out of the hysteria which threatened to take over. I could spend the rest of my life feeling sorry for myself and trying to figure out whether I could have changed anything. Right now, Lee needed me. I had to do something to help her.

She was right; she *did* need to get away from him. It was the only way she could escape the gravitational pull he exerted. I knew all too well how impossible it was not to get sucked back into him, even though you knew what a controlling dick he was. She'd become a shadow of herself. There was no way she could stand up to him the way she was now. If she didn't leave while she had the chance, she'd stay and be crushed into nonexistence.

I was different. I was made of stronger stuff and could handle it.

I thought about having her come and stay in our spare room. We could get my painting materials out of there and turn it into a safe space for her. But we'd be the first place Thayer looked. Lee's mom was an option, but she lived in Arizona and Lee hated it there. She loved bundling up in sweaters in cool weather, and her mother's new-age wackiness drove her crazy. It might be okay for a week or so, but it wasn't a long-term solution. Plus, it was too far for a quick getaway.

And then I thought of Aunt Hildy's house. It was the perfect solution. I could send her to Merrivliet.

When she pulled up and got out, I wrapped her in a big hug. She started to cry again, and my heart ached for her. Ached for us both.

"What am I going to do, Kristy?" Lee blew her nose and looked at me. Her face was so transformed by sadness that she looked almost elderly. "I'm scared."

I knew what she meant. I'd seen his face go rigid when he was mad. "We're getting you out of town. You're going to Hildy's."

The thought about it for a minute, and started nodding. "That could work." Then she let her head fall back, looking exhausted. "Wait. Thayer knows she left you the house, right? He'll obviously think I might head there."

I laughed, the sound jagged and slightly insane. Despite our sexual closeness, Thayer didn't pay attention to me or my life. He'd given me a cursory "Sorry for your loss," and "Death is inevitable. You just have to move on," talk. He never asked about her when I went to visit. He just told me to have a good time, and then complimented me on my tan while taking my bra off once I got back. "He doesn't know Aunt Hildy left me the house."

She looked confused. "How can he not know?" She paused to think, then rolled her eyes. "Of course he doesn't know. Good. I can go there."

"It's perfect. There isn't a better place for recovering than Merrivliet. You'll see."

Lee just stared at the ground, thinking. "That should work." She looked back at me. "Oh, Kristy. I'm so scared." It was the second time she'd said it.

"What do you mean?"

"I know you think you know him. But you also don't. There are things I didn't tell you."

"Well maybe you *should* have!" If she'd told me, maybe things could have been different.

"You're probably right."

"You can tell me now," I said, trying to be supportive even though I thought I might break into a million pieces.

"Actually, I can't. I'm too exhausted. And I have a long drive. How far is it?"

"About eight hours. Depending on how fast you drive."

"Okay."

I took my key ring out of my purse, pulled off the right keys, and handed them to her. "Put the address in your phone." I gave her the address and she tucked her phone back in her bag.

"He'll try to find me. He denied there was anything going on. But the things she said!" Lee shook her head in disbelief. "It was real. When I acted like I didn't believe him something changed. His eyes went all cold and..." She struggled to come up with the words. "I've seen that happen before when he was upset, but it was nothing compared to this."

I was very familiar with that gaze. I shivered.

"He acted like it was my fault for believing lies about him. Like I was crazy." She broke into tears again. "But that part I could handle. It was his eyes. I felt like if I didn't stop arguing with him, he was going to do something to me." She turned her face toward me again. "But I can't do it! I can't pretend I don't know! I should have left two months ago…"

"Were you fighting then?"

She blurted out a laugh so full of pain and derision that I cringed. "Were we fighting? No. We don't really fight, Kristy. It was… something else." My mind erupted with questions. It was Thayer after all, so it could have been so many things. She shook her head as if trying to shake off the weeping-induced cloudiness. "I have to get out of here. If he finds me and knows I tried to leave him, I don't know what he'll do."

"Do you have what you need?"

"I packed the stuff that seemed most important. I'm sure I've forgotten something though."

"Okay then. Let's get you on the road. I need hugs." I opened my arms for her. She bent to hug me. Her frame felt bony and fragile. "I love you, Lee. Everything is going to be all right in the end."

"Am I doing the right thing?"

I thought about how hard it was going to be without her; my closest friend. My throat closed. "Yes, sweetie. You're doing the right thing. Now get going."

She didn't release me. "I love you Kristy. I'm going to miss you so much."

My tears overflowed. "No you're not." I gave her a last squeeze then pushed her away. "I'm going to talk to you constantly and probably drive you crazy."

"Not possible." She took keys out of her purse and opened the car door. The back seat was piled with stuff. She climbed in. "Thank you, Kristy. You're the best friend a girl could ever have."

I choked down a sob. "Get out of here," I said, jerking my chin forward, playing the tough guy. She nodded, still looking at me, then closed the door. I knocked on the window so she'd roll it down.

"Forgot to tell you the house is empty. You'll kind of be camping. But the electricity is still turned on."

"That's okay. I don't care."

"Okay then. Better go."

"All right."

I could see the tears were about to fall again, so I stepped away from the car and raised my hand to wave. "Safe travels, sweetie." She started the car and pulled away. I felt relieved, filled with grief, and completely drained. My best friend was gone. My aunt was gone. Thayer had betrayed me.

I got in my car and wept.

CHAPTER 46

When the storm of emotion waned, I drove around for a while to clear my head and control my anger, wishing I was in Rochester and could drive out to the countryside where Ms. Hyslip had taken me. My mind was so blown by the day's news I wasn't sure what to think. If Thayer wasn't with Lee anymore, was it less bad to keep fucking him? If he was capable of cheating on us both, did I really *want* to fuck him? There was a lot to consider, but in the meantime, I had to come up with something to say to him once he realized she was gone.

You'd think with all the cheating I did I'd be good at subterfuge, but throughout our marriage, if Jimmy asked where I'd been I just told him the truth: that I'd stopped to see my cousin. I'd never needed to lie to Thayer. There was the stopping-birth-control thing but that wasn't so much a lie as an omission. Also, the planning to stop-having-sex-with-him thing, but again, omission.

Thayer was smart, and so... penetrating. I drove and thought about the way magicians used misdirection, considering how to deflect his attention. My fury lasted until I got home, which was helpful because it fueled my planning and resolve.

When Jimmy got there, I offered him the basic details. He assumed my rage was on Lee's behalf, and wrapped me in his arms when it manifested as tears. "Shh, baby, it's going to be okay. You know Thayer is basically a dick. She'll be better off without him." What he said was true, but there was so much more to it than that. He let me cry for a little longer before asking "So where'd she go?"

I'd prepared for the question, and now it was show time.

"I don't know. She wouldn't tell me." Jimmy was too honest. If Thayer interrogated him, he'd figure it out just by what he refused to answer. "She seemed really scared of him and said if I didn't know he couldn't make me tell him."

"Wow… something bad must have been going down if she had that kind of fear."

"I know. And that makes it worse. How did I not know?" I started crying again, half in actual sorrow and half in hope he'd stop asking questions.

"Let it out honey. You're going to need to be strong when Thayer comes to talk to you."

I nodded into his shoulder, knowing how right he was.

"Do you want me to go kick his ass? You know the boy's bugged me since the day I met him."

I gave a wet snort. "Your ass would be the one I'd be worried about. You've never been a fighter."

"I could learn. Watch some YouTube tutorials."

"In case I haven't told you lately, I love you," I said, gratitude and guilt doing battle for position in my heart.

"I love you too baby. It's going to be okay."

He was wrong, of course.

Thayer didn't call until first thing the next morning. "Let me talk to her," he said, not bothering with hello.

"Lee? She's not here."

Thayer laughed. "Good try. Of course she's there. Where else would she go? Put her on the phone. She's not answering hers."

"I'm serious Thayer. She's not here." I wondered if he could hear the coldness in my tone. Either way, he hung up. I stared at my phone until the screen went dark. It was kind of a relief that he'd given up that easily, but at the same time, I'd been braced for battle and my adrenaline was pumping.

The doorbell rang ten minutes later. Jimmy was closest to the door, so he opened it. Thayer stormed in and looked around. "Where is she?" he demanded.

"She's not here." Jimmy said.

Thayer stalked toward me. He stepped close and stared, hard. I could see the rage behind his eyes, well past the simmering point. His body vibrated anger. "Kristy?" He said, very, very quietly.

Jimmy appeared at my side and put his hand on Thayer's shoulder. "You need to back it up, son." Thayer glanced at him like he was a gnat, but stepped back. It was a relief to have him out of my air space. "I said she's not here," Jimmy wrapped his arm around my shoulder, and drew me in tight, his voice nearly a growl.

Thayer ran a hand through his hair. The muscles in his jaw clenched rhythmically. He turned away from us for a minute to look out the window. "I'll accept that she's not here. So where is she, Kris?" He turned his glare back toward me. "I know she talked to you."

"She did indeed. And she told me about that bitch you've been banging." His eyes flared with warning but the only way to get through it was to keep going. "So she bugged out. Packed some stuff and headed out of town."

"Where? Where'd she go?"

"She doesn't know," Jimmy said, still trying to be my shining knight.

"I have no idea," I said.

"Of course you do." Thayer kept staring me down. "Lee tells you everything."

"Not this time. She said if I knew, you'd find a way to make me tell you. And she was undoubtedly right."

His eyes flared again, warning and calculating.

Adrenalin was pumping in newly high levels. My heart pounded and my face felt like it was on fire. I was in full-on attack mode, but realized I needed to be careful not to go too far.

"She doesn't know where she *is* Thayer," Jimmy said. "If Lee wants to talk to you, she'll answer the phone. Otherwise, might be time to let her go. Sometimes a player has to pay the price."

Thayer cocked his head at Jimmy, looking a bit like a deranged bull.

"Is that right, James?" He looked my way, then back at him again. "Is that right?"

It was obviously time to de-escalate. "Look," I said. "When I talk to her again, I'll ask her to reconsider. That's really all I can do."

Thayer watched me. "You could call her now."

"Nope." I shook my head. There was no way I was going to call her with him there.

"I'm sorry for what you're going through, but Kristy and I have to go to work. Maybe work would be good for you too," Jimmy said. He moved to Thayer and put his hand on his back to move him toward the door. I was impressed by his bravery. Jimmy was taller and broader than Thayer, but he was a teddy bear. Thayer knew it, so I was surprised when he cooperated.

Before leaving, he turned back to look at me. "I'll talk to *you* later," he said.

"All right now. You go to your office. Get some distraction." Jimmy said. He closed the door behind Thayer. We looked at each other. "You all right?" Jimmy asked. I nodded. He shook his head and walked toward the bathroom. "Oh, what wicked webs." He looked back at me. I nodded, mute and exhausted from the exchange. "I'm sorry you have to deal with all this, honey. What a circus." He went in and closed the door.

It was a relief to have the initial encounter over, but I knew we weren't done. Thayer would never give up that easily. I was due to be interrogated again, and soon.

The smell of ramen and tuna fish in the teacher's lounge turned my nervous stomach, but I tried to force down a protein bar to offset the bad coffee I'd been drinking too much of. Seeing Thayer's name when my phone lit up didn't help. I told him I'd call right back, then went outside and ducked into a corner where two wings of the school met. It was out of the wind and away from the eyes of anyone using the side door. The grass was sodden and brown beneath my feet.

"You really want me to believe you don't know where she is?" he asked.

"What can I say? You picked a smart one. She might not know

everything about us, but she knows I couldn't keep a secret from you."

He was silent for a minute, but I could feel the tension traveling from his phone to mine. I imagined birds innocently flying through the waves of the call's transmission getting fried to a black frizzle and dropping out of the sky. He finally broke the silence. "FUCK!"

My body sagged with relief. It sounded like he believed me. And with the relief came a resurgence of my own anger.

"What, exactly, did you expect? You were screwing around on her. And on me. Did you really think we wouldn't find out?"

"You don't know what you're talking about."

"Lee told me what that skank said. You can try to lie your way out of it, but a woman doesn't say what she did without a darned good reason. Woman scorned, and all that. You were screwing her. Keep lying all you want to Lee, but I'm not going to buy your explanations, so just save your breath." For once he was quiet, probably shocked I was standing up to him. "Turns out you're kind of a man whore." I knew I should drop it, but I didn't seem able to.

"You should really examine your part in what happened, Kris."

"*Me*? What do I have to do with anything?"

"If it weren't for you, I wouldn't have cheated on her."

I couldn't wrap my head around the words he was saying. "But…," I stuttered.

"You're always putting yourself out there. Always looking at me with those eyes. Arching your back so your tits point at my face." I tried to picture myself doing those things. Of course I looked at him. but I didn't remember the back arching thing. "You're the one who made me believe fucking around was okay!" he continued.

I couldn't help it. I laughed out loud.

"Did you just *laugh*?" He sounded genuinely indignant. I couldn't answer. I was still laughing. "Fine. Guess we'll talk later. When you get your shit together."

I clicked the phone off and the laughter transformed into sobs. I doubled over from the pain and idiocy of his words, filled with rage, confusion, and sorrow. My lunch break was almost over. I had to get my act together before going back inside.

The poor students had to put up with a touchy, distracted teacher for the rest of the afternoon. All I could think about was whether what he said was actually true.

CHAPTER 47

We didn't talk for quite a while after that. I was glad he left me alone, but his words were like acid eating away at my insides. I felt tired all the time and the thought of food made me nauseous. Jimmy was as sweet as usual, and worried I was slipping into depression.

I couldn't let go of the idea that Thayer's cheating was my fault. People fell into patterns of behavior so easily. When you do the same thing a certain number of times it turns into a habit. I'd been the one who started pestering him for sex way back when he came to Lisa's house. I'd habituated him to it, so even when he had girlfriends, he'd grown to think it was okay. If I'd refused to have sex with him, he and Lee would have worked out.

Intellectually I knew that line of thinking was complete bullshit, but the certainty that it was my fault felt emotionally true.

There had to be a way to atone for what I'd done to Lee, though nothing could change what had happened. Eventually I decided to give her the house. Hopefully Aunt Hildy's spirit lingered there and would help encourage Lee's creativity. Maybe there her writing would flourish.

A fresh wave of grief hit. Merrivliet was my haven of safety and love; the place I'd been spiritually and emotionally nourished. The place I'd explored the arts and painting. It felt like the only treasure I'd ever have. But the sacrifice would offset my sins a tiny bit.

The decision felt agonizing but right. After I calmed down and allowed the idea to settle, I told Jimmy. He initially balked because we'd planned to use the house for summer vacations, but I told him it would be too painful. Then he suggested we sell it, but he saw my face and dropped it. All he ever wanted was for me to be happy.

Because of Aunt Hildy's careful planning, her house had transferred to me very quickly. I made an appointment with our lawyer and sent the paperwork to Lee. Sealing the envelope was like throwing the final shovel of dirt on Aunt Hildy's grave. But once it was in the mail, I felt better. Less burdened.

I wondered what it was like to be away from Thayer permanently. Part of me thought it must be fantastic; like a balloon let loose from a cranky child's grip, flying straight up without constraints. But the other part of me thought free flight would be terrifying. I didn't know if I could handle being so completely unmoored.

CHAPTER 48

It turned out there was a reason the idea of food made me want to retch. I'd gotten knocked up the very first month I was off my pills. Maybe even the first week. I did the stick test first, and then made an appointment with my OB/GYN who confirmed it. She also confirmed the timing, which freaked me out, because I couldn't remember having intercourse with Jimmy during that stretch. We'd traded oral once, but the time frame had been so fraught and emotional that sex with him hadn't been on the top of the list.

It had to be Thayer's baby.

I tried to consider the idea that there was some transformation of spirit from my aunt to the tiny being in my belly. I wanted to imagine raising a mini-Hildy. But for some reason I was certain the child was a boy.

When I broke the news to Jimmy, he was elated. He chastised me for not telling him I was going off the pills, but he was so filled with joy that he accepted that I'd wanted to surprise him. He couldn't stop touching my stomach and talking to it, even though my belly was still pretty flat.

"Let's not tell Thayer, okay?" I asked during one of the baby-whisperer sessions.

He looked at me, eyes wrinkled with questions. "We haven't been talking to him since Lee left. But are you sure you don't want to fill him in?"

"Yes. There's no reason he needs to know." He mistook the emotion in my voice as anger.

"Lots of people cheat, Kristy." Jimmy's sense of family ran deep, and even though he wasn't a Thayer fan, he was never comfortable with relationship rifts.

"I know that."

"How long do you think it will take before you want to speak to him again?"

The complexity of what I wanted made answering hard. "Our relationship is over," I finally said.

"I'm so sorry everything's gone down this way," Jimmy said. "You're a sweetheart, and he's a dumb shit to have done that to Lee. He doesn't deserve a cousin like you."

The lump in my throat was hard to talk around, so I just hugged him, resting my head against his chest where I could hear his heart beating. Jimmy was such a good guy. He would make a wonderful father.

The next time Lee called, I immediately started panic babbling. "You wouldn't believe how bad the traffic was around Orchard Park today."

"Good morning yourself!" Lee said.

"I thought I was going to shoot somebody. Maybe myself."

"Lucky you don't have a gun."

"Seriously. What's up?"

"I just wanted to tell you how fantastic the living room looks painted. It's glorious!" Lee was fixing up the place, one space at a time. I had mixed feelings about the changes, but figured it couldn't bother me too much as long as I never saw it.

"I'm so glad!" I said, feigning enthusiasm. "Which room is next?"

"The back hallway, I think. It's pretty gloomy back there."

"To hell with gloom. That's my mantra."

"I guess it should be mine too. How's Jimmy?"

"It's basketball season, so I'm a widow."

"I figured. Moscato keeping you warm?"

My silence went on for a beat too long. The time had come to tell her. "I'd planned to call and tell you," I said.

"Tell me what?"

"About the rabbit."

"What?" Lee sounded confused. "Did you get a rabbit for your classroom? The kids must be stoked!"

A sigh of frustration escaped despite my best intentions. "Don't be daft. I'm saying there'll be no more Moscato for me."

"Is it Lent already, or are you just worried about that beautiful butt of yours again?"

"There are other reasons people stop drinking cheap wine than losing weight Lee. Are you being deliberately obtuse?"

Lee fell silent, and then it hit her. "You're... pregnant?"

"Bingo!" I wondered if my jocularity sounded as forced to her as it did to me.

"How far along are you?

"Three months," I said.

"How are you feeling?"

"My boobs are weird. They look puffy and I have to wear a bra all the time because anything brushing against my nipples hurts like crazy. Jimmy's pissed because I've banned him from the fun bags." Jimmy had been nothing but sweet and attentive to the sensitivity of my breasts, but I couldn't seem to stop faking it.

"Poor Jimmy," Lee said. "Any morning sickness?"

"A little? But it hasn't been too bad, thank God."

"Jimmy must be over the moon."

"He's insufferable. Already found a miniature Buffalo Bills jersey for him. Or her."

"Do you have a preference?"

"I'd like a boy, I think. Someone to keep Jimmy company because you know how I feel about sports. Not that a girl couldn't be a fan. God, listen to me. I'm in a gender box."

"At least you recognize it. First step to recovery and all that."

"The victory is mine," I said, feeling the opposite of victorious.

"I'm happy for you sweetie." She didn't sound all that happy, which was odd. But it was hard to focus on anything other than getting the conversation over with.

"I'm so glad! I figured it could go two ways. You could either be happy about hearing some good news, or be sad because you won't be here with me as this creature takes over my body."

"I'm probably both."

"That makes sense."

"Are you taking care of yourself? Got the vitamins? Cutting down on the crack?"

"No crack, no sweet Moscato. Just horse pills which make me constipated. No wonder I'm a bitch."

"Well, you're my bitch, and I love you." The words were funny, but her voice wasn't humorous.

"I love you too," I said. "You sound odd though. Are you all right? Have you heard from my dear cousin?"

"It's going okay. And no news on that front. The calls have slowed down."

"I wish you'd get a new phone. I'd feel a lot better if he had no way of being in touch with you."

"Me too. Unfortunately, all my business contacts have that number, and there's still a chance I might need to get a real job." Lee was working as a waitress in a diner and seemed to like it. She'd befriended the elderly owner of a junk shop and hung out there regularly. Life for her seemed to be settling down.

"Might be time to reinvent yourself. Completely. Isn't that what your old lady friend has been telling you?"

"What are you, Maria's echo? Listen, tell your handsome husband I said congratulations. And hug yourself for me." Lee's voice hitched a bit on the last phrase.

"You sure you're okay?" I asked.

"I'll be fine. I mean I AM fine."

"Sounds like you're the one who could use the Moscato."

"You know I can't stand the stuff."

"That's because it takes someone this sweet to handle something that sweet."

Lee snorted. "All right Sugar. I'd better go."

"Okay. Talk to you soon." I hung up, feeling like the lowest rank of vermin that ever crawled out of a sewer.

The days passed, and I tried not to panic about the baby being born blonde, pale, and obviously not a product of Jimmy's loins. I decided I'd better keep on the good side of Thayer in case I ended up needing his help, so I told Jimmy we were talking again. When Thayer texted me our booty call code word for the first time since the blowup, I decided to go ahead and meet him. With Lee gone there didn't seem to be that much reason *not* to sleep with him.

That first time, he joked about my boobs seeming bigger. I wriggled to move his attention elsewhere because they hurt, and tried to concentrate on pleasure rather than the future. It worked, for a few minutes.

After that, things went back to our old pattern. I made him promise he wouldn't cheat on me, which, looking back, is pretty hilarious. But Thayer was a little weird about where we had sex. He didn't want us to use the bedroom when I came over. He didn't even want to go upstairs. I figured he viewed it as some kind of shrine to her memory. We generally stayed in the living room where he turned on cheesy Elvis songs. I was okay with everything but the music.

CHAPTER 49

Thayer texted me around 11:00 one night.

I need you to come over. Right now. It's about Lee.

Jimmy had just fallen asleep. "Jimmy? Jimmy."

"Whah?"

"I have to go to Thayer's. Something happened. Something about Lee."

He started to sit up. "I'll go with you. Just give me a minute to wake up."

"No, honey. You have to get up early. Go back to sleep. I wouldn't have bothered you except I didn't want you to wake up and find me gone."

"Are you sure? Because I can be ready in two seconds." The last part was a stretch. Jimmy woke up groggy and came to life slow.

By that time, I'd slipped on my shoes and was zipping up my sweatshirt. "Thank you. I know you would." I walked over and kissed his cheek. "Go back to sleep."

"Okay, if you're sure. I love you baby. Tell him I said hello."

I was relieved it had gone so easily.

Thayer answered the door right away, like he'd been waiting for the bell to ring. I followed him to the living room and sat down.

"So what's up? Why the command appearance?" Thayer's hand shot toward me, waving a piece of paper. I took it. It was a statement from a women's health clinic, addressed to Lee. The service listed was for a vacuum aspiration.

Lee had had an abortion.

"Oh my God," I said.

"You're going to pretend you didn't know?"

"I had no idea."

"Lee is your best friend. There's no way she did this without telling you. You had to know she was pregnant."

"I swear Thayer. I didn't." My brain was moving so fast it could barely form sentences. No wonder she'd acted odd when I told her my own news. "You know I don't lie to you! That's the one good thing about our fucked-up relationship." Saying I didn't lie to him was a lie, which scrambled my mind further.

He ranted for a few minutes about women's intuition and how could I possibly not know, and a bunch of other stuff. Then he started talking about finding Lee. I couldn't let that happen. His tone was ominous.

"You should give up on finding her," I said. "She's gone. You should just move on."

"There's no way I'm giving up on hunting that cunt down. No way in hell." His face was contorted with rage, and it scared me. I looked away, trying to control my thoughts, then remembered how he accused me of luring him. An inch of cleavage peaked out of my neckline, so I turned toward him and arched my back to see if it really did push my boobs up. His expression shifted. "Fuck her," he said, then picked up his phone, and turned on some music. Elvis again. I was beginning to hate Elvis. He came and stood right in front of me, with his crotch almost in front of my face.

I reached for his zipper.

CHAPTER 50

By the time I finished up with Thayer and went home, I'd worked up a pretty good head of anger at Lee, though for entirely different reasons than his. My mind kept circling around the same set of thoughts and questions. Why didn't she tell me? Why didn't she want to keep it? If she'd told me I could have talked her into keeping the baby. And if she'd kept it, I would have been able to stay away from Thayer so he could be a good daddy. I wouldn't want to risk his child losing their father the way I lost mine, but through divorce. It would have given me the reason I needed to kick my Thayer habit.

I called her at 6:30 the next morning, right after Jimmy left for his workout.

"You never call this early. Is everything all right?" Lee asked.

"You had an abortion!" I wondered again if it had been hard when I'd told her I was pregnant. Unlike me, she'd always talked about wanting to be a mother, which made her decision all the stranger. It was out of character all the way around.

"Kristy, I..."

"That was my second cousin! Or cousin once removed. Or something!" I'd not gotten a ton of sleep, which was never good for my thought processes.

"Listen..."

Images of her child playing with mine popped into my mind; the two presumably cousins but actually half siblings. I could tell how tired I was when I had those thoughts, recognizing the preposterous horror of the whole situation. "Don't say another word. I don't want to hear it."

"I couldn't figure out..."

"I'm not calling so you can try to explain it. I just wanted to let you know that I know. That's all. So bye." I hung up the phone, wishing for the days when you could slam a handset down into a cradle like in the old movies. It must have been so satisfying.

She hadn't told me, which meant I hadn't stopped betraying her. She hadn't told me which meant we weren't the friends I thought we were. It felt like I'd lost Lee all over again.

CHAPTER 51

Pregnancy takes over your life. Your back aches and your relationship with food alters. You can't drink alcohol, and you have to drape an herbal tea-bag string over the edge of your coffee cup to avoid dirty looks from your co-workers. Your boobs hurt when the shower hits them.

Jimmy was sappy ridiculous. He liked to lay his head on my stomach and listen. Mostly I think he heard my stomach processing the Cheerios I couldn't seem to get enough of. I wasn't sure how to tell Thayer, but it was inevitable that he'd figure it out.

The sky was dark on the March evening when I'd stayed late prepping for parent teacher conferences. The parking lot was almost deserted, but a BMW was parked right next to my old Toyota. Thayer got out when I got closer.

"Aren't you a sight for sore eyes," I said. The other thing about being pregnant? It made me horny, which doesn't make evolutionary sense. If a woman is already knocked up, why should she be hungry for more sex? Maybe orgasms were good for babies. "I've missed you." I stepped up close enough to catch his scent, which made the blood leave my brain and head south. He scanned my body up and down, which made the blood pound harder.

"It *has* been a while." Thayer said. "You must be raging by now. Did you have to take it out on Jimmy?"

"I channeled it all for you, baby." My words sounded phony and slutty even to my own ears. I slid into the space of his open car door so I could be closer to him. "Where can we go?" I asked.

He stroked my cheek with uncharacteristic gentleness. It seemed odd, but I leaned into the touch, wanting more of it. His hand slid under my chin, and he grabbed my jaw, hard. "First, we have something to talk about," he said. "I've been thinking about your body today. Your tits are huge. And you haven't gotten fully undressed for me in a while." He pulled up my tunic and ran his free hand along my belly which had begun to curve outward into a distinct baby bump. He pushed me away and I bounced back against the car door. It hurt where his fingers had pressed. My heart started pounding, hard.

He stepped back and started pacing like he did when he was upset, talking about how I should have been using birth control. "I *thought* we had an agreement," he said. Anger flew from his eyes like arrows tipped with poison. He was scaring me again. He scared me a lot over those months. I drew my bag over my stomach.

"I'm... sorry Thayer. But seriously?" I was frightened, but he was also pissing me off. "Sex is a two-way street. You could have used a condom."

He stepped up to me again and pulled my hair into a fist, making me gasp from the pain.

"Put your bag down."

He'd never gotten physical like that. I tossed the purse in the car, and he opened the back door and pushed me in so I was bent over the seat. He lifted my dress and yanked down my tights and though my mind was screaming that the whole thing needed to stop my body was clamoring for him. Somehow the fear and my anger at him and my body's sexual hunger all merged together. He was in me and moving and the tide was rising when suddenly it was over. He pulled away and started zipping up.

"Thayer... wait... why... come on!" I was panting in frustration.

"Fuck you. Get up."

"That was just mean. Now what am I supposed to do with myself?" I fixed my clothes and tried to get my body to calm back down.

"Shut up about that. We need to talk." He sat down in the driver's seat, throwing my purse to the floor. "Get in." I got in. "So, what are we going to do?" Thayer asked. "How likely is it the kid's mine?"

"Pretty likely."

"There will have to be consequences you know."

"Consequences? What do you mean? You aren't planning to tell Jimmy, are you? Please Thayer, don't..."

"No. We won't tell your blind dope of a husband."

I sighed with relief.

"Besides," Thayer continued "It will be more fun to watch him think it's his. If it comes out blonde, he'll just assume it comes through the family line, dumb schmuck."

"That's what I was thinking," I said. "We can say Grandpa William's genes won out." I felt awful talking about it.

"But you will have to pay. Make no mistake. Now get out of my car."

I grabbed my bag and climbed out. Thayer started the engine while I was half out the door and drove away fast. I had never felt so loathsome.

Little did I know how much worse I was about to feel.

CHAPTER 52

Lee called the next day. "I know you're still mad at me," she said. "But I had to call you. You'll never believe what just happened."

"What is it?"

"I got a message from Thayer. He says your baby is his. Can you believe he'd go that low?"

I tried to come up with words in response but failed.

"Kristy?"

"He can't be sure of it!" I finally said. "There's no way to prove it."

"Wait." The confusion in Lee's voice was obvious. "What do you mean he can't prove it?"

"Lee, I…"

She was speechless for a minute, but her breathing picked up pace. "You mean it's true? You've been *fucking* him?"

"I told you years ago that I slept with him."

"But you never said it was actually sex. And you were just kids!"

"I was 11. He was 17."

"Oh my God. 11? Isn't that rape?"

"It was consensual." Why was I trying to protect him?

"How is that possible if you were 11?"

"Regardless. I told you it happened. I just didn't tell you it wasn't the only time."

"You sure didn't!"

"It's been going on forever Lee. It never really stopped. Every once in a while, there'd be a break of a year or two, but then it would pick back up." My voice was apologetic, nearly panicky, picking up speed as I pushed the sentences out.

"Why, Kristy?" She was nearly gasping now. "How could you do that to me?"

The words were like a punch in the gut. Not that the reality of hurting her was anything new, but now she knew about it. My defense mechanism kicked in. "You know how he is! He's powerful. He's sexy. He's the epitome of the bad boy you want to tame." The words didn't come close to explaining the complexity of my connection to Thayer, but I didn't know how to form the deeper parts into sentences.

Lee made a deep sound of pain and disgust.

"It's like he had some kind of power over me," I continued. "I'd tell myself never again, and then bam, it was happening."

"Bam." Lee spat the word.

"That was a stupid choice of expressions. But seriously. I couldn't help it!" Lee didn't respond. The silence built for a few moments. "It's not like you wanted him!" I finally erupted, defensive again. "You told me you didn't want to have sex with him." I sounded disgusting even in my own ears but couldn't seem to stop. "Why are you so surprised he'd look for it somewhere else? I was kind of doing you a favor. Helping him let off some steam."

"You were doing me a favor?"

"Yes! If you look at it the right way."

Silence fell again, a silence as full and pregnant as my stomach.

"Well, I just thought I'd check with you," Lee choked out the words, her voice soft, stunned. "I assumed he was just mind-fucking me when he said the baby was his. Ha. Ha ha."

"I'm sorry, Lee, I just…"

"Don't bother Kristy. Don't bother."

"I've always loved him you know. I would have married him."

"You would have married your *cousin*?"

"Obviously I *couldn't* marry him. But I loved him that much."

"Does Jimmy know about any of this?" Lee's fury rolled through the phone and straight into my panic zone.

"I suppose you'll tell him and ruin my life the rest of the way."

"I have no idea what I'm going to do. Except say goodbye."

"Lee, wait! I need to know if you're planning to…"

"Goodbye Kris." Lee hung up.

CHAPTER 53

For the next two months I pretended Jimmy and I were in some sort of 1950s family sitcom where everything was beautiful and we were about to become the perfect family. Until school broke for the summer, I pretended I was a good teacher and tried not to think about how thin the line was between my sanity and my world crumbling into rubble. At night I lay awake listening to Jimmy's rumbles and trying to figure out how to fix everything, but never came up with answers.

The only thing that helped was Thayer. I used him like a mood-altering drug, and he made himself available for several doses a week, despite the looming cloud of his threat. I experienced all the heights and plummets of an addict as I lost myself in physicality and then plunged into feelings of self-disgust and shame.

Things went downhill when Thayer stopped answering my calls and texts. I had no way of compensating, no way of self-soothing. I thought I was going to have a nervous breakdown and end up in a psychiatric ward. I finally just went to his house one morning in July right after Jimmy took off for his fitness club. Once he let me in, I immediately started stripping, trying to be sexy, and lay back on the couch, opening my knees in invitation, feeling vulnerable and very, very needy. I held my arms out and tried to channel vixen. But when Thayer looked at me, his face screwed up in what could only be called revulsion.

"I can't do it," he said.

I slammed my knees together and hauled myself back to a sitting position. "What are you talking about?"

"Maybe after the baby. When you are back in shape. But now…" He waved a hand toward my torso, which was distended and stretched from the growing child. "Ugh!"

I was shocked. While my body had changed a lot, I thought the changes were strangely beautiful. I wanted to paint myself and other pregnant women and find a way to highlight the amazing fecundity we radiated. While I felt like crap about myself as a human being, and while many of the physical changes were uncomfortable, my body was kind of a masterpiece. Jimmy thought so too. He couldn't stop touching me.

I started to cry.

"Dear God. Let's not have tears," he said.

I babbled for a few minutes about how he used to like my softness in comparison to Lee's boniness.

"Lee might be bony, but at least she looks human," Thayer said.

"How is this not human?" I asked, gesturing toward my baby bump. Thayer threw his head back and looked at the ceiling. His expression was a mixture of disgust and impatience, and it broke the thin wall of my self-control. "Maybe you should go remind yourself of exactly what she's like." My voice jerked as I tugged on my socks.

"What are you trying to say?"

"I'm saying I know where she is." He came to stand in front of me, more menacing than I'd ever seen him. But I was beyond caring. "In fact, I gave her the place to go." I cackled while pulling my shirt over my head.

"You… gave her the place?" He shook his head as if he couldn't process what I was saying. "Where is she?" He grabbed my shoulders and started shaking me. All I could think of was the old ad campaign about never shaking a baby. I laughed at the grotesqueness of the situation. I laughed that I was somehow, weirdly, in control.

"She's in Massachusetts. I gave her Aunt Hildy's house. But you were too stupid to figure it out."

He let go of my shoulders, then lifted his arm and backhanded me.

My head bounced off the couch. My brain felt ricocheted, physically and emotionally. Thayer stormed into hallway, grabbed his keys, and headed toward the door.

"Bye-bye Thayer. Say hello to Lee for me." I don't know how I managed to choke out sarcasm given the black hole of devastation which was expanding in my chest. The look he threw back felt like another punch, but he kept going.

When the door slammed, my sorrow burst out as a swooping blast of sound, filling the room and my eardrums. The unfairness of his response was part of it. I didn't understand how he could find my body ugly when he knew it carried his child.

But I also wondered if maybe I'd been wrong to hide Lee's location all that time. Maybe it hurt him too much. Maybe having Lee in his life helped him be human while my presence just made him a monster.

A monster like me.

CHAPTER 54

Once the tears were spent, I pulled on the rest of my clothes, mortified that the whole exchange took place while I was partially naked. By then my mood had swung back toward anger. I decided to go upstairs and poke around, primarily because it would piss Thayer off if he knew.

I checked out the bathroom first. It was filthy. He must not have cleaned it in the months Lee had been gone, which wasn't surprising. Thayer "joked" about cleaning being women's work, and apparently he'd rather live like a pig than pick up a toilet brush.

Lee's office was next. It was unremarkable, other than that her chair was missing. Her desk was still there though, with its neat collection of supplies, an altar to her orderliness.

The guest bedroom came after that. I didn't expect to see much in there, but man did I get a shock when I saw what was in the closet. It was like a pop-up sex shop. There was lingerie of every color and degree of tackiness. A row of stands held wigs in various lengths and hair shades. There were falsies, drawers of hosiery, and an epic collection of stripper boots and FMPs.

"Holy shit," I said. The trip upstairs had certainly been worth it. I was pretty distracted. I wondered if the outfits were his idea or hers. It was hard to picture Lee suggesting it, and even harder to imagine her in a cup less black-pleather bustier.

The whole thing started to creep me out, and I backed away, then bolted from the room. It was more than I'd expected to see. No wonder he didn't take me upstairs. No wonder he missed her and didn't want me; they'd had some sort of costume-fueled passion fest. I couldn't compete with that.

The sorrow rose again, because I knew things were never going to get back to normal for Thayer and me. For so many reasons. I figured I might as well finish the self-flagellation and check out their bedroom, expecting some sort of weird S&M hardware attached to the headboard, or maybe an alarming collection of dildos. I braced myself for whatever it was I'd find.

But there was no bracing for what was actually in there.

The tan office chair I'd helped Lee pick out was pushed into a corner. A transparent white negligee was arranged on the back rest, with the spaghetti straps over the top edges, and the skirt draped down to rest on the seat.

"What the hell?" I said it out loud. I walked closer and saw the straps were attached with staples. A pair of matching filmy white panties was stapled to the seat. But the cushion was the most disturbing part. It looked like it had been attacked by an angry badger; cream-colored foam peeked out from a central tear, and there were stab marks all around it.

The lingerie was positioned the way a woman would wear it if she deflated to the thinness of nothing and then disappeared. A clothing hanger was duct taped to the headrest. A chunk of Styrofoam stuck up from the top of the hanger, presumably skewered on the curving part that normally hooked around a closet pole.

My mind tried to make sense of what was in front of me, but couldn't. It was too bizarre.

And then I saw it. A Styrofoam wig head lying on the floor by the window. I crept over to it, somehow afraid. Afraid of what it might do. Afraid of what I would see. Its face was turned away from me. Its neck had been broken off from the base, which must be what was still on top of the chair. I pushed it with my foot. The head rolled to look at me.

I'm pretty sure I screamed.

The hair was bad enough; it was a cheap blonde wig, but the locks had been crudely chopped off in a parody of a pixie cut. Worse, it had weird electric orange stripes as if a toddler tried to color it with a marker. But the face...

He'd drawn crude facial features on the indentations and outward pushings of eyes, nose, and mouth. There were black tears falling down both cheeks. He'd used a Sharpie.

How did I know he'd used a Sharpie?

Because the marker was imbedded halfway into one of the thing's eyes.

Its mouth was the worst part.

He'd carved a hole in the lips, and then shoved something in it. I didn't know what was in there. It was brown and deep red and crusting over. I bent closer to try to figure it out, before realizing I didn't really want to know.

For the second time in just a few minutes, I backed away, mind whirling.

He'd made this thing. The head must have been skewered on the top of the chair's headrest at some point.

It had short "red" hair.

It was supposed to be Lee.

I'd always thought skin crawling was just a phrase but turns out it's a real thing. It felt like there was an army of ants under my flesh trying to lift it up and carry it off, my skin fluttering like a flag.

Thayer had done this.

Thayer was scary.

Thayer might even be insane.

Thayer was on his way to find Lee.

CHAPTER 55

I thought about calling him but remembered how his eyes looked when he hit me. It was unlikely he'd stop. Plus, I was afraid of him now. Almost terrified. I knew I had to warn Lee though.

A message reported that her phone was out of service. I tried again and got the same thing. Perhaps she finally changed her number. If so, the timing sucked.

I waddled out of the house as quickly as my hugely pregnant belly permitted, and jammed into my car. I'd have to act fast to get to Lee before he did. He was probably already driving east, but he'd need to get the address from Lisa, and that would slow him down. Navigation systems always took you the slower route into town, so if I drove like a hellion, I might still be able to beat him.

I called Jimmy and told him Lee was in some kind of a panic and needed me. He was in the dark about what happened between us because of Thayer. He wasn't thrilled I was going, but because he's Jimmy, he didn't complain. Just told me to take care of our baby.

Driving such a long way while eight months pregnant was extremely uncomfortable. I held my pee for longer stretches than I should have, speeding and praying I didn't get pulled over. But with that much weight resting on your bladder, you don't have much choice and I had to stop more than I wanted to. Thayer's car never passed me on the road though. I didn't know if that was a good thing or a bad thing.

What I'd seen upstairs kept flashing through my mind. The closet full of costumes. That gruesome head. Lee's ravaged chair.

I drove faster.

There were two cars in Hildy's driveway and a third pulled up in front. One of them was Thayer's BMW. Seeing the house made my heart lurch with sorrow for Aunt Hildy. Even with all the tension and the driving need to get inside and try to stop him from doing whatever he was going to do, the pain of losing her still hit me.

The porch and front doors were both open, so I flew inside. There was someone in the kitchen, but it wasn't Lee. It was an old woman, sitting in a chair and holding a rolling pin. Something was lying on the floor next to her.

I walked closer, scared at what I was about to see.

"And now you? Kristy?" The woman asked. A cat mewled at me from beneath her chair. "This is what happens when you forget to lock the door, Lelita," she called toward the back hall. "Every kind of annoying comes flying in." Lee had told me about the old Italian woman who befriended her, so this had to be Maria.

Thayer was on the ground, with blood pooling under his head. For some reason cat food was spilled all around him. He looked dead.

I plopped awkwardly to the floor and took his face in my hands. "You stupid son of a bitch. Now look what you've done." I wrapped my arms around him and broke into tears.

"You should never move an injured person. You might make him pulverized," the woman offered.

She must be insane. "What? Pulverized?" I noticed blood on the rolling pin.

"It's something to do with his neck, I think. Or his spine. I do not know. But you shouldn't risk it, in case he lives."

I just shook my head and hugged him tighter, thinking he was already dead, that he couldn't have survived being beaten by that ferocious lady who'd probably been some mob boss' wife. That's when Lee emerged from the hallway. She had blood on her neck and around the scoop of her tank top.

"I heard you talking and thought maybe he was coming to," Lee said to the old lady. "Obviously that wasn't the case." She turned to me. "What the hell are *you* doing here?"

"I was going to try to stop him. I drove as fast as I could, but he had a head start." Thayer's chest moved up and down. He was breathing. Lee just stared at me, standing in the doorway with her arms crossed. "I shouldn't have told him, but I was so upset." I didn't know where to begin explaining the whole thing. It was so wide, and deep, and filled with murky alligators.

"You will have time to tell your story," Maria pronounced. "To the polizia. For now, you will shut your lying face." The sound of sirens wailed in the distance. Help would be there soon.

My tired eyes turned to Lee again. She resembled the girl I'd first known. Gone were the short hair, Oxford shirts, and khakis. In their place was the softer femininity I remembered. But all that stopped at her face and her motions. Where she'd been graceful and smooth before, she now moved in jerks and slams, and her face looked like it was etched from rock, as if she'd been turned into some sort of war memorial. Her eyes were equally hard as they looked at Thayer, at the mess on the floor, and at me.

The ambulance arrived first, with the police close behind. I wanted to ride with Thayer to the hospital, but the officers demanded I stay and provide a statement. Everyone seemed to know Maria. The cops asked her what happened and took some notes. Then Lee told them her version of the story.

She'd been making cookies when he walked in. He zip tied her to a chair and ripped out her earrings. She gestured toward her ears, and I could see the flesh was torn which explained the blood. "He was going to rape me, and then kill me with one of those." Lee pointed at the row of knives lined up on the counter. She kneed him in the nose and knocked him out momentarily when he'd bent to go after her cat, and that's when Maria got there. Apparently it was Maria who'd beaten the shit out of him. With the rolling pin.

I explained who I was, what I knew, what I'd seen in their bedroom, and why I'd shown up. Lee and Maria listened, which was nice because I didn't have to tell my story twice. Maria was still holding on to the rolling pin, and when I got to the part where I was describing the grotesque Lee creation in Thayer's bedroom, she lifted it and started tapping it in her palm. That's when the police officers realized they should probably take it away from her.

They finally wrapped up and talked about contacting the police department in Buffalo to have them check out the house. They asked for emergency contact information for Thayer's family. Then they finally let me go.

Maria told me how to get to the hospital.

"Listen," she said. "If that bag of merda wakes up, you tell him he is going to jail. And if he gets out of jail when he is old, with his cazzo shriveled to the size of a pinkie," she waggled her little finger as she said it "you tell him if he comes near to her, I will kill him."

The statement made no sense. By the time he was old she'd be long dead. But I just agreed. "Okay. I'll tell him."

"Bene." She nodded her head, then tipped her chin up to assess me. Her eyes softened. "It was a good thing you did. To try to stop him." I gave her a weak smile. Exhaustion from the drive and all the emotion was winning out. "All the rest is another story. You should be on your knees begging God to forgive you. But for coming? It is a bit of atonement." She looked at Lee as she finished speaking, and I wondered if she was saying it for my benefit or Lee's.

Either way, it was time for me to go. "I'm so sorry Lee. For everything." My words were trite and meaningless, but they were all I could offer. Lee just lifted her eyes to the ceiling and shrugged. I'm sure she had no idea how to respond. She must have been in shock from all that had happened. My apology was probably insignificant at that point.

The hospital was easy to find. I had to wait in the emergency room until they finished doing all the tests they needed to figure out how far from death he was, which gave me plenty of time to think. Plenty of time to roil around in my feelings of guilt and betrayal. Plenty of time to hyper focus on how obsessed he'd been with Lee when I thought I was the real love of his life. How much of my own life had centered around that false reality, and been perverted by it.

Once they got him settled into a room, they let me in to see him.

CHAPTER 56

The nurses came and went. I amped up his morphine. The beeping and whooshing receded as I watched Thayer's face and waited for him to die from the drip, drip, dripping. I wished there was a more painful way to do it. His eyes shifted from a clear understanding of what I'd done, to what was about to happen to him, and then to a hazy drifting. Finally, they closed.

His breathing slowed.

My rage slowed.

I'm not sure how long I waited. It was kind of like the time I spent with Daddy, after he died. It might have been thirty seconds or thirty years. In reality it couldn't have been terribly long, because Thayer was still breathing when the scent of roses snapped me out of it. The smell was strong and sudden, like one of those ammonia snappers you break under the nose of someone who fainted, only made of flowers. I jerked back to the IV stand and returned the morphine drip to its previous setting.

I stayed and watched for an hour, then two, just to be sure. I left only after the nurse came in and checked Thayer's vitals.

I never saw him again.

PART FOUR

PART FOUR

CHAPTER 57

Cheating on Lee with Thayer all those years made me feel pretty shitty, but murder was a whole new low. There probably wasn't any way to trace what I'd tried to do, but I had to live with the new knowledge of who I was.

Images kept replaying in my mind: the Lee-thing in the bedroom; the line of knives on the counter where Aunt Hildy assembled peanut butter and jelly sandwiches to take to the beach; the blood on Lee's neck. So did memories of times he'd been angry at me: the threat I saw behind his eyes and in the irritated tic of muscles in his jaw. I had no idea Thayer was *that* crazy. But those memories were syncopated with flashes of tenderness when he touched me, and the scent of him which acted like atomized opium.

Hildy's house was transformed forever. Thayer would always be on the floor, in a pool of blood and cat food. The kitchen had been a haven of pots bubbling with good smells, where discussions about books and music took place. But now it was stained bright red.

I started thinking suicide might be a pretty good option.

I forced myself to call Jimmy, who'd been leaving me increasingly frantic messages when I didn't pick up. I didn't tell him about what happened at the hospital of course. There was enough to focus on by just venting the horror of what I'd seen. I sobbed through the description of how grievously injured Thayer was. My skills for subterfuge were at an all-time low though, and he asked a lot of questions that I stumbled through. He was angry I hadn't told him Thayer was going to find Lee. He ranted for a few minutes about having put myself in danger along with the baby, and about having always known something wasn't quite right with Thayer. I just let him rant. Finally, the conversation drew to a close.

"I'm so tired, Jimmy."

"Do you need me to come out there?"

"No. I want to come home."

"Go check in to a hotel. Get some rest. Then come home to me."

The hotel bed felt like a tiny piece of heaven despite my belonging in hell. I slept for ten hours straight.

CHAPTER 58

Contractions started the day after I got back to Buffalo. The baby probably couldn't wait to eject from my murderous body.

Jimmy was joyous and patient throughout the labor. He plumped up pillows and lifted ice chips to my mouth. I was a miserable wreck from the trauma of what happened, the terror of giving birth, and the worry about what would come next. My misery distressed Jimmy, though he didn't comprehend the fullness of it. He watched from the foot of the bed as the baby ripped me in two on its way out, and then cut the cord, his face transformed by wonder and joy.

Jimmy stroked my head while they weighed and measured the infant, pricked his heel, and cleaned him up. "I'm so proud of you," he said. "That was rough. You're a champ."

I was mute with trepidation.

They handed the swaddled child to me as if not registering that he was a ticking time bomb. The baby was blonde with eyes the kind of blue that don't change color. Eyes like mine. There was no hint of mocha in his skin, and no hint of curl in the hair. Just straight, shining, blonde silk.

"Well, well, well. Would you look at that?" Lisa had appeared like a Dementor at the side of my bed.

"You called her?" I asked Jimmy. My voice trembled. Her presence raised my panic level another several notches.

"She's your mama, Kris." Jimmy always hoped we'd find a way to reconcile. He must have thought the sight of her first grandchild would push a magic reformation button. He was wrong.

"Isn't he the spitting image of Thayer?" She said. I remembered how her eyes assessed me the last time we'd all been together at a family event. Mistrusting. Judging. Accusing. She was looking at me that way again, and Jimmy saw it.

I fumbled for the words I'd practiced "Grandpa Williams would be proud, ha ha!" I choked the laugh out, the sound sick and hollow.

Lisa's eyebrows rose. "Right," she said, stretching the "I" out for three beats.

Jimmy's head pivoted from her face to mine and back again, his expression transforming from vague confusion to concern then to something else. "Kristy?" His eyes begged me to save him.

I was mute, my expression also pleading, though for something different. My exhaustion was too profound to maintain the subterfuge.

"I'll just give you guys a few minutes." Lisa smirked as she turned away and left the room.

I was alone with him and the baby, the three of us, perched on a cliff. His expression nearly toppled me over the edge. "Jimmy, I…"

He stared at the child, and it was clear that puzzle pieces were clicking into place. "How could I have been so stupid?" he said.

"You aren't stupid!"

"Stop it." He shook his head as he spoke. "All those times you went to see him." He paused, and I couldn't fill the silence. "I trusted you!"

"I know you did. I'm so…"

Jimmy cut me off. "He's your *cousin*." His expression twisted into disgust. "He's *family*."

"Maybe if I explain how things were…"

"The last thing I want to hear is details." The disgust on his face morphed into sadness. "I thought I was going to be a dad." Tears spilled over, trailing sorrow toward his chin.

I wanted to take away his pain; to shift time magically backward three days, before I'd seen what I'd seen and told Thayer where Lee was. Before this child escaped my body. In that re-lived time, my actions would be different. Jimmy would know the truth and could choose what he wanted to do. Lee would know Thayer was a psychopath. There would be no secrets. I started crying along with him.

"I have just one question," he said. "Did he force you?"

I shook my head. "No. No, he didn't."

Jimmy nodded, slowly. "I'm an idiot." He turned to pick his phone up from the window ledge.

"Please, Jimmy. Can't we talk about this?"

"No. At least, not right now." His eyes were filled with hurt and a rising, rare anger. "If I stay here, I'll say or do something we'll both regret." He walked to the door. "Good-bye Kristy."

My tears kept falling after he left, which was surprising because I felt dead inside; a brittle husk, empty and waiting for a giant hammer of justice to come slamming down and shatter me out of my misery.

When the nurse came to check on us, she knew something was wrong. "I'll just take the little guy to the nursery so you can get some rest." She scooped the child up and nestled him into her shoulder. "Have you decided on a name?"

I just shook my head and curled into the bed, wishing it were Hildy's shoulder and I could tuck in and pretend none of this was happening.

Thank God she took the baby. Thank God a grownup was in charge.

It didn't take long for exhaustion to win out. I slept, my dreams populated by hospital sounds and sorrow.

CHAPTER 59

I wobbled to the bathroom the next morning feeling broken and hopeless. A collection of grooming supplies invited new moms to get spiffy before going home. A cheap orange razor offered a different invitation.

Twin blades sparkled beneath the razor's cover.

Aunt Hildy's G clef tattoo was ugly in the harsh hospital light. The skin on the underside of my wrist was so thin and tender blue veins shone through it. I clenched my fist and twisted it back and forth to see what position pushed the veins closest to the surface, away from the tendon that wanted to create a skin tent over them. The blades slid smoothly across the surface at first. I had to change angles and press harder, pulling and sliding to force my skin to catch beneath the edge of the steel. I cut myself three times, then tried to do it on my other wrist, but it was hard because my hand was shaking, and I've never been ambidextrous.

Cutting myself was creepy and fascinating. It hurt, and I wish I'd done it a long time ago. The blood didn't flow like it did in the movies though, and I worried about how long it would take before the end came.

That's when I must have passed out.

CHAPTER 60

Bandages wrapped my wrists when I woke up. I'd miraculously slept through the commotion of being moved to the psych wing but chalked it up to exhaustion. The trip to Merrivliet followed by 12 hours of labor left me drained in more ways than were countable.

A doctor came and announced he was putting me on something for post-partum depression. I just nodded, not bothering to explain that it was a whole lot more than that. He told me they'd tried to get in touch with Jimmy, but he wouldn't answer.

The hospital kept me in the loony wing for a week, during which the baby was brought to me for visits. My breasts ached as the milk came in, and they poured out with their own form of grief when he was there. They said I could breastfeed while taking the drugs, but I didn't want to contaminate the poor thing any more than I already had.

My friend Theresa from school drove us home when I was finally discharged. She offered to stay and help me get settled, but I shushed her back out the door then walked around the house noticing what was gone. Jimmy's man cave was cleared out. So were his clothes, bathroom stuff, and the recliner he loved. He'd left a few new things behind. The crib was assembled and made up with the set of monkey linens and bumper pads we picked out together. Curtains were hung, and the furniture was all arranged. He obviously scrambled while I was in Merrivliet, wanting to surprise me.

The baby was a welcome distraction. We fell into a rhythm of sleeping, bathing, and eating which worked together as a soporific, dulling my senses and the pain so that it was survivable. He was a content little thing, crying only when something was wrong, and staring up at my face, trying to teach his eyes to focus. I liked that he couldn't see me clearly yet, imagining all the years ahead when his vision would be steeled on all the things I'd done wrong. As the days passed, we grew to be buddies, cocoon mates, him in his swaddling of infancy and me in my swaddling of grief and self-pity. We binge watched cooking shows and ignored phone calls from friends and Lisa. I was surprised she bothered calling. Steve must have been behind it.

The drugs kicked in, which helped further insulate my cocoon. Floaty numbness was an improvement over the agony of before. The torture of envisioning a future receded to a background throbbing.

The baby remained nameless, but I had to call him something, so he went by Little Guy. The rhythm of our life together was soothing, but it couldn't completely block the memories. I was hungry to be forgiven.

In a moment of desperation, I decided to call the old woman who sat in Lee's kitchen holding the rolling pin. Her eyes had offered encouragement, despite everything that happened. Lee said they met in the junk shop on Market Street, so I googled the number and dialed, nervous about what she'd say. More nervous about what *I'd* say.

"Hello, this is Good Goods."

"Maria?"

"Yes, it is me. Who else would it be?"

"Hi. This is Kristy. Lee's friend. Er... Lee's..."

"Ah, it is you. I wondered when you would be calling."

Why had she expected my call? "How is Lee?" I asked.

"Lelita will be fine. It is not an easy thing to go through what she did, but she is strong. She will be all right. I will make sure of it."

"I'm glad. She's lucky to have you."

"I am the lucky one."

I fell silent after that, trying to figure out what I wanted to ask.

"Now what is it I can do for you?"

I still didn't know what to say but had to come up with something or she'd hang up. "I was hoping you could help me."

She laughed then. Not a happy laugh, but a sort of cackle. "You? You want me to help *you*?"

"I know it sounds crazy, and I won't blame you if you hang up. But I just don't have anyone else to talk to, and it feels like this whole thing is going to kill me." Maria was silent, so I kept going. "Lee told me what a good listener you are. How you encourage her. I really need a little bit of that. I really, really do."

Maria's sigh traveled down the telephone lines and into my ear, but it triggered hope. She didn't sound frustrated, she sounded resigned, as if I was just one in a long line of homicidal lying women who called her requesting some sort of spiritual clemency.

"Madre mio, you ask me to do such hard things."

"Excuse me?"

"I wasn't talking to you. I was talking to the Blessed Mother."

"Oh. I see."

"I will listen to what you have to say. But I am no priest. You must first go to a church. Lee said you were Cattolico, no? Find a priest. Make your confession."

"I'm not really Catholic. My aunt had me confirmed, but I don't practice."

"Any kind of Catholic can go to confession. There is no special kind. You go."

The thought of spilling my guts to a priest was kind of terrifying, but if it meant Maria would keep talking to me, it would be worth the torture. I couldn't imagine explaining all my ugliness to Theresa or any of my other teacher friends, and Maria knew most of it already.

"I... I guess I could do that."

"Of course you can. Call me once your soul is washed and then we can work on your psicologia."

"All right. I'll go."

"Goodbye then?"

"Yes. Goodbye." I hung up the phone, and stared at it, running through confession scenes from movies and books. I hoped there'd be a screen so I wouldn't have to look at the priest.

Google reported the church a few blocks away offered confession Saturday afternoons and Sunday mornings, so I went that weekend, waiting my turn and watching people go in and leave again. Watching their faces to see if they were transformed. Mostly they looked the same.

Finally, it was my turn. "Forgive me Father, for I have sinned." I followed the opening script, as best as I could remember it from Hollywood. And then I spilled my guts all over the wooden walls of the little booth, the blood and darkness of my sin adding to the layers accumulated there from countless other confessions, like smoke and grime from the pit of hell. I told him everything, or as much as I could remember. He didn't seem fazed, which made me wonder about the people of Buffalo. Were murderous, incestuous, fornicating liars a dime a dozen?

I fell silent after telling him about breaking Jimmy's heart.

"Is there anything else?"

"No Father. I think that's everything. That's enough, right?" I forced a chuckle, but he didn't laugh.

"Dear child, my soul weeps for all the pain you've described in yourself and in those you've loved. You need help. You realize that, don't you?"

"Yes Father. I do."

"And you will seek it?"

"Yes. I've already begun." Maria would help me.

"Your contrition seems sincere. As penance, say three Hail Mary's, and pray for the healing and restoration of each of the people you mentioned."

"Yes Father."

"I will keep you in my prayers. Please come back to the Mass and feed on the one who loves you."

I nodded, not wanting to commit to anything prematurely. He said some closing prayers and told me to go in peace. I left, though not particularly in peace, and called Maria once I got home.

"So, you went to the sacrament of penance?" she asked.

"Yes. I did."

"And?"

"I don't feel much different. Getting it out was sort of a relief. I felt purged for a few minutes, but now I feel pretty much the same."

"This is normal. Confession is not about feelings. What did the priest give you for penance?"

I told her.

"Today's priests are pushing overs. That is not enough," she said.

"I thought I was washed clean?"

"The priest's absolution returns your soul to the cleanliness of a bambino. But your body? Your mind and your heart? Your memories? They are covered with scars. To heal those takes more work."

"More work?" I thought about how scarred I felt, and looked down at the G-clef on my wrist which memorialized Aunt Hildy and so much more. I turned my wrist and saw the healing scabs from the cut marks. I didn't see how any of it could be erased. What work could possibly repair my damage? "What kind of work?" I asked.

"That is what we will find out." She was a very confusing conversationalist, but the sound of her voice was comforting. "We will talk again soon," she continued. "I will pray and call you when I have heard what comes next."

I'd hoped for more than that, but she was in charge. "Okay," I said. "Hope you hear soon."

"Addio, Kristy. May God be with you."

"Goodbye." I hung up, feeling disappointed.

I took Little Guy out to a diner that night. The waiter offered ketchup for my French fries and the sight of it after all the recollections forced by confession brought back the memory of that day in the trailer with Daddy. That first time he'd forced me to have sex with him. Bile rose in my throat, and I swallowed hard, shook my head, and looked at the baby to try to get the image and the thought of the ketchup out of my head.

After the baby fell asleep that night, I dragged my easel to the dining room because it had the best lighting. I found a blank canvas and arranged tubes of acrylic. I painted, for the first time in months.

It was simple and stark, done all in red paint against the white of the gessoed canvas. In it, a little girl who looked like me was standing with her mouth wired shut. Daddy stood in a corner, being hugged by a priest.

CHAPTER 61

My penance was prayer for the people I'd hurt, and so I started with Jimmy. The prayer went something like this:

I'm sorry.

Please forgive me.

Please don't hate me.

Let me explain.

But they sounded more like things I should be saying to him than prayers.

He wouldn't pick up the phone or respond to the messages I left. I finally decided to just keep dialing over and over again, and it finally worked.

"What do you want, Kris?"

"We need to talk. Don't we?"

"I don't think there's anything to talk about."

"Of course there is. I need to explain."

His laugh was a short bark. "Explain?"

"Yes. It's a lot more complicated than you think."

"Here's the thing Kris. I don't care."

"How can you not *care*?"

"It doesn't matter. Whatever justification you've engineered doesn't matter. You fucking around on me is bad enough. But he's your *cousin.*

That's just sick."

"It *is* sick. Just let me…"

"No. I don't *care*. We're done. I can't do it. I can't look at you the same way ever again. I can't look at that baby without seeing him. Without knowing what you did. How you lied. All those times we got together with Thayer and Lee. All those times you were gone for hours."

"Please, Jimmy…"

"We're done, Kristy! I've already seen my lawyer. Please just answer the door when the papers are served, okay? Can you at least do that for me?"

By then I was crying. I knew I never loved him the right way, but he was good to me. He was the only thing left of everything I loved.

"Will you, Kris?"

"Yes." It was hard to speak around the sobs. "Yes. I'll do it."

"Good." He clicked off the call.

The worst part was knowing he really meant it. Jimmy was a softie overall, but once he made his mind up there wasn't anything you could do to budge him. I couldn't really imagine life with him under this new model anyway. Couldn't imagine taking turns feeding the baby and handling the stresses of parenting without Thayer as my fix. Couldn't imagine Jimmy overcoming his devastation in order to be super dad to someone else's kid. He was a good guy, a really good guy, but the thing I'd proposed in my own head was just too much. Too ridiculous.

I was on my own. Fully, completely alone.

CHAPTER 62

Time on maternity leave was loose and stretchy, so it could have been days or decades before Maria called back. Seeing her name of the screen made me feel excited for the first time I could remember. "Hi Maria!" I said. "Have you figured out what I should do?"

"Yes."

"Great! What is it?"

"You need to pray. You need to do a lot of praying."

When the priest told me to pray, Maria said it wasn't enough of a penance. Now she was reversing her stance? "I did the praying I was told to do."

"It is not enough. You must pray more."

"But how does prayer help any of this? It's all too late. I did it, and it can't be changed."

"I have been thinking much about this. I have been hearing things."

"Like voices?"

"Here is what I heard: Time is the blue gown of a sorrowful woman named Wisdom."

She was obviously crazy. "I have no idea what you're talking about."

"I was told to look to Joshua ben Sira."

"Who?"

"He is the author of the Wisdom of Sirach in the Hebrew Scriptures.

Listen to this. It is in the fourth chapter, about she who is Wisdom:

> "Wisdom teaches her children
> and admonishes all who can understand her.
> Those who love her love life;
> those who seek her out win the LORD's favor."

The woman spoke in riddles. I wondered how Lee was able to translate. "That was lovely. But I still don't get it," I said.

> "And this one, from chapter fourteen:
> Happy those who meditate on Wisdom,
> and fix their gaze on knowledge
> Who ponder her ways in their heart,
> and understand her paths;
> Who pursue her like a scout,
> and watch at her entry way;
> Who peep through her windows,
> and listen at her doors;
> Who encamp near her house
> and fasten their tent pegs next to her walls;
> Who pitch their tent beside her,
> and dwell in a good place;
> Who build their nest in her leaves,
> and lodge in her branches;
> Who take refuge from the heat in her shade
> and dwell in her home."

I had no idea what to make of any of it, but figured the smartest thing to do was play along. "So, we should all seek to be wise. I don't mean to be rude, but isn't that obvious?"

"You must listen beyond what your brain tells you. Do not dismiss the words as symbolic. These are instructions."

"How can they not be symbolic? Wisdom isn't a person. It's a state of smarts. There's no house to camp next to. No walls."

"Did you know that many believe Wisdom to be also Mary? The mother of our Lord?"

"No. I didn't know that."

"I will tell you where to find the verses I read to you, and others. You have a Bible, no?"

"Yes. Somewhere."

"All right then. Write the verses down. Read them again later as you contemplate what I am telling you."

"Let me grab something to write with." I pulled a receipt and a pen out of my purse. "Ready." She read off the chapters and verses and I captured them as she spoke. "Got it."

"Bene. So. Wisdom is what you seek. And Wisdom is a she. And she is Our Lady."

"Okay?"

"To seek her, the easiest way is the rosary. You are familiar with this prayer?"

"My Aunt Hildy used to pray it all the time. I remember some of it."

"It is Mary's prayer. As you pray and work your way through the beads, one by one, ten by ten, you will peep through her windows. You will ponder her as you consider the life and sufferings of Gesù Cristo."

I thought about what she was saying, trying to figure out how such prayer could possibly help. What did any of it have to do with the scars I'd accumulated on my heart and psyche?

"For nine days you will pray the mysteries," she continued.

"Nine days?"

"Yes. A Novena. And I think you should always be praying the sorrowful mysteries. There will be time for joy and glory later on."

"I'm not sure what that means."

"You young Cattolici. They teach you nothing. Do you have an internets?"

I snorted at the phrase. "Yes. I can get on the web."

"Then use the goggles to find it. You will see. It is the way you focus your contemplazione. The things you think about. The internets will explain."

"All right. I'll check it out and give it a try. But I'm still not really sure what you expect to come of it."

"Shh… Obedience is all that is required. Do not worry beyond that."

I thanked her and we ended the call. She might be crazy, but our conversations were soothing and brought me to an odd state of peace. The baby lay content in my arms, his tummy full from the formula he guzzled while Maria and I talked. He had a sweet radiance that turned my heart to mush.

Google revealed the mysteries, just as Maria had said. I read through the five sufferings of Christ that made up the sorrowful set, and when the Little Guy fell asleep, I prayed the first real rosary of my life. I had to read the prayers on my phone, but I did it, using the beads Aunt Hildy had given me all those years ago. When I was done, I felt accomplished, but like with confession, there wasn't any kind of fundamental internal shift.

I thought maybe I was doing it wrong.

CHAPTER 63

The sound of banging and the doorbell ringing woke us. The Little Guy slept in a basinet in my room when he wasn't lying next to me, and the cacophony startled him into crying. I picked him up before going to the door, wondering who it could be and why they were so aggressive. I peeked through a front window to make sure it wasn't some wandering madman, but just saw Lisa standing there, pushing the bell and hammering on the door with her fist.

"What's wrong with you?" I demanded once it was open.

She stormed past us, then turned around to look me. Her face was a tear-ravaged mess of smeared makeup. She'd never looked so bad.

"He's dead, Kristy. Congratulations."

"What?" I was baffled, but only for a few seconds. She must be talking about Thayer. "Dead? I didn't…"

"Yes, you did. You killed Thayer."

"No, mama! I made sure…"

"Oh, please. You set the whole thing up. Just *had* to introduce him to Lee. Needed some kind of cover for Jimmy. Was that it?" She was raging and pacing. "And now he's dead. Dead!"

"But what happened? Tell me what's…"

"Why couldn't you have just left things the way they were Kristy? It was good, wasn't it? You had him when you wanted him."

"You knew?"

"Of course I knew! Do you think I'm stupid? I knew you were a little whore from the day you came to live with us."

"I'm not a whore! It was just Thayer. He had some kind of power…"

"I know all about his power, you stupid little bitch."

"What?"

"We could have kept it going indefinitely, but you had to go and screw up everything." Her eyes were full of sorrow and disdain, and her face with all its melted makeup looked old for the first time I could remember. "He would have just stuck to the blonde bimbos if it weren't for you."

I couldn't figure out what she was talking about. If she'd given me a few minutes to process the idea of Thayer being dead, I might have had a chance to figure out the rest. But it was too much to take in at once.

"Oh, God, Kristy. He's dead!" She slumped to the couch and broke into deep, ratcheting sobs. The Little Guy's cries grew louder in response. "I should have found a way to be with him again," she said. "I could have talked him into it if I'd just known. And now… never again? Never again?" Lisa looked up at me with heartbreak filling her eyes, eyes which didn't look like mine, but which held the emotion I knew would hit me any minute.

And then what she was really saying finally hit me. "Wait. Were you two…"

"Sleeping together? We had been since before you showed up, you little twit. And it didn't stop until last fall."

"Last fall?"

"Once Lee was gone he came back a few times, but it was nothing like before. Nothing. Oh, why did you have to introduce them?" I thought she might hit me, her sorrow and rage were so consuming. "You were a dream smasher from the minute you implanted."

Her words hurt, but I was still thinking about what she'd said. About Thayer ending it with her in the fall. Fall was when Lee got the phone call that propelled her out of town.

"He tried to break it off with you, didn't he?" I asked.

"Yes, but he wasn't serious! He said he was going to focus on his marriage, which was a joke. I'm sure you were still sticking your greedy little claws in him whenever you got the chance."

"Did you call Lee? Was it you?"

Her face transformed into an ugly mask of calculation and humor. "Did she tell you about that?" I nodded. "Ungrateful little bitch deserved to be shaken up. I never expected her to take off though. Didn't think she had the backbone." Her face fell again, and she looked absolutely ancient. Thayer didn't like his women large with child or etched by time. Lisa had always been beautiful, and her ageing was undoubtedly the cause of his defection.

But now Thayer was dead.

I couldn't envision him dead, despite what I'd done to the morphine drip. Couldn't get it to make any kind of sense. Meanwhile, I'd just found out that my mother and I had been fucking the same man for the past twenty years. My mind was completely blown.

"Get out," I said, surprised my voice was so calm.

"What?"

"Get out of my house. I never want to see you again."

"How dare you? After all Steve and I have done for you." She rose and walked close to me, her eyes thunderous and threatening. But I was beyond caring about her threats.

"Get. Out." I could feel my own face shifting into a mask of fury and malicious intent. I took a step toward her. Her gaze faltered, and she raised a hand to touch her lips as if deciding what to say further. "*Now*," I demanded.

She lifted her chin in vague defiance but headed toward the door. "Sure, kick me out. But it doesn't change anything. Thayer is dead. And it's all your fault." She turned and left.

I dropped to the couch. The Little Guy began to cry again. He was wet and dirty from the night, and undoubtedly wanted breakfast. The sight of blonde hair so like his father's pushed me over the edge, and I wept.

CHAPTER 64

I didn't have much time to contemplate the news because the bell rang again a few hours later. This time it was two police officers.

"Can I help you?" I asked.

"Are you Kristina Alexander?" A tall Latina asked the question while her short partner glared at me with crossed arms. His gaze doubled the guilt I was already carrying.

"Yes. That's me."

"I'm Detective Vera, and this is Detective Burke," she said. "We'd like you to come to the station and answer a few questions."

"Is this about Thayer?"

"And just why would you think that?" Burke might have looked like a drunk leprechaun, but his voice was devoid of either accent or humor.

"Am I under arrest?"

"We just have a few questions. Would you mind coming with us?" Detective Vera asked.

"Be happy to offer you a ride." The dick couldn't keep his mouth shut. I decided I'd only talk to her.

"Yes, I'll come. Just let me get the baby ready." I wasn't sure what etiquette demanded in this situation and decided to opt for basic niceties. "Come in." They followed me inside. "Have a seat." I gestured toward the couch.

"We're fine standing right here," Burke said.

"Is there someone who could watch the child for you?" Detective Vera asked.

"No, there's no one. All my friends are at work right now."

"No family?"

I choked back a frantic laugh. "No family."

Meanwhile, my brain was whirling. I hadn't asked Lisa what happened to Thayer, but assumed his death was related to what I'd done with his IV. I didn't know if I should try to make up something to try to cover my ass, or just confess and get it over with. Serve my time as penance for all the wrongs I'd done.

I made sure the diaper bag had what it needed and grabbed a sweater in case the questioning room was cold. "Do I have to ride with you?" I asked, hoping for a bit more time to think.

"Yes," Burke replied at the same time Detective Vera said, "Of course not."

"Great. Car seat and all." I tilted my head toward the Little Guy, who was trying to focus his gaze on the voices he heard.

"We'll wait for you. Just to make sure you get there okay." Burke said. I wanted to smack the smirk off his broken-capillaried face.

"All set?" The woman gestured toward the front door, as if it were her house rather than mine.

"Let me lock the kitchen entrance, and I'll be right out."

They complied, though Burke looked reluctant. I breathed a few deep breaths and went to face the music.

PART FIVE

CHAPTER 65

Burke sat across from me when they finally returned from their extended coffee run. Detective Vera sat at his right. "So. You asked if this was about Thayer. Why would you assume that?" Burke said.

"My mother told me this morning that he was dead. So it seemed logical." I noticed a camera in the corner near the ceiling. It made me even more nervous.

"Why would we need to talk to *you*?"

"I assume because you think I might have something to do with it."

"Good guess."

"When's the last time you saw him, Ms. Alexander?" Detective Vera finally spoke.

"In his hospital room."

"In Merrivliet?"

"Yes. It was right after he was… beaten." The memory of him lying on Aunt Hildy's floor, bloody and broken, made me feel ill.

"So you haven't seen him since he's been home?"

"He came back?"

"Are you saying you didn't know he was here?" Burke asked.

"No. I didn't know. What hospital was he in?"

"He was staying with his *parents*? They were *caring* for him?" His exaggerated pronunciation made it clear he didn't believe me.

"I'm just surprised!" My mind spun from all the news, and I scrambled to keep up. "I didn't think he'd be able to leave the hospital for a long time."

"We understand that he was doing well physically, but there could be long-lasting cognitive issues."

Oh God. Was it the morphine?

"Apparently his injuries resulted in some pretty significant brain damage." Detective Vera offered.

Maybe it wasn't the morphine?

"Guess the douchebag messed with the wrong women, eh Kristina?" Burke asked.

I nodded, unsure of a proper answer.

Detective Vera looked at her notebook. "We understand that you and Thayer had a… special relationship. Is that correct?" she asked.

"Heard you were banging your cousin." Burke interjected.

"We were close. Yes." My face blasted heat from the shame of it.

"We saw the dummy he set up in his bedroom. How'd it feel to fuck a creep like that?" Burke looked like he was enjoying himself.

"It must have been disturbing for you to find those things," Detective Vera said. "And to learn he was planning to kill your friend."

I'd always thought the good cop/bad cop thing was just for the movies, but she was doing a great job playing the nice one. I felt the pull of her illusion of safety.

"It was… horrible." There were no words that could capture the enormity of the past few weeks.

"Did it make you jealous? Knowing he was obsessed with her?" Burke offered.

I tried to control my face muscles. Jealous wasn't exactly the right phrase, but it was close. Close enough to describe the emotion which drove me to push the button on the IV drip.

"Yes. It bothered me. A lot." I figured I'd be honest, but only answer what they asked. Kind of like how you're supposed to handle it when a young child asks questions about sex.

"So jealous you wanted to kill him?"

There it was, dangling right in front of me, ready to grab like the golden ring on a carousel. Offering a free ride to prison. I nodded. "For a few minutes, yes. I *did* want to kill him."

"So, you waited until he got back here, then smothered him," Burke said. Detective Vera shot him a "shut up" look.

"What?" I asked.

"Where were you last night between 10:00 and midnight?" It was Detective Vera's turn.

"Home. I was home. Watching TV."

"Was anyone with you?"

"No. It was just me and the baby. Do you mean he died last night?"

"Can anyone verify that?"

"Maybe the neighbors. They might have seen my car."

Burke made a note. "Did you think it was some sort of irony to kill him in bed?" he asked.

"What?"

"You know. Poetic justice?"

"But I didn't do it. It wasn't me. I haven't seen him since Merrivliet."

"Are you sure there isn't anything that could prove you were home during that timeframe, Ms. Alexander?" Detective Vera's voice was an oasis of calm in the lunacy. I tried to think.

"Is there some kind of history when you stream movies to your smart TV?" I asked. "I watched a few different shows. Changed my mind a few times. Can you check that?"

Burke tipped his chair back on its rear legs and tapped his pen on the table, assessing me. I wished he'd fall over backward, but no luck.

The TV thing was all I could come up with. "If it's on the TV, I would have had to be there to get it going. And change shows, right? Plus the neighbors?"

They were both silent.

"I wanted to kill him. I admit it. But I didn't do it. I swear I didn't." They were still silent, watching me. "There's no way you can prove it was me, because I wasn't there, I was home. There will be no evidence that links me to it." Their silent stares rattled me, even though I was innocent of the murder. My nervousness started changing to anger "I don't have to answer anything. You never read me my rights!"

"You aren't under arrest. We didn't need to read them." Detective Vera's voice was quiet, but a hint of irritation created ripples in her calm.

"If I'm not arrested, then I should be able to leave. Can I leave?"

"Yes. But you might want to stick around town. Just in case we have more questions. You wouldn't want to look any guiltier than you already do. Am I right?" Burke ended with a question, but I wasn't sure if it was directed to Vera or me. I realized it didn't matter. I stood and picked up the diaper bag.

"Thanks for coming down, Ms. Alexander." Vera said. "We appreciate your time."

"Yeah, thanks." Burke's voice was heavy with sarcasm. "And sorry about the loss of your fuck buddy."

"Detective!" Vera's voice had turned into a reprimand, but I was heading out the door.

"Incest. Sick bitch," Burke muttered. I walked out, trying not to cry in front of the people gathered in the hall.

CHAPTER 66

Thayer's death didn't seem real. Despite having seen his body looking lifeless on the floor. Despite having tried to kill him at the hospital myself. Somehow none of that connected with the reality that he was dead and not just off somewhere unreachable due to the atrocity of what we'd both done.

Dead was different.

When Thayer was hospitalized, I could pretend I'd maintain my outrage and find a way to live without taking a hit of him. But his death showed how flimsy that pretense was. With him truly gone, a bottomless chasm of need cracked open.

I wondered if some other person could fill it, and what that person would need to be like. Would they have to look like him? Would they need to talk to me the way he did? Was it his sexual moves that created such a dependency?

Examining the texture of our relationship didn't reveal anything which would make it repeatable. The individual pieces didn't add up to his psychotropic power. He was just…Thayer. The hero of my pre-teen years. Distraction and safety in the toxic atmosphere of Lisa's home. There could be no replacement.

It was almost as devastating as Daddy's death. Or maybe it was more devastating.

The world had been surreal for weeks, but now the dislocation from reality grew more distinct. I retreated into the Little Guy. Babies are consuming, and I desperately needed to be consumed. Despite trying to distance myself, I was falling in love. The stunning simplicity of his beauty inspired me to paint, and I tried to capture the light of his soul gazing out through his eyes, the impossible pink curve of his upper lip, and the tiny fingers which seemed surprised by the things they accidentally encountered. I longed to capture the pure innocence of him on canvas.

The days slipped by as I wove in and out of grief and wonder, forgetting to eat and not caring to shower. I'm not sure how much time passed. Eventually, Maria called to check in.

"So. The novena. How does it go?"

"It doesn't."

"What? Why not?"

I filled her in on Thayer's death.

"I cannot say that the world will miss him very much. But I am sorry you should go through more sorrow."

"Thank you." Her sincerity was humbling. She was Lee's friend and knew what I'd done, yet she made room to offer compassion.

I thought about what the sarcastic cop had said. He'd called what I had with Thayer incest. Of course I knew what it was, all those years, but I'd somehow managed to not think about it. "Can I ask you something?" I said.

"Of course."

"How could I not have known that sex with Thayer was so wrong? I mean I did, but I also didn't."

Maria was quiet for a moment, then said "It is like this. Put a hand over one of your eyes."

"What?"

"Just do it."

I cupped my palm in front of my left eye. "Okay. It's covered."

"Make sure both your eyes are open. Now, what do you see?"

"I see the closet door across the room."

"You do not see the skin of your palm, correct?"

"No. I don't see it."

"Both eyes are open, both are seeing. The brain receives both images. But it chooses to focus on what is beyond as more important."

"How is that like Thayer and I?"

"The hand is too close."

"Okay?"

"It is like that, this situation with Thayer. It was too close. Your brain could not handle to process it. Your brain said, 'No. Look at this thing over there instead.'"

I kept my hand up, urging my eye to focus in, to see the lines of my palm. But it wouldn't do it. I pulled my hand away a few inches, and could start to make out wrinkles in the flesh. A few inches more and the whole thing came into focus. Perhaps I was in that in-between stage now. Maybe with a little more time I'd see even more clearly. "What if I can't handle being able to focus on it? What if I can't survive it?"

"You can do it, Kristobella. With God's help."

"Why would God want to help me?"

"He loves you. He loves us all. He loved you when you were a tiny bambina and will love you when you are an old signora like me."

I sighed, pushing out the weariness of the situation. "I just wish I could go back and change things."

"That brings us around to the beginning again, no?"

"What do you mean?"

"To the rosary! It is what I have been trying to tell you."

"I prayed it once. The sorrowful mysteries, like you said. But I didn't feel anything. I don't think it helped."

"It turns out I was a hasty pudding. I heard that I was wrong about all the sorrowfuls straight from the start. You must begin with the glorious mysteries. They will introduce you to her."

"To Mary?"

"Yes! You must get to know the mother of Gesù. Queen of Heaven. Queen of Time."

Her speech was puzzling and largely nonsensical, but I wanted to be carried along by the force of her belief.

"So, I need to get to know her. The Queen of Time."

"Si! Exactly! And when you know her, she will help you fix things. You will tell her. You will pray it. In the rosary."

"How can I possibly pick what things to fix? There was so much…"

"Life moves along and we do many things we regret. Then when we decide we need to fix them it is like pushing a cooked spaghetti through the hole of a colander."

I laughed at the image. "Exactly. It feels impossible. And there's too much."

"Just pick three things then. Three is a good number."

"Three."

"Si. Now go and do your work."

"Okay. I will."

"Call me when you have met her, through the glorious mysteries. Capisci?"

"I think so."

We ended the call, and I thought about what she'd said. I was to tackle three memories. Three transgressions. I googled the glorious mysteries.

For a minute, it felt manageable.

CHAPTER 67

Given the lackluster outcome of my first attempt at the rosary, I thought I'd try adding some sacramental oomph to the experience. The Little Guy was happy to go for rides and walk around with me trying to look at things, so we went to the grocery store to find candles, and selected one in a tall, slender jar with a picture of Mary on it. We also needed diapers.

Back home the Little Guy was ready for a nap, which meant I could try again. I settled at the kitchen table so I wouldn't get too comfortable and fall asleep myself. The candle sputtered in front of me, burning scentlessly though I'd imagined it smelling like incense. I pulled up the rosary prayers on my phone again and then dove in.

The prayers were uneventful until the mystery about Mary being named the queen of heaven, when something clicked. I suddenly saw her; a woman who filled the sky. The moon was under her feet. She wore a crown, and I counted the diamonds shining from it. Or maybe they were stars. There were twelve of them. She wore a cloak and gown of the deepest blue, midnight blue, velvet midnight, with the constellations scattered upon it like twinkling crystals.

She held out her arms and I swept into them somehow. I melted into her presence and felt her lifting me into an embrace so engulfing and comforting that I wanted to weep. She smelled like oceans and dust and something sparkling, and like the roses Aunt Hildy and I walked past when we went to the beach. I blinked away tears and watched her lift the edge of her cloak and carry it toward my face. A memory suddenly clicked of *A Wrinkle in Time* when Mrs. Whatsit explained tessering. And I almost understood it as Meg almost had; the fabric of time and space being foldable. A star was right in front of my eyes, and she drew the velvety darkness closer and closer until I saw it wasn't a star at all, but a hole that light was coming through. Closer and I could see through it. Closer still, and then I passed through the hole and into the scene on the other side.

It was one of the beautiful spring days when JB and I hung out in the field at the bottom of the trailer park. The clover was in bloom, so we sat on a carpet of green and white, watching the bees travel from one white orb to the next. JB had just found a four-leaf clover and I already had three, and it was the strangest thing. I remembered it as that young girl, but I was also *there*, separate and watching. Seeing the impossible beauty and innocence of the girl and the purity of her joy in JB's find. I watched him too, and marveled at what a good friend he'd been, and the way his smile came from deep within his eyes as he watched me back.

We heard Daddy calling my name above the bouncing of a basketball, the buzzing of bees, and the hum of the sewage treatment pump, and got up to go home. Before I entered our driveway, I looked across the street and one door up, and saw her. The woman with the blue scarf, looking out her front window. Watching and smiling that sweet, sad smile.

That's when I started pulling away again; the light of the day narrowing and tunneling first around and then in front of me until it became just a pinprick of brightness in velvet blue, before swirling away. I felt myself released from the blue velvet embrace, and a whoosh as I pulled away from the scene.

When I blinked my eyes open, I was sitting in my chair at the kitchen table, the final bead of the final decade between my fingers, the last "Holy Mary, mother of God" trailing from my lips.

I wanted to stop and ponder what I'd experienced but decided to say the concluding prayers and finish the rosary.

And all the while, I smelled beach roses.

CHAPTER 68

Buffalo might be a city, but it was very much like a small town, and salacious news traveled fast. Theresa was the one who called and told me Thayer's murderer had been arrested.

It was his father.

The news was shocking. He'd been an imposing man, very much concerned with the impression he made on others. He worked in finance, like Thayer, and put a lot of pressure on his son to achieve career success. Lee was terrified of him, and I understood why. He had all of Lisa's negative traits, multiplied by testosterone.

Although I didn't want to call Mama, I figured I had to. After all, her brother was in jail. It would be heartless not to express concern. I also wanted to find out more. I hoped she'd pick up the phone, given our last interaction.

"Hi Kristy," she said, answering after the third ring.

"I just heard the news about Uncle Thomas. I'm shocked!"

"*You're* shocked? Imagine how I'm feeling."

"Do you have any idea what happened?"

"I know exactly what happened. Lillian told me. She's a wreck and a bitch, but she couldn't stop blabbing. She's the reason he was arrested."

"She is?"

"Apparently she couldn't live with what she'd seen and eventually she crumbled."

"What did she see?"

"He smothered him. Put a pillow over his face and smothered him." Lisa began crying. "Oh, Kristy... how could he have done it?"

The image was gruesome. It was hard to wrap my mind around the words she was saying.

"But why would Uncle Thomas kill Thayer?"

She regained her composure enough to continue talking. "They were taking care of him, and he was getting better. But apparently, they've been having money problems. Something to do with bad investments."

"That makes no sense. He's a whiz!"

"I know. But they'd been arguing about the cost of in-home care, because of course Lillian didn't want to get her fingernails dirty nursing him."

I was sure that was true. The woman was always impossibly coiffed and polished. "So, he killed him because of money? Didn't Thayer's health insurance cover it?"

"I don't know the details, Kristy! My God. Do you want to hear the story or not?"

"I'm sorry. I do want to hear it."

"Then stop interrupting."

I forced myself not to scream at her, because I needed to find out the rest. "I will," I choked out.

Lisa's sigh was long and exaggerated. "There was the issue with money. But apparently that wasn't the big problem."

"Well what was?"

"It looks like, because of *you*, Thayer was going to face attempted murder charges, assuming he'd come through the injuries. Lee and the crazy old woman who beat him up concocted some sort of story about how he came after Lee and was going to hurt her."

"That's true! He had knives lined up. Lee was injured."

"He was probably just trying to scare her!"

"No, Mama. He was deranged. You should have seen the thing I found in his bedroom…"

"I don't want to hear it!" she interrupted. "I still hold you accountable for this. Now let me finish talking or I'm going to hang up."

"Okay. Go ahead."

"*God.*"

"Please. Tell me the rest."

"As I was *saying.* The police believed those two lunatics in Merrivliet and were following up with attempted murder charges. And maybe some others. That's what tipped Tom over the edge."

"Why?"

"He couldn't take the embarrassment. He was already having financial problems and apparently thought if the news got out that his son was a murderer, he'd lose the rest of his clients. So he gave Thayer some extra meds before bed, then took a pillow and smothered him while he was sleeping."

"My God…"

"It's horrible, isn't it? I mean, I could understand if it were a mercy killing thing. Because we didn't really know if Thayer was ever coming back to himself. He wouldn't want to live if he was going to be some kind of vegetable." I cringed at her phrasing, while she steamed ahead. "And I hope that's what it really was. Because otherwise, it's pure selfishness."

"Didn't he know he'd be caught?"

"It sounds like they wanted to blame it on you. Apparently he tipped the police off about you and Thayer."

"They brought me in for questioning. I wondered how they knew."

"It was him. Lillian said he pretended to be heartbroken, and implied that you were crazy and jealous. He thought it was the perfect defense. He even had an old pair of panties you'd left behind. Gave it to them as evidence." I tried to remember the last time I'd had sex with Thayer at their house. It was years ago. The thought of Uncle Thomas saving my panties gave me the creeps, deep, deep down. I must have made a sound because she said, "Disgusting, isn't it?"

I gurgled some kind of response.

"I can't believe you were too stupid to take your underwear with you. And why did you do it at their house? Do you have no self-control?"

There was no point engaging in discussion about my panties. "I guess I don't."

"Obviously not." She said. "So he turned in your nasty underwear and hoped for the best. But it turns out his wife can't keep a secret. Even for her husband."

"She saw him do it?"

"Apparently she walked in at the end and tried to stop him, but it was too late. When they sat her down without Thomas, she spilled her guts."

"What a story... I don't know what to say..."

"I'll bet you don't."

I couldn't reply.

"I blame you for all of this. Thayer being dead. Now my brother being incarcerated. And for the shame you brought on our family name."

"I'm sorry." She didn't deserve apologies from me, but I agreed with her words. "But don't you think I've suffered enough, Mama?"

"Don't call me that. Why can't you remember not to call me that?"

I couldn't answer. There *was* no answer.

I hung up the phone.

CHAPTER 69

After recovering a bit, I called Maria and filled her in on what I'd found out.

"The wheels of destiny, they turn in strange ways," she said.

"You said a mouthful."

"I suppose I am grateful to him. The padre."

"Grateful? What do you mean?"

"Well, I had to worry, a tiny bit. About the damage we did to Thayer."

"He deserved it!"

"Sì. He did. But that is not the point. Sometimes the ones who do the crimes they come back after you. I do not care so much for myself, but I worried he would find a way to keep hurting Lelita."

"I could see him doing that."

"He did not recover enough. But once he did? Perhaps he would sue her or sue me. Perhaps he would find a way to put me in jail. Or maybe come and kill her for good this time. These people, they are determined when they are angry."

Images of the things I discovered before I drove to Merrivliet came to mind, and I shuddered. "Determined is a good word."

"Now Lee does not have to worry. She does not have to go through a trial to convict him of what he tried to do to her."

"That's true."

"So, I should be grateful. To a murderer. It is a strange wheel, destiny."

"It is *so* strange." I paused for a moment, thinking about how complex the whole situation had become. "I'm not sure where this all fits in to what's happening to me. There's been so much confusion, and loss, and guilt..."

"He was close to you, this man? This murderer?"

"No! Not at all. But it adds to my guilt. My mother said it should."

"From what I can comprehend, your Madre is no madre, and you should listen to exactly none of her words. You did many things wrong, for many reasons. As we all do. But you did not cause Thayer to come and try to kill Lee. You did not cause Thayer's father to kill him. Murder must swim in their pool of genes. These crimes do not rest on your shoulders. Do not pick them up. You have burdens enough to carry."

Her words were comforting, and though the two women were nothing alike, they brought Aunt Hildy to mind. I felt the warmth of her presence and the pain of her loss simultaneously.

"So. You keep up your work. You do what you can to address your own mistakes."

"I started on the prayers." I suddenly remembered the amazing experience of that last rosary. "I didn't get to tell you! I figured out what you were trying to say about Mary!"

"You did?"

"Yes! It was during the glorious mysteries. Just like you said."

"Tell me!"

"At the coronation mystery, I could see her. She was part of the sky, sort of, only so much bigger. Like part of the universe." I explained the rest of the vision. Her sigh at the conclusion was full and satisfied, as if she'd just finished a good meal.

"Grazie Santa Madre for being faithful to your promises. It is a joyous day! We should be having a celebration! Do you have wine? You must toast."

Her joy was temporarily infectious. We laughed and talked about how amazing the whole thing had been. But eventually my mind turned back to Uncle Thomas.

"The prayer with Mary was profound. But finding out what happened to Thayer feels like I went backward."

"This is a pilgrimage. It is not meant to be easy. Some pilgrims climb mountains on their knees. Some walk across entire countries. Why for you should this be an easy thing? All you are asked to do is pray."

"I know. It's just hard to get up the courage to remember the things I need to pray about. It hurts."

"You must do what is difficult. You must face the monsters who have pushed you down along the way. You must thank those who have helped you. You must accomplish your work."

"How will I know what I'm supposed to accomplish?"

"You will know. Your heart will tell you. And do not take back up this mantle of guilt over what Thayer's padre did. It is not yours, Kristobella."

"I'll try not to."

I meant what I said, but I couldn't imagine how to do it.

CHAPTER 70

I prepared for the next rosary by reading the scriptures related to the sorrowful mysteries. The agony in the garden. The scourging at the pillar. The crowning with thorns. The carrying of the cross. The crucifixion. And because there were five, I decided to choose five things in my life to return to, rather than just three.

I prayed the opening prayers, trying to push through the recitation and think about Jesus' loneliness in the garden after the last supper, feeling abandoned by those who claimed to love him. I remembered my life with Daddy in the trailer park before everything fell apart, surrounded by trees and clover, and visited by turtles and bunnies. It had been the Garden of Eden in my life; a place of pure and simple pleasures before everything changed. Maybe Daddy would have become an addict even if Mama stayed. I couldn't know for sure. But one thing I did know was that she'd abandoned us both. Rejected us. Rejected me, though I'd done nothing wrong.

I mumbled the prayers with all those memories swirling through my emotions, and imagined Mary sweeping her cloak toward me. Once again, one sparkling star became an opening and surrounded me, whooshing me into the past. This time, I transpired back into that first trailer, with Mama cleaning up after breakfast while I watched cartoons. The air was heavy with the scent of breakfast sausage and cigarette smoke. I heard the knock on the door, and watched the younger me startle and turn toward Lisa.

"Mama? Someone's here."

My grandparents walked in. "Get out of here!" I screamed into their faces. But no one heard me.

"Are you ready? Is he gone?" Grandpa said before spotting me on the floor. "So that's the little hell-spawn."

"Papa..." Lisa said.

"If it weren't for you, my daughter would have finished University and be advancing in her career by now."

I wanted to smack him. He was glaring down at the little girl/me as if we were lower than dirt.

"My. She looks just like him, doesn't she?" Grandma piped up. "Those eyes are just not normal. You should have known nothing good could come of someone with irises like that." She finally seemed to realize the tiny me was sentient. "Keep your peepers to yourself, young lady!" she snapped.

"And this place! You've been living in a dump," Grandpa said.

"Hey!" The young me was finally brave enough to say something. We'd *loved* that trailer. As an adult, I could see it was tawdry. But I was just as offended as she was.

"Let's just go," Mama said. "We'd better hurry."

I remembered then that she'd sent Daddy out to the store. They were trying to leave before he got back.

"Mama?"

Lisa turned to look at the young me, said goodbye, and left. The adult me followed, trying to stop her but she pushed right through me. She couldn't hear it when I screamed in her ear. Her face remained cold and rigid until they started to pull away. Then it went slack with what looked like relief.

I was filled with impotent rage at their callousness toward a fragile child. The little me was still inside the trailer, watching TV in her flowered nightgown. Alone and vulnerable. My heart twisted, and that's when I began to pull back out, back through, back into the present.

Tears ran down my face, though I hadn't known I was crying. I thought for a long time about what I'd re-experienced. The young

Kristy had felt Lisa's leaving as a kind of relief. The adult me saw how alone the little girl had been and knew what was coming because of it.

Something broke as I thought it all through. In a good way. Some kind of commitment or responsibility to Lisa that I'd carried. Reliving little Kristy's experience snapped it, hopefully for good. She may have given birth to me, but she wasn't my mother. She was never my mother. She probably only came to get me after Daddy died because she couldn't think of a way out of it. Not because she felt responsible. Not because she wanted to make amends. She'd never cared for me and didn't now.

It was freeing and exhilarating to feel the weight of that chain drop. I contemplated what family meant and realized that blood has very little to do with it. Blood relationships can be caustic and can even kill you. Family is made up of those who take care of you. Steve had tried to be family. Aunt Hildy was family. Jimmy was more family than anyone I'd ever known, but that relationship was done. I knew I needed family, but he wasn't coming back. I thought about adopting Maria into my life, but it wouldn't be fair to Lee on top of everything else I'd done. She shouldn't have to share her. I'd have to find others.

Mama broke our lives wide open by leaving, even though I didn't know it while it was happening. But it had some good results. With her gone, I got to explore nature, and make poetry with Daddy, and practice wonder. None of those were present once I went to live in Mama's house.

The brushes and canvas called to me again. I painted a circle with young Kristy in the center in a garden of green clover and blue skies. On one side of the circle a car pulled away carrying three fiendish figures, heading into a ball of red and yellow flames. On the other side of the circle was the adult me at the kitchen table, with my head down and rosary beads between my fingers. That same ball of flames floated above the Mary candle.

CHAPTER 71

That prayer kicked off a period in which time began to morph further, not only because I was going back and forward to my past, but also because the days melted into one another as the Little Guy and I lived a liturgy of infanthood interrupted by rosaries. It felt like I'd entered some sort of convent and was deep within the steps of novitiate, immersing myself in silence, food, diapers, and prayer.

I knew what had to come next, and I didn't want to think about it. I'd avoided it for decades, and if there was a choice, I wouldn't have thought about it ever again. But it had to be done. It was the work set before me; part of the penance Maria assigned. It was my scourging at the pillar.

I settled into my accustomed place at the table and lit the candle, still wishing it smelled like incense. The lack of scented smoke didn't seem to matter because it happened fast. Moving through the beads of the rosary seemed to pull together folds in the fabric of time. I sunk through the space between the threads, from one now to an older one. And there I landed, in our trailer kitchen. Watching the eight-year-old me licking ketchup from a paper plate.

Young Kristy doesn't look how I pictured myself at the age. She'd begun the transition to coltish; her limbs were stretching so much that her bones stuck out. Her skin was pale and ethereal as if lit by an internal moon. She looked magical and beautiful, awkward and alone. It was hard to believe the creature was me despite the sharp, disgusting taste of ketchup on my tongue.

When she finally finished, we walked to our bedroom, the older me dreading what was to come. We got ready for bed and climbed in, pulling up our beautiful Strawberry Shortcake comforter. Then Daddy came in. He was so drunk or high he couldn't think straight. I felt the trust and adoration shining from the girl's eyes. I heard her thinking "Poor Daddy!" I saw her simple obedience, and her purity.

I had to do something.

When he got close to the bed, I slid in between him and the child, urging my adult body to take form in this past time, despite not having been able to stop Mama from leaving. Our young face was so vulnerable in the mirror over the dresser, and it looked like she could see me. I whispered to young Kristy to think about tessering somewhere beautiful, and it was as if she heard me, because she obeyed. She imagined Mrs. Whatsit, and I felt her drifting away. It was as if Daddy heard me too, because his eyes squinted like he saw something for a minute. I was in front of young Kristy and I took it instead of her. I took him into my mouth instead of hers. We smelled the funk of him that was both like and unlike the scents of the other men I'd been with, and I wished I could block her nose. She didn't understand what was happening, but I did. I knew the full depth of its wrongness, the violation and the assault. I took into myself the horror of it, hoping to shield her innocence, to protect and hide her from it, to receive the weight of his sin so she could walk forward from it unharmed.

He finished and left. Young Kristy sat up and we vomited on her beautiful Strawberry Shortcake comforter. We cleaned up in the bathroom, then went to Daddy's room because we heard him crying. I wrapped my arms around him. He was sick and an abuser. I was angry and revolted and loved him anyway. We both did.

After Kristy fell asleep, I kept watch over her; filled with horror for what had happened. Then with a blink and a whoosh, I found myself back in my kitchen. Back in the now, gone from that time, but the horror was still raging. Horror for the act which had shaped my view of sex and relationships. Horror for my father. Horror for the child.

She'd been surprisingly naïve about sex, so Daddy must have sheltered us until that moment. But from the point at which she sat with the plate of ketchup right up until she finally fell asleep, the child's purity was still fully there. Still fully intact. What was done to her didn't make her corrupt. It merely made her bruised.

We'd gone through life not realizing we felt dirty. It should have been obvious, of course, but I hadn't permitted myself to think about it. There'd been too much pain. I'd chosen to love Daddy because there was nothing else.

Until Thayer.

I'd walked in silent, unconscious shame from that day on. But now I knew I wasn't dirty and never had been. I was injured. The child me had been injured.

I took a deep breath and went back into prayer revisiting each time I could remember Daddy assaulting us. And I took it, each of the times, so she wouldn't have to.

And even then, I wasn't tainted.

I was transformed.

CHAPTER 72

Maria said I needed to thank people who'd helped me, which was confusing. Aunt Hildy was dead, and she was the person to whom I owed my sanity. Lee tried to be a good friend to me, but I could hardly expect her to be receptive to thanks. I could thank Steve, though he certainly hadn't put up much of a fight when Lisa pulled her assorted bullshit. There were miscellaneous friends and acquaintances who were helpful throughout the years. And there was Ms. Hyslip, who also tried to take care of me.

How was prayer supposed to help me do any of it though? How could a rosary be an action of thanks?

I gave up thinking about it and figured it was best to just jump in and see what happened. As the hole of light widened around me, I found myself in the trailer park again, this time walking up the road behind young Kristy. She glanced at the trailer across the street and one door up from ours to see the woman peering out the window. But the woman wasn't looking at *her*; she was looking at me. Straight at me. The invisible, adult me.

I wasn't sure what to do, but remembered Maria's instructions to offer thanks and figured I could thank this woman who'd been a presence for young Kristy. I pressed my palms together and bowed slightly to her, offering a Namaste. The woman's smile grew, and she tipped her head in return.

It was the shortest of the leaps so far. I bowed, she nodded, and then the road ahead of us tunneled and transformed to my kitchen table again. I wondered who the woman was, and how she could see me.

I spent the rest of the day thinking about it, and about the timing of the leap. It had happened during the crowning with thorns which made me consider how the agonies of life offer us a chance to choose what to do with them. We have to choose how to move forward, and whether to wear our injuries as a hair shirt of shame, hidden beneath our clothing but driving us crazy with the itch. I wondered about how to transform that shame and pain into a crown instead, and what wearing a crown like that would mean.

The questions flowed from my paintbrush. A teenage me stood in the center of the canvas tearing a strip from the bristle-covered tee shirt I was wearing, lifting the frayed end toward my forehead. As the strip got closer to my head, the bristles lengthened and sharpened, turning into thorns. My young eyes were filled with fear and hope.

Painting didn't provide answers, but I figured that was part of the work that was still to come.

Recovery could be a long road.

CHAPTER 73

The next prayer session involved multiple leaps. First I transpired into the night I'd gone to Thayer's room shortly after he'd moved in with Lisa. I walked with young Kristy up the stairs and through his door, then over to the bookshelf, and finally, up on the bed. I hovered over her again and willed my body to achieve mass and block her from what was happening. We touched him and the wrongness of it hit me like a punch in the gut. For the first time I felt it rather than merely knowing it. When it was finished, I watched Kristy pick up the book and we went back down to our basement sanctuary. She tucked it under her pillow, and I lay down and wrapped my arms around her hoping she could feel my presence.

I zipped away again, and a series of zooms in and out of darkness and light and days and years followed. Each one was a time I'd had sex with Thayer. I think it must have been *every* time I'd had sex with him. It was dizzying, the sense of motion and the sheer number of occurrences. I didn't stay long at any of the interludes, thank God, because I wasn't sure I could handle the emotion of reconnection with him or my horror and shame at desiring it. As we got older, the sense of Kristy's obtuse participation diminished and shifted, becoming increasingly tinged with shame and guilt. Each time felt grosser than the time before. The last one was the worst: the pregnant me hunched over the back seat of the car with my ass sticking out the door, and him using his hold like a weapon.

When I came back to the present, I vomited all over the table. Then I cried as I cleaned it up, thinking about what happened.

The leaps began during the mystery of the carrying of the cross. My life seemed to have been spent carrying a cross I'd had no choice but pick up when I was eight. A cross of sexual disruption and distortion and inappropriate attachment. I'd been handed that cross the first time Daddy molested me, and the burden of it traveled with me from then on. The burden of having sex with a relative. The burden of having sex with someone who is in a relationship. The burden of having my identity formed in an atmosphere of toxic sexuality.

Until that moment I'd felt guilt for what I was doing to Lee and to Jimmy. But for the first time, I realized the wrongness of what was happening throughout all of it, to *me*. I'd known it in the abstract, of course. But I knew it the way you know how gravity works; it doesn't mean much until you jump out of an airplane. It hit me that this was the cause of so much that happened later. It didn't excuse anything I'd done, but my actions were transformed into an understanding of cause and effect rather than simply self-blame. I imagined myself as the fulcrum of a teeter totter with the weight of these initial actions plunging down on one end and all the atrocities I'd committed flying up into existence on the other.

Revisiting those times with Thayer doubled the realization that recovery would be slow. The longing wouldn't simply disappear just because my recognition of the wrongness of it had intensified and clarified. It was just like any other addiction. I had to simply push through the longing, hoping it would eventually dissipate.

I turned to canvas again, this time painting an adult me dragging a cross, bigger than I was. The cross was made of Thayer and Daddy combined, their faces fixed in the rigid grimaces of climax and their penises jutting out like weapons. I dragged them by the cross bar of their outstretched arms, their muscle and meat stiffened into wood, and heavy. I dragged them over the wailing bodies of Lee and Jimmy.

It was torture, and it was necessary.

The days of the novena were winding down, and I was running out of sorrowful mysteries. The only one left was the crucifixion. I wasn't looking forward to what would come out of that one.

I fell through time quickly when it happened, this time landing in Thayer's living room, sprawled on the couch, naked, with his baby almost ready to be born. My belly was huge and swollen; I could see blue veins through the skin stretched to near transparency. She was so vulnerable, this other me, so close to the now me. Similar in many ways, and utterly alien in others. She was still the before me, and I was the after. The flesh of my stomach now drooped against the emptiness beneath it, in contrast with the hope that still filled her in the shape of that pre-born child.

Her naivety was stupefying.

Just as when we were a child, I wanted to shield her. She was about to be crushed, nearly destroyed, and I wanted to prevent it, prevent her from telling Thayer about where to find Lee. But I didn't know what to do.

We were there, on the couch, knees open, asking for him. I moved to stand between them, willing myself to take form, willing it harder than ever before, and for a minute, I thought it was going to work. I faced her rather than him, because I didn't want to see the revulsion in his face even though I couldn't block out his words. Nor could I block her from seeing him. Her face crumpled at what she saw, and she began to cry.

"Dear God. Let's not have tears," he said.

I turned around to punch him. My fist just swung through his face, of course. His eyes flared for a second as if he felt something, but he kept talking, the two of them throwing verbal jabs at each other.

This was the last chance to change things. I dropped to my knees in front of where she sat on the couch. "I'm saying I know where she is," the younger me said.

"Where is she?" He grabbed her by the shoulders and started shaking her. I tried to push him away, and the frustration of not being able to make contact was excruciating.

"She's in Massachusetts. I gave her Aunt Hildy's house. But you were too stupid to figure it out." I wanted to stop her but at the same time, was weirdly proud of how brave I was being. Stupidly brave, now that I knew what he was capable of doing, but still.

And then he hit us. I watched the skin of my cheek turn red beneath her cradling palm while we listened to him leaving. All our bluff and bluster collapsed the minute he went out the door, and she broke into sobs so deep and heart-rending I thought our soul was being pierced.

It was a kind of death for us both. A death to everything that had come before, because nothing would ever be the same again. It was the death of my relationship with Thayer, and my younger self somehow knew it even though she didn't know all that was still to come. It was the end of the girl who had a coping mechanism, leaving her naked and alone. What she didn't know was that it was also the death of our whole history of lies and sexual misconduct. She couldn't see that part yet.

I had to leave her there, crying. I couldn't stop her from going upstairs and seeing what she had to see, couldn't stop her from going to Merrivliet and being in that hospital room with him. There was no choice but to let it play out.

Maybe everything had to unfold the way it did in order for me to be free. Maybe I would have clung to my ideation of him forever if it hadn't. Maybe the whole tawdry mess was a way of releasing me in the only way I would permit freedom; through lack of choice.

This time the painting came painfully. This time the cross made of Daddy and Thayer was stuck into the ground, and the naked, pregnant Kristy was nailed to it, ravaged by tears. Blood flowed down her thighs, and I waited beneath her to catch the child that was about to fall from her womb.

CHAPTER 74

Once the fever of painting passed, I called Maria. The Little Guy was awake and gurgling happily around his bottle, his little face so purely perfect that it took my breath away. I couldn't let myself stare at him too long or I was afraid I might dissolve into wonder and never come back out again.

Maria's voice tore me out of it. "Buonasera Kristilita! How does it go there?"

"Painfully."

"I am guessing that would be so. But there is progress?"

I thought about the experiences I'd relived and the realizations which resulted. And also, the paintings. "I think so. Each time I prayed I traveled back in time again. Just like I described to you before. And each time there were some pretty major revelations."

"Molto bene. It sounds like good work is being done."

"I think I'm finished, actually."

"The novena is complete?"

"I'm only on seven. But I got to the end of my crap, so I must be done."

"If you are only on seven then you are not done. A novena is nine. You must complete it."

"But I revisited everything! I even experienced the crucifixion. I painted it afterward. I've been doing a lot of painting. Do you like art?

I wish you could see them."

Maria's sigh was loud and exaggerated. "You young people and your impatience. You should be grateful enough to follow through. And who doesn't like art?"

"Grateful? For reliving all of that?"

"Are you not grateful when a doctor washes the dirt out of a cut before he stitches it closed? Are you not grateful for the light that shines when it is dark, and you cannot see?"

"Of course."

"Well then, why are you not grateful for this cleaning? This light?"

"I am, I guess. I mean, I really am. But it's hard."

"Here we are going again."

"I'm sorry. I *am* grateful. Truly. Full stop."

"What is this 'full stop'?"

"It means 'period'. Like, that's all."

"Okay. So, you are grateful. It is good. And how are you doing with the forgiving?"

"What forgiving?"

She sighed again, and my gut clenched at disappointing her. "This journey you have been on. The praying. Did you really not know it is about forgiveness? Could you have prayed so much and not realize?"

Once she said it, it seemed obvious. But I genuinely hadn't thought about it. I'd mostly just hung on as hard as I could to try and survive it. "Forgiveness," I whispered.

"Sì. You can get nowhere forward without it."

"I'm supposed to forgive them."

"Sì."

"How?"

"It is simple. It is just decision. You decide to forgive and blam! Forgiveness."

"There is no way I can forget what's been done, Maria. I can't forget what they did, and I can't forget what *I* did. It's just not possible."

"Who said anything about forgetting?"

"How can I remember and forgive? Every time I think about it, I'll be upset again."

"You are confusing in your head. There is no need for forgetting. There is no need for not being upset. There is need only of one thing. You choose forgiveness. That is all! It is simple!" Her voice was filled with optimism and hope. Even joy. She made it sound so easy.

"I just *choose* to do it? Despite how everything feels?"

"Yes! That is it. Di preciso."

"It feels false. Like I'm cheating." The encounter with Thayer was still fresh in my memory, my flesh crawling from the recollection of the Lee Thing he'd created and what he'd tried to do to her. How could I forgive him?

"Forgiveness is not about feelings, Kristobella. It is about deciding to take an action. It is about releasing."

She gave me the space to think for a moment, and although I could still feel the horror and anger, I decided to just do what she said. "All right then. I choose to forgive them."

"Them who?"

"Daddy and Thayer. Who else?" Maria was silent in response. "Oh! And Mama. Okay, I forgive her too."

"There is one more you must add to this list."

"Who? Lee? She didn't do anything to me."

"It is you. You must forgive also yourself."

I laughed out loud when she said it. My guilt was so interwoven with the reality of my being that to sever it would cause my DNA to unravel.

"When you are done with the novena this will be your new work. To find a way. To keep forgiving. To move forward and live a good life. And to love yourself."

I couldn't imagine what all that would look like, but I tried to make agreeable noises before ending the call.

CHAPTER 75

The rosary on the eighth day felt empty. There was no leap of time, no revelation about someone else to forgive, no insight into what else I needed to forgive myself for. Just repetition. Hail Mary, full of grace… I felt a bit smug about how I'd been right and debated mentioning it to Maria.

I went into the ninth day with low expectations. Nothing happened right up until the final prayer tumbled from my lips:

Hail, Holy Queen, Mother of Mercy, our life, our sweetness and our hope. To thee do we cry, poor banished children of Eve.

The words resonated. I was a banished child, banished from my home, and banished from the love of my father when he was lost in addiction.

To thee do we send up our sighs, mourning and weeping in this valley of tears.

I remembered the tears I cried; when I had to leave, when I was stuck at Lisa's, and when I lost Lee and Aunt Hildy. The more recent tears I shed for Thayer.

But mostly I remembered the tears which gushed when Daddy died.

I didn't want to go there, to that time. Reliving it would be torture. But the queen appeared adorned as ever with her crown and swept me up in her arms as she had that first time. She breathed a "shhhh" into my hair, as if trying to soothe me in advance. But there was no soothing. I tried to push the fabric of time away as she drew it toward my face, but my arms pushed through the air and stars as if through water.

The golden dot of the day of Daddy's death was dimmer than most had been. I wanted to close my eyes and shut it out as it grew closer, but the vision didn't come through my eyes and the point of time grew larger and larger until it slipped around me. And then I was in.

Young Kristy was asleep in our bedroom at the back of the trailer. She was tucked under our Strawberry Shortcake comforter, looking sweet but troubled. The wind from a late season storm rattled the windows. Thunder rumbled long and low, as if an ancient cart full of bones was being pulled through a bumpy sky by Thanatos himself. Lightning lit up the room and I dropped to her side, wishing a strike would hit close enough that the bang would rouse her.

I wanted her to wake up and go out to the living room so we could save him, hoping there was time and possibility.

The lightning flashed but the thunder was muted, and she slept on. I tried yelling but she couldn't hear it, and tried to shake her, but my hands just slipped through her flesh as it had each time, without matter and useless.

But the fleshless sliding gave me an idea.

I sat on the bed, but this time right on her, right through her. I lay back on her, into her, so that my head was lined up with hers, my skull sinking into hers, my body conforming to her shape. There was a pop as if my ears were adjusting to a pressure shift the way they did when an airplane dropped through the clouds before landing. And then I was inside. "Wake up!" I yelled. Miraculously, she did.

The young me started to panic when she felt my presence, but I whispered to calm her, letting her know she was safe. It was the strangest feeling; she was alien and yet we were utterly the same, and I could feel her experiencing the same strangeness. It was as if we were internal conjoined identical twins, and I was an elder sister to my earlier self.

"We have to get up. We have to hurry," I told her in thought.

Young Kristy nodded, and began to sit up, swinging her legs over the edge of the bed. I stayed within her, trying to shield her from my memory of what was happening in the living room just in case we could somehow change it and stop him from dying. I'm not sure if she heard all my thoughts, but she definitely picked up on my urgency. It might not be possible, but we were both willing to try. We hurried out to the living room.

Daddy was in bad shape. The smell of vomit was ripe and stomach-turning. "Daddy!" she cried. She was starting to panic again, and my own panic was rising. We went to him and felt his forehead. He was burning up. He opened his eyes and tried to look at us, but his focus was on something else, somewhere else. His hands were wrapped around his chest like it hurt, and he was gasping for breath. I didn't know what to do.

But young Kristy did. She looked at him and her heart was so full of love and pain that I didn't know how she could stand still and survive it. How she didn't just collapse. I felt her mind turn into my knowledge and realized she knew the outcome. Our heart clenched and I wasn't sure if I would be able to handle it, wasn't sure if I should beg Mary to let me transpire back out of this horrible scene. But the Queen of Heaven didn't rescue me, so I tried to pull myself back together to be there for the girl.

She grew calmer, gathering decisiveness, and thought about Daddy's talk earlier that night, when he spoke of death and God's appointed time. I'd forgotten the conversation. I felt her absorb the knowledge that he was dying and wanted to shield her but couldn't.

She stood up straight and looked away for a moment, thoughts whirling along with the sound of the wind outside. And then, having decided, she walked us to the bookcase, pulling out Daddy's old copy of *A Wrinkle in Time*. She held it in both hands, and we gazed down at it. My heart was saturated with love and missing it and joy at seeing the worn copy again. She led us to the door and opened it. The wind tore into the house, driving rain through the doorway, and tossing Daddy's newspapers over the top of the couch and into the kitchen. She held the book like it was holy, walked us back to stand in front of him, and I suddenly heard what she planned to do.

So I helped her.

I willed my hands to work with hers as she opened the book. Daddy's head listed to the side and his mouth was open. His face was a mask of agony. We lifted the book high, and tipped it so the pages hung down, fluttering open and swinging in the wind that buffeted through the room. And suddenly the air was filled with tiny flying bits of green; four-leaf clover swirling and dancing around us and around him. There seemed to be hundreds of them, perhaps even thousands, though it wasn't possible that we'd found so many.

Together we remembered the stories he'd told about four-leaf clover; how Eve had taken some with her when she'd been forced to leave paradise, and how it was magical protection from evil. I felt her worrying about Daddy's soul and hearing my later memories of Lisa saying he was going to hell. Our heart surged with pain and grief, and a desire to save him so profound that we shook the book even harder, urging every last bit of clover out into the air. I remembered Aunt Hildy explaining the concept of Eucharist for the dying; viaticum; food for the journey, saving food, and felt young Kristy listening to those memories, understanding but not understanding. And as we thought these thoughts and watched the clover whirl around us like a papery green tornado, we saw a clover fly into his open mouth. Perhaps we willed it. Perhaps the power of our desire for him to be safe, whole, and protected turned into a force which moved the wind. Two more pieces flew between his open lips and startled him. He shook his head, confused, and then swallowed. We shouted together in victory, mine silent, then stayed, watching him.

We watched as his breathing slowed, and then stopped.

The wind slowed with it. Some of the clover blew out of the room. Others fluttered to land on tabletops and the floor. We gathered it up and carried it to the bedroom, where we slid handfuls beneath the mattress. When we were finished, we went and kissed Daddy goodbye. I convinced the young Kristy to go back to bed, and lulled her into sleepiness, whispering fantastic stories about heaven where the animals talked, and Daddy chatted with the rabbit who used to live in the side yard. She sighed and smiled in her sleep, and I stayed and kept watch.

When morning came, she woke, not quite remembering. She

stumbled out to the kitchen and the rest unfolded as it had the first time. We called 911. The ambulance took a long time to get there because tree branches were down all over the roads. The EMTs apologized, and I took charge of talking to them, through her.

"He's dead." I said. "It was an overdose. It's not your fault."

Mary chose that moment to pull me back out. I would have stayed with her until Lisa finally came to get us. I would have lived the rest of my life with her to try to help.

But nevertheless, I left.

Turn, then, most gracious Advocate, thine eyes of mercy toward us, and after this, our exile, show unto us the blessed fruit of thy womb, Jesus. O clement, O loving, O sweet Virgin Mary. Pray for us, O holy Mother of God. That we may be made worthy of the promises of Christ.

The words fell from my lips as I returned to the kitchen and the now, sad that the young me had to face her future alone. She didn't deserve any of it.

But co-existing with that sadness was a sense of peace, deeper than any I'd ever known.

CHAPTER 76

There was a lot to process about what had happened during the novena, and painting seemed to help consolidate my thinking, so I decided to set up a studio. The Little Guy was using the room originally intended for the purpose, but I'd never been thrilled with that space. I thought about transforming the master bedroom. The memories there weren't exactly heartwarming. But it was really too big, and the light wasn't much better than the baby's room. I walked around the house, evaluating each space, and finally decided to use the sunporch which opened to the backyard. There were a ton of windows, and it was cozy but not tiny. It would be chilly during the winter, but I could worry about that when the bad weather hit. I strapped the Little Guy to my chest in a flowered baby wrap and got to work. I sang him songs and dragged furniture out. His eyesight was improving, and his neck was gaining strength. My heart lurched with love for him and sadness about what he'd been born into, and from. But I didn't let the sadness stop my progress.

I hauled in my supplies and completed paintings, along with a small desk and chair from the guest room so there'd be a place to sketch. The last items were a comfy armchair for dreaming, and a portable crib for the baby.

Together we hung up some of my finished paintings, and it was like a tour through the revelations of the novena. I felt on fire to work, to paint, to breathe out my heart onto the canvas.

Once everything was set up, the Little Guy tried to watch as I gessoed five canvasses in preparation for work to come. He was patient and sweet: the polar opposite of his father.

We ended the day tired but satisfied. And ravenous. I couldn't remember the last time I'd been hungry. The cupboards were close to bare, so I fried a couple of eggs and made sandwiches. The smell seemed to ignite Little Guy's hunger, because he started to complain while the eggs sizzled. I prepped him a bottle and tried to safely feed him while cooking, marveling at the dexterity of mothers and wondering how long it took to master the mommy juggle. I wolfed down the sandwiches and couldn't imagine anything tasting more delicious. We fell asleep on the couch with the television on. My sleep was deep and dreamless.

CHAPTER 77

The novena had done amazing things, but I knew the work was still not done. I needed to see a counselor. The healing had begun but I was an emotional wreckage, the Edmond Fitzgerald of psyches. I figured with all my attachment issues I'd probably try to fuck a male counselor, so it had to be a woman. Theresa saw a female psychologist, so I called her to get their name.

When I arrived for my first appointment, I waited in the lobby and tried not to look at the people who waited with me. I wasn't sure what etiquette was called for, and so went for a "let's pretend none of us is actually here" approach. It was lonely without the Little Guy, but Theresa had offered to watch him because she said I needed to focus. I'm sure she was right, but he would have been a welcome distraction from the awkwardness of the wait.

"Ms. Alexander? You can go in now." The smiling receptionist had kind eyes. I put down my magazine and smiled back.

The counselor met me at her doorway with her arm extended. "Hello. I'm Eta Bhatti." I took her hand, and we shook as if kicking off a business deal. She had a short black bob, and a slender body, with graceful motions.

"Hi. I'm Kristy Alexander."

"Come in." She gestured toward a chair. "Have a seat." I perched, and she sat down across from me. A coffee table was between us, equipped with a clock, a box of tissues, and a jar of hard candy. Something for every emotional need.

Her office was full of ferns. I'd heard that ferns are hard to maintain, and so I felt safe. If this person could care for them, I figured she could care for me. A fountain bubbled on her desk and the room smelled wet and woodsy. The effect was like having a waterfall nearby.

"What brings you to see me?"

I liked that she cut straight to the chase. I gave her the basic rundown and explained that my goal was to get my shit together so I could have a chance for some sort of reasonable life. She listened carefully, taking notes and asking questions periodically.

"Do you think you can help me?" I finally asked.

"Here's what I see. I see a young woman who has had a lot of emotional stuff to deal with her whole life. That's not uncommon. Unfortunately, too many of us are dealt hands that are painful and destructive. But we're given choices in what to do about it. You're making a choice. You're choosing change and healing."

I nodded because it was indeed what I wanted.

"That means we have a very good chance of making progress together."

I smiled, relieved, realizing that I'd unconsciously thought she might kick me out. "Great. That's just great!" I gushed.

"Let me tell you about my process." She explained that we'd start by developing a family diagram to map out the emotional context into which I was born.

"You might need Xanax before you're done listening to that," I joked.

But she just gazed at me, serene. "I've heard a lot, Kristy. We all have stories. You aren't alone." She continued describing her process, and then wrapped up. "Next time you come, let's talk about your goals."

"What kind of goals? For my life?"

"We'll start with your goals for our time together. That may overlap with your life goals, or it may not."

"Okay."

"So that's your homework. Think through what you want to

accomplish. Emotionally. With your mental health. With your relationships."

I laughed. "At this point, I don't really *have* relationships."

"Well then, perhaps that is one of your goals?" She glanced at the clock. "Our time is up for today." She stood. "It was a pleasure to meet you." She walked to the door and turned to look at me. The lines around her make-up-free eyes crinkled as she smiled her gentle smile. "Walk in hope, Kristy. It's going to get better."

I thanked her and left, thinking about that phrase: "walk in hope." My heart felt semi-buoyant and optimistic. My steps down the hall even felt lighter than they had when I arrived.

Maybe that's what she meant. Maybe that's what walking in hope felt like.

CHAPTER 78

One of the things that came out of my sessions with Eta was the need to apologize. She helped me realize that this wasn't so that relationships could be resurrected, but because it was a good psychological, spiritual, and emotional practice.

"It cuts a sort of cord that runs between you, tethering you to each other in an unhealthy way. It makes forgiveness easier on their part. And forgiveness is healthy for everyone involved. Especially for them, in this case. And you want them to be healthy and free, don't you?" she said.

"Of course." I thought about what Maria said about forgiveness.

The idea of apologizing for wrongdoing is as basic as it gets. But still; I was terrified to face Lee. I called anyway. I was getting better at doing things that were hard.

"Hi Lee. It's Kristy."

"I recognized your number."

"Thanks for answering my call," I said. I paced around the dining room and kitchen as a way of coping with my nervousness.

"How'd you get my new number?"

"Maria gave it to me."

I heard her sigh. "Figures. She told me you've been talking."

"Yes," I said. "I can see why you like her. She's amazing." My voice sounded odd. Too chipper.

"Is there a reason you've called?" Her voice did *not* sound chipper.

I sighed. I knew this wouldn't be easy, and it wasn't. "Yes. First, I wanted to make sure you heard about Thayer."

"You mean that he died? Yes. Maria filled me in."

"I'm sorry." I stopped pacing, held the phone to my cheek with my shoulder, and started picking at my cuticles.

Lee laughed, a sad, short laugh. "You didn't kill him. *We* almost did, but you didn't."

"I almost did too."

"What?"

"Never mind. It's not important at this point. What I really called about was to apologize. For everything."

"I don't know what to say, Kris. I'm only talking to you because Maria asked me to play nice when you called. Which is why I haven't hung up yet."

"I understand. I wish I knew how to make it up to you, but I ruined your life, and I'm not sure what I can do about it. You have the house and I'm glad. But I know it's not enough." Lee didn't say anything, so I kept going. "There are things I didn't tell you. Things that happened in my life."

"Maria told me some of it."

"I didn't know how to talk about it. There was so much, and it all started when Daddy died. It was a drug overdose. He was hooked on meth. I found him, like I told you. But it wasn't AIDS. It was drugs."

"That's rough."

"There's more. He… sexually abused me. I was so young. I didn't really understand how wrong it was. And then after I moved in with Lisa, I was so alone. Until Thayer came." She made a strange gurgling sound, but I kept going. "So I transferred that whole sexual thing to him. I just thought that was how you interacted with males."

Lee was quiet, and I gave her some room to think. Finally, she spoke. "I guess that explains how it started. But it doesn't explain how it *continued* all those years. Or how you betrayed me. Or why you even introduced me to Thayer."

I pulled at a hangnail too hard. "At first I hoped if the two of you were together, I'd have the courage to resist him." I watched the blood welling. "My intentions were good, believe it or not! I thought you guys would balance each other out. I knew he was kind of a dick, but he was also charming, and smart, and sexy. I thought your... purity would pull him into goodness, and my love for you would keep me away from him sexually." The drop of blood swelled, and Lee was silent, so I talked faster. "But it didn't work. I kept trying and trying, but I couldn't stay away. I'm sick, Lee. Really sick. But I'm trying to get better."

"I can't believe neither of us saw how much of a monster he was. Until it was too late."

"I tried to get to you as fast as I could. I tried to stop him. I really did."

"I believe you."

"I'm asking you to forgive me. I don't expect your friendship; I know I ruined that completely. But I just want you to know that I always loved you and still do." I expected her to interrupt me, but she didn't. "I know it doesn't make any sense. That's not how you treat people you love. But I did love you. I'm just really fucked up. And I wanted you to know what really happened."

"I'm trying to process it. And part of it is that I'm mad you didn't tell me. When I look back, I can see that Thayer was always Thayer. I saw it from the beginning, so I can't entirely blame you. He started treating me like crap early on, and I should have dumped him. I shouldn't have been surprised by any of it with him. But you were my *friend*. I thought you trusted me. You could have told me about what happened with your dad. And with Thayer. At least some of it."

"I'm sorry. I should have. Maybe it would have helped me escape. But it was just all so... perverse. I was ashamed."

"I get that," Lee said, then paused. "Part of what I'm struggling with is realizing that I'm such a terrible judge of people," she continued. "I can't tell when they're lying to me."

"That makes sense."

"I feel like I have to learn a new set of skills around that. And I don't know how to do it."

"At least you have Maria. I think you can trust her.

"I think so too."

"Can I ask you a question?"

"Sure," she said. Her voice sounded tired. Resigned.

"Why didn't you tell me you were pregnant?"

"I knew you'd want me to keep the baby, and I just couldn't. Thayer as a father was just... inconceivable."

"You're right. I would have tried to talk you out of it."

"You sure would have. But if I'd known he was cheating on me, I would have kept the baby and left him."

We were both silent for a moment, thinking our separate thoughts about all that had transpired, and feeling the weight of regret.

"I guess I should let you go. Just wanted to tell you I'm sorry," I said.

"I don't really know how to respond."

I started pacing again. "You don't need to say anything," I said, even though I hungered to have her tell me she forgave me.

"I know I don't *need* to," Lee said. "But I can at least tell you this: I've never been happier. I love it here"

"Merrivliet is wonderful! I'm so glad you love it like I did." My enthusiasm sounded chirpy even in my own ears, but I was just so relieved I had to let some out.

"I love not waking up to Thayer every morning. I'm getting stronger all the time, and I'm writing like crazy. I'm going to help other women recognize when they need to get out. That doesn't mean what you did was okay. It just means some good ended up coming from it."

I nodded, thinking about her words. But then I realized she couldn't see me. "Good. That's really good," I said.

"So, you just work on you. Listen to Maria's advice; she's a miracle worker. Try to have a good life."

"I will try."

"And thank you for the house," Lee said.

I didn't know how to respond.

"Take care, Kris."

"You too, Lee."

She disconnected the call, and I was left to think about what she'd said. I felt better than I had in years.

CHAPTER 79

I cornered Jimmy in the parking lot of his building when he came out at the end of the day. Waves of heat rose from the pavement in the distance, and I wanted nothing more than to break into a run and seek an oasis.

He came to a halt when he saw me standing by his car. "What do you want?" The words were short, but his face just looked tired.

"Hi, Jimmy."

"I asked what you want."

The darkness in his voice felt alien to the person I knew him to be. The knowledge that I'd done that to him stabbed straight through my heart. I felt for the rosary beads in my pocket and ran them through my fingers as a way to vent my nervousness. "I just needed to say I'm sorry. About everything."

Jimmy was quiet for a minute before answering. "That's it?"

"Yes."

"You think that's supposed to make everything all right? Put all the pieces of my life back together again?"

"No, I just…"

"You broke my *heart*, Kristy. I adored you. I trusted you."

"I know." I began to cry. The pain in his voice was naked, jagged.

"You *don't* know."

"You're right. I'm sorry."

This time he laughed. "Sorry." His voice broke. "How could you do that to me, Kristy?"

"I could try to explain, if you want! Would you let me explain?" I fumbled, hoping he would listen. Hoping my story could somehow expiate me.

"No. I don't want to hear it. It doesn't matter. I don't care what sort of victim trip you've created for yourself to justify it."

"I'm not trying to…"

But he cut me off. "That's enough. Is there anything else?" He reached for the car door handle.

"No, Jimmy. I just wanted to apologize."

"Well, you did. Congratulations. I hope you feel better, because I sure don't."

He got in, slammed the door, and drove off. He hadn't wanted to hear any of it, and that just had to be okay. I couldn't force him. Maybe in a few years he'd be able to forgive me. Maybe I could tell him my story then.

I'd felt better after my call to Lee but felt a whole lot worse after talking to Jimmy. I remembered Maria's words about doing the hard work, and Eta's words about the freeing action of forgiveness. I didn't know how long it might be before Jimmy could forgive me, but prayed that it could be as fast as possible.

For his sake.

CHAPTER 80

Eta told me I was too isolated and needed friends, but I wasn't sure how to function within a friendship after what had happened. I didn't feel like I was safe yet, for others, or for myself. My story consumed my mind and life, and I didn't know how to have coffee and talk about the latest celebrity romance or political imbroglio. But she was right. The baby was consuming in many ways; his needs were a gorgeous distraction from the thoughts that wanted to drown me. But there had to be more. I needed to engage.

She answered the first time I called. "Ms. Hyslip?" It had been surprisingly easy to find her number.

"Yes?"

"You were right."

"Who is this?"

"Kristy. Kristy Alexander. I mean Lamberton."

"Well, hello Kristy! What a surprise! How are you?"

"I'm hellish, to tell you the truth."

"I'm so sorry to hear that."

"You were right."

"About what?"

"About everything, Ms. Hyslip. About Thayer."

"Please. Call me Sandy."

"Do you think we could get together?"

"Of course! Where are you living these days?"

I explained that I was in Buffalo, and we arranged to meet for lunch that weekend halfway between our two cities. The Little Guy fell asleep on the drive, but his presence was still comforting company. She was already there when we arrived, looking the same as she did in high school though more silver shine in her dark locks. She hugged me once I'd set the baby down, and her embrace felt so good I thought I might cry. She smelled spicy and clean, and I wished I could stay in that warmth forever. But she pushed me to arm's length and lifted her chin to assess me.

"You look like you've been through hell."

I laughed. "I guess you could say that."

"Introduce me to this handsome fellow."

"He doesn't have a name yet. I call him Little Guy."

She gave me an odd look, as if calculating whether to ask more questions, but then dropped it, probably figuring it would all come out when we talked. "Little Guy it is. Sit down! You obviously need to eat. A whole cow, maybe."

I laughed and looked down at myself. My clothes hung loose, my bare arms were more bones than flesh, and I knew my face was gaunt. "I haven't had much of an appetite." I slid into the booth next to the baby's carrier and picked up the menu. The smells of the diner finally hit me; coffee and fried food and something rich and roasty. "It smells amazing in here!"

She sat down across from me, her eyes appraising.

"I'll order first, and then fill you in on… everything."

"Sounds good. I'll do the same." We made our selections and placed our orders. "I'm glad you called me," she said. "I've wondered how things have gone for you."

I covered my eyes with my hands and rubbed them, hoping to push the tiredness out. "Are you sure you want to hear it?"

She nodded, her gaze gentle. The waiter brought us our drinks. I slurped mine as a delay tactic, even though I wanted to tell her, but then I jumped in and told her everything. It felt like confessional again, with a different purpose. She had to know so I could have an honest relationship for once. Time with Aunt Hildy was safe and special, but it had been tainted by my secrets. I wanted a friend who knew my whole story. If Sandy couldn't handle it, I wanted to know right away.

The waiter brought our food, and I was suddenly ravenous. We ate and I kept talking. Our plates were cleared, and the Little Guy woke up so I gave him a bottle and kept talking. She didn't seem shocked. She just listened to it all, asking questions periodically.

When the words ran out, I felt purged and empty, in a good way. The baby rested on my shoulder as I patted his back to encourage a burp. "So that's it. My life in a nutshell." She was silent, twisting the paper from her straw. "Are you shocked? Appalled? Sickened?"

"Kristy. I'm so sorry. I'm so very sorry." Her eyes glistened with tears.

"Thank you." My throat tightened in response to her emotion.

"I wish I had known more. I wish I could have helped you." She looked increasingly distressed. "I should have reported it."

"You didn't know anything was going on."

"I did though. You remember I tried to warn you. I knew."

"But you had no proof."

"No. I didn't." She looked out the window, but her gaze seemed interior. "I had nothing to report, but I should have told your mother."

I laughed out loud. "She was sleeping with him too." That seemed to shock her. She shook her head, her face dismayed. "There was nothing you could have done," I continued. "That's not why I'm telling you."

"I'm so sorry." Her sorrow on my behalf did something to my insides. Something shifted and released. The relief of it was overwhelming.

"Thank you." Emotion made it hard to speak.

"How can I help you now?" she asked.

"Will you... will you be my friend?" The words sounded ridiculously adolescent, pre-adolescent even, but I kept going. "I really need a friend."

"Of course!" She looked confused for a moment but recovered quickly. "I'd love that." She smiled and I smiled back.

"Great! That's really great." I turned my face away to hide the intensity of my relief. "So now I need to hear about you." I'd had enough of my own stuff. "You're still teaching?"

She filled me in on what her life was like; she was still married, still working with high school students, still making ceramics. I told her about my own work in the classroom. She told me she'd never had children and that it had been painful, but she'd made a good life regardless. We talked about the paintings I'd been working on lately and how they connected to the exploration of my life.

We stayed for several hours, talking. It was the beginning of a friendship that flowered and grew. A friendship in which I was no longer embarrassed about the trailer park, or my father's addiction. No longer hiding all the ugly things that happened. I finally had a friend who knew everything about me and liked me anyway.

CHAPTER 81

Maria called once in a while to see how I was doing. I no longer called her, out of respect for Lee, but I was grateful when she contacted me, and it was usually at the perfect time.

"Something else happened while I was praying the rosary," I told her during one of these calls. "I've been thinking about Mary going through all that with Jesus. Being a mother to him. And I'm not sure I can be a mother to this baby." I'd been thinking about it a lot, but it was the first time I'd verbalized my fears.

"No? Do you not love him?"

"I'm desperately in love with him." My throat started to close as I said the words. "But I see Thayer in the child already, and with my attachment issues, I can't imagine he can turn out okay."

"It sounds like you have been giving this much thinking."

"I have. I was pretty screwed up from being raised by a single parent who was addict, and I don't want to inflict the same thing on someone else. I'm an addict too, just a different kind."

She was quiet for a moment. "We have two chances to experience parenting. Once when we are the bambini, and once when we are the parents. Because of that, we can change our broken experiences and make them whole."

I thought about what she said. It sounded logical, but I wasn't sure of her point. "I *do* want to be a parent. Someday. But I have to finish my healing first."

"This is good. This is what I am saying to you. We have two chances. Your first was merda. You do not want this one to be shit as well. You do not want to pass along the shitting."

I laughed. "Exactly! The Little Guy deserves to have a chance."

"Sì. Good."

"Plus, it just doesn't seem right to burden a child with the weight of my story. The weight of his *own* story, now. He should have a life with a mom and a dad who are emotionally healthy and who can love him. I know there are no guarantees they'll be perfect, but at least he'd have a chance of that." I started to cry in earnest. "His messed-up beginnings weren't his fault."

"Shh, Kristobella. It will be okay. All will be well. You are growing in wisdom. It is a good thing you are thinking, this adoption."

"I don't know how I'll do it, though. I adore him already. And I'll be all alone."

"You will find a way. It is the first step in being a good parent for him already. Sacrificing yourself. Doing what hurts for the sake of the little one you love."

"Is it?"

"Tell me. Which would be easier on your emozioni: to keep the child or to give him to a family to love?"

"Keeping him. Keeping him would be a million times easier."

"Then this would be sacrifice."

I sniffled in response.

"You are doing well, little Kristobella. I am very proud of you."

Finding out how to give a child up for adoption turned out to be super easy. There were a lot of companies which connected childless couples with unwitting or unwilling mothers. I chose one and initiated the process, filling out questionnaires about Thayer and me. I decided not to have contact with the child as he grew up. I thought it would be too hard, and that the kid had the best chance of thriving if he was completely disconnected and didn't have a chance to ask me questions to which he didn't really want answers. But I hoped for a day in the future when he might try to find me as an adult. Maybe I could tell him a few things when he was thirty. Maybe that would be enough time for us both.

I watched dozens of videos of prospective couples who all seemed like they would be wonderful parents. It was moving and heartbreaking how eager these people were to have a baby. I settled on a family who'd already adopted a sweet-faced little girl with Down syndrome, figuring that if they had enough love to take on the challenges required for her, my Little Guy would be safe.

It all felt terribly risky, passing off a child. My child. Thayer's child.

I first met them at a park. Theresa watched the Little Guy for me so their attention to him wouldn't color my evaluation. But they were as lovely in person as they were in the video. And the little girl was even sweeter.

They acted like I was giving the baby up because his father had died. I figured it was easier to let them think that. I must have looked too shattered to raise the child, and that part was certainly true. I know I still looked horrible, even though my appetite was returning. My face was still shadowed from lack of sleep and poor nutrition. They probably wondered if I'd been doing drugs, which was funny, because my drug of choice died months before.

I liked them. I said yes. There were papers to sign and lawyers to meet with. It all happened fast.

Two days later, I gave them my baby.

CHAPTER 82

Returning to work when school started wasn't easy. I qualified for family leave even though the baby was gone, but the emptiness of the house without the Little Guy in it was more than I could bear. I needed the distraction and the purpose.

Sandy was my cheerleader. She came to my classroom to help make some organizational changes before the kids' first day, and gave me some ideas for projects that worked well for her when she was feeling creatively tapped.

Teaching turned out to be good therapy. I found myself engaging with the children more deeply than I had before and was able to identify a few who showed special artistic passion that I could foster, the way Ms. Hyslip fostered mine. Theresa and I had dinner or drinks once a week, and I joined a book club.

Meanwhile, I kept painting.

It had taken a few months after reliving Daddy's death before inspiration finally came. Paintings from the other time leaps happened immediately, but this piece was a little bit different. It didn't include me. I knew right away that it was for her.

For Maria.

The painting was of Mary. She was full of majesty; smiling her serene smile with the moon under her feet and her head adorned with a crown of twelve stars. Her skirt and cloak were a velvety midnight indigo, scattered with pinpoints of golden light.

She was smiling, surrounded by a swirling cloud of four-leaf clover.

I wrapped it carefully, then boxed it up and took it to UPS, hoping she'd like it.

CHAPTER 83

The school year passed surprisingly quickly. When summer break arrived, I decided to take a road trip. Counseling had progressed well, and I felt stronger, saner, and more at peace than seemed possible. It had been almost a year since my world exploded, and my new life felt like it was being built on solid ground. The pain of losing the Little Guy still throbbed, but it was a better kind of pain. A right kind.

Before leaving I needed to find out where Daddy was buried. I'd cut off ties with Lisa so couldn't ask her. Besides, she probably didn't know. After some internet searching, I discovered he'd been given an indigent's burial. Apparently no family member had been found to take care of his remains, which meant Lisa hadn't bothered to call Aunt Hildy until she wanted to dump me on her doorstep that first summer. Hildy must have been heartbroken and furious that his body was given so little attention and respect. I was shocked she never told me after all those years, and proof of how much she wanted my relationship with Lisa to have a chance.

The drive to Missouri gave me plenty of time to think. In a way it was like another form of time travel, through more mundane methods. I thought about the progress I'd made with Eta in accepting my conflicting feelings about Daddy rather than trying to get rid of them, finding a way to co-exist with the horror, longing, dismay, anger, and love.

I checked in to a hotel then drove to the cemetery. It was armadillo season in Missouri and the roads were peppered with carcasses. As a child I'd been fascinated by them, wondering if God thought he made a mistake with the weird creatures who were always born as quadruplets; four identical babies split from a single egg. A cross between classes; reptile and mammal. Aztecs called them "turtle rabbits." My thoughts tumbled across a landscape of information collected through the years. I wondered if JB ever ended up keeping one as a pet the way he had that turtle.

The cemetery caretaker showed me where to go. The simple marker noted the dates of Daddy's birth and death, but nothing else. I knelt beside the grave.

"Hi, Daddy." I set down the pot of flowers I'd brought along. "I'm here. I came back." I'd forgotten to bring something to dig with, so used my hands. "I wanted to tell you something." Recollections of life with him swirled through my mind. Memories of when things were good, and he wrote me poems or told me stories. Memories of when things were bad, and he was sick and touching me. I thought about the role he'd played in what happened with Thayer, and my own culpability in Thayer's death. But I'd come with a gift to give him, and a gift to give myself.

"I forgive you," I said.

I prayed for him then, prayed backward in time for his brokenness to be healed, for his freedom now, away from the pain of his life and his addiction. I prayed for him to be able to dance in joy and wholeness. I prayed he'd be able to forgive himself. I prayed that Aunt Hildy would take care of him. And I prayed for myself, and my own future, asking Mary to pray for us all.

The wind picked up by the time I got back to the hotel, and that night lightning shattered the sky and thunder boomed loud and long just as it did back in my childhood. It would have been great to listen to storm updates on our old radio rather than watching relentlessly excited reporters on the television weather channels.

The storm blew through quickly, so I joined the smokers in the courtyard and gazed up at the Missouri sky, looking for constellations. They looked both the same and different from the ones my memory held. I remembered the wonder of recognizing the dippers that first time, and it felt like it might be possible to experience wonder again.

On the second day of my pilgrimage, I went to the trailer park. The second park, where Daddy died. I drove around, surprised by how little and how much things had changed. Trailers had aged. Some of the older ones were gone, and new ones had arrived. Trees were taller. But otherwise, it was essentially the same, though smaller. I parked my car in the driveway of a lot in which no trailer was located and walked the streets of my youth. Kids still played basketball, and the thwack of the rubber on asphalt was a kind of nostalgic music.

I walked to the end of the park, toward the sewage treatment system and the empty field in which JB and I hunted for four-leaf clover. A street which was formerly populated with trailers was now empty and overgrown. A gaslight-style streetlight was being overtaken by the edge of the encroaching woods, like something from an old C.S. Lewis story, where talking animals congregated to plan the overthrow of an evil queen. Trumpet vines twined around the trees and bees buzzed in and out of the orange horns. Nature was taking over. One of the lots had housed a man who beat his wife, but time had wiped away the ugliness and subsumed it in its endless cycle of growth, blossoming, and dying.

The buzzing of the insects was louder than I remembered, and the heat was more intense. I smiled at the groups of skeptical kids on bikes and playing basketball, remembering when I'd been one of them. I'd saved our trailer for last. It was still there, just looking more faded and dirty than when we'd lived there. The deck had been replaced and expanded but was already dilapidated. I imagined Daddy's bunny hopping down the strip of shade from the neighbor's trailer, toward the road.

The old trailer across the street and one door up was also still standing, and I could swear I saw the curtain drop back to cover the face of a woman in a blue veil, smiling.

CHAPTER 84

On Friday night I set the alarm to go off before sunup. It was crazy, really, but I rose and got dressed, too nervous to eat anything. I just grabbed some coffee from the hotel lobby and went out to the car, then drove to the creek as the sun rose. I parked and approached the creek bank. A man was there, fishing. He didn't notice me coming because he was busy pulling a catch out of the water. I watched him for a few minutes until I got a good view of his hands.

JB jumped when I sat down next to him, his pupils flaring wide with surprise. I think he could read my own eyes, and his expression transformed from surprise to recognition to pleasure before he turned back to the fish he was trying to get loose from the hook. "Took you long enough," he said.

A smile grew from my heart and spread until it encased my stomach in warmth and burst out through my face. He got the fish loose and dropped it in a bucket of water. He leaned into me. I sighed, deep and long, and tilted my head to rest on his shoulder.

"I'm a few decades late," I said.

"Just glad you finally came," he responded.

A dragonfly touched down on the quiet water near the creek bank, creating circles of ripples. The sun sparkled on them like the golden light on a crown of twelve stars.

"I have something for you," JB said.

"You do?"

"Yup."

"What is it?"

"A bunch of poems. Some assholes tore your house up after you left. I went in afterward. Your mattress was flipped up against the wall and there were little bits of paper all over the floor. There were a ton of those four-leaf clover we collected too. I gathered it all up."

For a moment, I was stunned into silence, shocked at the gift he'd offered. It didn't seem possible. But then I remembered the woman's smiling face beneath its veil of blue.

"I would love to have them," I said. "Thank you."